THE KEYHOLE

GIGI STYX

AUTHOR'S NOTE

This is a dark psychological thriller with graphic and sexually explicit scenes. For a full list of trigger warnings, visit www.gigistyx.com/keyhole

For readers who like it spicy, dark, and impossible to put down.

ONE

When this plane lands, I'll either disappear into a nanny job on Helsing Island or end up cuffed and bleeding in a holding cell. There'll be no makeup for my mugshot, no mercy at the trial. They'll probably pour drinks after they throw me in the electric chair and send me straight to hell.

The judicial system doesn't exactly go easy on cop killers. Not even those who didn't murder by choice.

My gaze shifts to the window as the plane drops below the cloud line and the island comes into view. Even through the dark, the vast expanse of forest gives me hope that this will be the perfect place to hide.

The seatbelt bites into my hip bones. The cabin stinks of coffee, old sweat, and that sour chemical tang of recycled air. And the man sitting in the aisle next to mine hasn't stopped staring at me since takeoff.

But so has everyone else. They know what I've done. Know where I'm going.

Mom told me I was damned. Dad called me a sinner. The old bastard they married me off to said I was a demon. Maybe they were right.

The tiny plane lands, taxis, then shudders to a stop, its propellers winding down with a metallic whine that cuts through the night air. Eight passengers file past toward the exit, their gazes boring into the side of my face.

My chest tightens. Each breath grows shallower, thinner. Countless nights of sleep deprivation have frazzled my nerves, but if I jump at every stare, I'll blow my cover before I even land.

I fumble with my duffel's zipper and rifle through the stolen cash, spare clothes, and the prepaid phone holding WhatsApp messages from a man named Edward Rochester.

That's why I came to Helsing Island. In the hope that whoever's behind the Facebook Marketplace ad really is a widowed father seeking a nanny and not a psycho setting a trap. But I'm desperate enough to answer the kind of ad no sane person would trust.

Mr. Rochester's employee is meeting me at the airport. I turn on the burner phone to email him that the plane is late, and every one of his replies is replaced with a box that says: *This message was deleted.*

My messages remain, hanging in the void, but his side is scrubbed clean. When I click the Facebook Marketplace link, the ad no longer exists.

Shit.

The seatbelt snaps back like a whip as I rise, my legs shaky. My knees feel unsteady, not from the flight but from the weight of being a fugitive on the run about to hide out in a stranger's manor.

Bottom line: I've run out of options.

The terminal is nothing more than a single room with plastic chairs bolted to the floor and fluorescent lights that hum like dying insects. Everything smells of bleach and jet fuel. The walls are stained yellow from years of moisture and neglect, and somewhere outside I can hear gulls crying like they're mourning the dead.

There's no café, no gift shop, no place to hide. Just vending machines humming in the corners and the hollow echo of footsteps on linoleum.

I clutch my duffel bag tighter and keep my head down as I walk toward the exit. My boots squeak with every step, screaming my presence. Through the glass doors I can see the parking lot with three cars and a pickup truck that's more rust than metal. Paranoia has me crossing the empty space feeling eyes drilling into the back of my skull.

Legs trembling, I push myself toward the doors, pretending I'm not dying inside.

I'm halfway down the concourse when there's movement in my periphery. A strange man shifts against the wall near the exit, his eyes raking up and down my form. He rocks on his feet, watching me walk toward him with a patient smile.

What if he's a cop or FBI?

Shit.

Shit.

Shit.

My throat closes and my breath comes in panicked gasps as I imagine his hands on my wrists, the cold bite of cuffs, the way everyone back home will shake their heads and say they always knew this was where I was headed.

But I keep walking because I have a plan. Not really. He's probably the driver my new employer said would meet me at the airport. But why isn't he holding a sign? I hold my features in a neutral expression, pretend I'm not wanted for murder, and keep my gaze on the glass doors.

When I reach the exit, he leans forward and whispers something obscene. He wasn't FBI. Just a fucking creep. I freeze for a second, too stunned to speak, flesh crawling like it's trying to leave my bones. The automatic doors slide open with a pneumatic hiss, and I sprint out into the night.

The wind hits my face like a slap, driving rain through my jacket in seconds. It doesn't matter that my boobs hurt from not wearing a sports bra, or the air tastes of salt and wet stone, or that I'm near the ocean though I can't see it through the darkness. I'm grabbing this chance to escape that perv before he decides to take chase.

Up ahead, a single car idles at the curb, a vintage limousine from what I can tell by its shape. Chrome bumpers catch the yellow light from the terminal, and everything about it whispers old money. Some might call me a gold digger for moving toward it. I call myself a survivor. Better to risk safety with one powerful man than end up prey to every predator on my tail.

"Hey, baby," says a male voice from behind.

I'm still looking back for that guy when I collide with something solid. A wall of muscle wrapped in wool. A scream catches in my throat.

Large hands grab my shoulder, triggering my fight-or-flight. Just as I'm about to reach for his junk, my captor says, "Are you Annalisa Burlington?"

The voice is cultured and low. I crane my neck and notice two things at once, despite the broad shoulders and chiseled jaw. He wears a black chauffeur's uniform with a cap pulled low over features I can barely make out in the shadows. Definitely not FBI.

"Annalisa Burlington?" he repeats, releasing my shoulders.

Burlington. That's the name I gave the guy from Facebook Marketplace. I nod because my voice has abandoned me somewhere between fear and relief.

"Um... Yes?" I croak. "That's me."

"Rochester Manor awaits." He opens the car door with white-gloved hands.

I glance back toward the terminal one last time. That weirdo is nowhere to be seen. I grind my teeth. Guilt has me seeing predators in every stranger's face. Either way, this car is my only shot at disappearing, and standing here in the rain won't save me from arrest.

"Thank you," I mutter, and step into the limousine's interior.

The leather seats are worn soft with age and smell like tobacco and cedar, masculine scents that remind me of the old man I once hooked up with from Casino DeMartini. Wood paneling lines the interior, and the windows are tinted so dark I might as well be in a coffin. I clutch my duffel on my lap and try not to think about how many bodies have disappeared in cars like this one.

Seriously, I need to shut the fuck up. A woman facing the electric chair can't afford to worry about being whisked away by maniacs.

He pulls out onto the access road and continues along the flyover. I lean against the window, my gaze fixed on the exit signs.

"Where did you work before?" His voice breaks me out of my thoughts.

I meet his eyes in the rearview mirror. Black. Unblinking. Probing. Shouldn't he already know all this? I shake off that thought. Of course, he wouldn't. I was emailing Mr. Rochester. This guy is probably just making small talk. Shit. He wants to know where I worked.

What the hell did I say in that fake résumé? Was it Milwaukee? Damn it, why did I have to be so extra?

"Um... Chicago," I mutter. "Private family."

"How long?"

"A year."

"Why did you leave?"

"They moved to Europe." My throat dries. "Wanted a nanny who could teach them French."

"Where before that?"

I swallow. "Milwaukee."

"And before that?"

"Um... Indiana."

Silence. Then: "No luggage? Or did you leave it on purpose?"

My hackles rise. My fingers tighten around the duffel. What the hell is this interrogation? I clench my teeth. "Airline lost it."

"Or are you traveling light because you're on the run?"

"I'm not—" My voice cracks. Prickly heat crawls up my neck, threatening to brand my face with a confession. Who the hell does this guy think he is? A chauffeur doesn't get to ask if I'm a wanted woman.

"Excuse me?" I snap, trying to regain some ground.

"What address did you give for them to return it?"

I freeze. "I... didn't."

"Why not?"

Because I have no home. Because I'm a fugitive. Because my last living blood relatives would kill me if they knew I was still alive. My tongue darts out to lick my lips. "My bags weren't valuable."

"Cut the bullshit. Now isn't the time for lies."

The words hit like a punch to the throat. Breath hitching, I try not to shriek, "It's the truth."

The man pauses long enough to make me squirm. "No friends? Family? Surely there's someone out there to send your luggage."

"I didn't want to bother anyone," I say, my voice dropping.

He studies me through the rearview window. "Mr. Rochester values discretion. If you plan on sharing his business with people at home, tell me now. He's given me orders to return you to the airport."

My pulse hammers. I sit up straight in my seat. They can't send me back. I have nowhere else to go. "He has nothing to worry about," I blurt. "There's no one. I'm all alone."

He nods and drives on in silence, seeming satisfied with my answer. I stare at the tinted glass, my reflection pale, ugly. Why the hell did I allow myself to get so desperate? A knot forms in my stomach at the realization. I just told him I was all alone in the world. That nobody would ever come looking.

The driver pulls into a road, which narrows in less than half a mile, with trees closing in overhead like the ribs of some enormous beast. Fog rolls between the trunks, thick enough to swallow our headlights whole.

I glance through the divider at the back of his head. This silence is making my skin crawl.

My gaze darts toward the tinted windows. Somewhere during that interrogation, we left the highway and are now racing through a narrow country road bordered by tall shrubs. I fumble with the duffel's leather handle, not quite realizing Helsing Island could be so vast compared to how it looks on the map. What if he's taking me to the middle of nowhere?

"How far is the house?" I ask.

"Sixty miles."

"What's the place like?"

"Cliffs to the west. A thousand acres of forest to the east."

My stomach drops. I wipe my sweaty palms on my jeans. This is what I wanted, wasn't it? Isolation? A place where I wouldn't be found?

The Facebook Marketplace ad promised a live-in nanny gig, discretion essential. In my right mind, I would never work with kids. Two years of being a teenage stepmom to that old bastard's brats is enough for one lifetime, but I don't have any other ideas.

I try not to think about what I'll do if something goes wrong with the job. I'll just have to make it work until I can figure out a plan B. We drive for what feels like hours through cliffside roads and dense forest. There are no streetlights, no turn-offs, just this endless expanse of road. Just as my eyes start to droop, the headlights catch iron gates rising from the fog like the entrance to a graveyard.

I sit up, my breath catching. "Is this Rochester Manor?"

He nods.

We crawl along a winding path where hedges grow wild and trees lean in like they're whispering secrets. I suppress a shudder and tell myself it's going to be okay.

An old mansion rises ahead, a black mass against the storm clouds. Every window is dark, like a skull with empty sockets. Wind howls through the trees with a sound like something dying.

The car stops. In the sudden silence I can hear my

pulse hammering in my ears like a countdown to something ominous.

"Congratulations. You've passed your interview." He tilts his head toward the house. "Mrs. Fairfax will take it from here."

My stomach drops through the leather seat. "What interview?"

The divider rises, sealing him off. All traces of fatigue vanish, replaced by creeping dread. I clutch my duffel, shove the door open, and flinch as the rain hits my face like freezing fingers.

I step onto gravel that crunches under my boots like broken bones. The chauffeur drives away, leaving me alone in the fog with whatever waits behind those dark windows. A shiver runs down my spine and settles in my gut. I've escaped prison, so why does it feel like I'm no longer free?

TWO
THE KEYHOLE

You're more beautiful than the others. A rare gem.

Blonde hair, blue eyes, breasts large enough to smother me until dawn. You don't know it yet, but you're already mine.

I see how your sins cling to your skin, how you bite that plump lip and scan the grounds as if someone might rescue you.

They will not.

I imagine all the ways I'll ruin you. The whimpers, the pleading, the way your body will tremble at my command.

Your pretty features will look exquisite contorted with pain. You might even make a lovely corpse.

Welcome to Rochester Manor, my sweet Annalisa. Enjoy being my plaything. The others never lasted, but you might last long enough.

THREE

A shiver runs down my spine as the limousine rounds a corner, taking away the light. Rochester Manor looms ahead, a three-story building that could easily be the set of a movie about a wicked duke who ruins young women for sport. I cross the gravel courtyard, squinting against the wind and rain.

Even the doorbell feels wrong. Not a ding or a buzz, just a deep, echoing chime like Big Ben calling the dead to rise. I've never been to London, but I've watched enough BBC murder dramas to recognize the sound of doom. I huddle against the doors, waiting for footsteps or chains.

But there's nothing.

Just the wind.

Just the rain.

And me, shivering like a wet dog left on the porch.

Rain beats down my back like a vicious husband on his wedding night. I shiver, my teeth clacking, and switch my thoughts to the reason I'm standing outside a creepy old house: Gil. My ex was more loyal to his underworld bosses than to the love of his life, but when we met, he was a warm blanket. A lifeline. And he never left me unsatisfied.

At least not until the end.

I wait. And wait. And wait. I tell myself that the distant howl is the wind and whatever's lurking in the forest. When nobody answers the door, I ring the bell again and press my ear to the wood.

When I hear nothing, I crouch down and peer through the keyhole. It's dark, so I close my eyes and listen. Minutes pass, maybe half an hour, and a spasm seizes my back. I bang on the door with fists, and yell for attention.

Finally, footsteps approach, slow and heavy, as if the mansion's interior is cavernous. Drawing back at the jingle of keys, I pick up my duffel and straighten. The locks turn, their mechanisms sounding rusty even through the heavy rainfall, and whoever's behind the door slides one bolt, followed by another.

I back away, already having second thoughts, when the night sky brightens with forks of lightning, followed by a roll of thunder.

The door groans open, and the woman answering is large enough to fill its frame. Broad shoulders, thick neck, black dress starched like cardboard. A matching mask covers the lower half of her face.

I step back.

"Annalisa Burlington?" Her voice is rough, like it can't decide whether it's male or female.

"Y-Yes?" I squeak.

"You'd better come in." She steps aside, leaving barely enough for me to cross the threshold.

I have to squeeze past her bulk into a vast foyer. It's silent as a cathedral with stone floors stretching into the shadows, and the ceiling tall enough to give me vertigo. On the wall are sconces. Not fake ones with electric bulbs, but actual flames that flicker in the draft, making the shadows dance. I inhale a sharp breath, taking in the scent of beeswax and something medicinal that catches in the back of my throat.

The door slams shut with a thud that makes me flinch. The woman I assume to be Mrs. Fairfax brushes past, her black dress rustling against an impossibly bulky frame. Following, I shiver at the eerie silence, broken only by our footsteps echoing off the stone. I try to take in details—mahogany paneling, oil paintings in heavy frames, a grandfather clock ticking somewhere in the darkness—but she moves too quickly, and I'm too busy trying to keep up with her long strides.

"How long have you worked here?" I ask, my voice small in the vast space.

"Long enough." Her voice is gravel and smoke.

"And Mr. Rochester? What's he like?"

She doesn't answer. Just continues walking toward a staircase that curves up into the shadows like a spine.

We climb to a grandiose landing, illuminated moonlight streaming through tall windows. Then up another flight, where a cobweb brushes my cheek like a curtain. I shudder, distracting my revulsion with portraits of men in uniforms, women in gowns, children with dead eyes watching us pass.

My thighs burn, but Mrs. Fairfax charges ahead without slowing. A painting of a woman with pale skin and blonde ringlets catches my attention. Her eyes seem scratched out in the flickering light. I stop following long enough to lean closer.

"Keep up," she growls without turning around.

The next floor feels different from the one before. Smaller. Darker. Crumbling. Even the ceiling is lower, pressing down like it's designed to crush spirits. This has to be the servant's quarters. Before I can ask how many of us live here, Mrs. Fairfax stops at a door at the end of the hallway and produces a key.

"Your room," she says, turning the lock. "Breakfast is at seven sharp. Do not be late."

The door swings open to reveal a space that's both a prison cell and sanctuary. Moonlight streams in through French doors, illuminating the dark wood floors. A huge bed dominates its center, its posts reaching toward the ceiling like fingers. The room is sparse and basic, apart from the velvet curtains around the bed and the balcony doors.

Mrs. Fairfax shifts aside just enough for me to enter. "The wardrobe contains everything you'll need."

I step inside, my shoulders sagging with relief. After a week of paranoia, of feeling like everyone within glancing distance was a cop waiting to drag me to justice, all I want is to be alone to catch my breath. I never thought my life would turn to shit at the age of twenty-five, but hiding out in the middle of nowhere as a nanny is better than the alternative.

"Burlington?" She asks from behind.

I turn, finding her still looming in the doorway. She stares down at me with an intensity that has me rooted to the spot. My fingers twitch. My breath shallows. I wait in agony for several heartbeats, expecting her to ask the same awkward question as the chauffeur.

"Yes?" I finally reply.

"Welcome to Rochester Manor." I swear that she

smiles beneath that mask before pulling the door shut behind her with a thud.

With a final exhale, I turn the key in the lock.

The first things I explore are the French doors. They need to open, so I'm no longer breathing air saturated with medicine and polish and rot. I turn the handle and step onto a stone balcony that overlooks the grounds. A cool breeze fans over my fevered skin, and I fill my lungs. The rain has stopped, leaving everything glistening under silver light. Below, formal gardens stretch away from the house lined by hedges in perfect geometric patterns and pathways that lead nowhere. Everything here seems too orderly, too controlled.

It feels like the set of a period movie, and I'm an actress who's forgotten her lines.

My nipples tighten with the cold, and my skin prickles into goosebumps. I rest my hands against the stone railing, cursing Gil for leading me into an ambush, letting those people make me a murderer, and then casting me out.

Mom said God cursed women to desire men but be crushed under their feet. It was Eve's punishment for tempting Adam into eating the forbidden fruit. When she and Dad married me off to Brother Matthew, my belief in the scripture crumbled. There was nothing attractive about a bad-tempered old man who stank of horse piss.

I used to think she was full of shit until I met Gil.

He was everything—a change from the rich old guys I'd pick up in cigar bars or casinos. An upgrade from the assholes who'd make me earn my rent money. He was handsome, charming, attentive, and had the body of an athlete. Even if our relationship didn't last more than a month, he was the sweetest, strongest, kindest, most generous man I'd ever met. Until he wasn't.

Fuck that bastard.

And his boss.

With a shiver, I hurry back through the doors and head for the wardrobe. There's a single black dress hanging inside, pressed and waiting like it's been expecting to be worn. Arranged on the shelf underneath are white aprons, cotton nightgowns, and underwear still in their packaging. The Facebook Marketplace ad wasn't exaggerating. Everything really is provided.

I lift the dress off the hanger and grimace. It might fit my waist and hips, but there's no way in hell it'll handle my boobs. The only saving grace is the line of buttons down the front. I can wear it open until they find something that actually fits.

Fugitives can't be fashionistas.

With a sigh, I explore the attached bathroom. The walls are tiled in white subway brick that reflects the moonlight in fractured patterns. When I flip the switch, the bulb flickers once before settling into steady illumination. Probably because no one updated the electrics since the master of this mansion learned to channel lightning.

I turn on the shower, cringing at the groaning pipes sputtering out brown water. As I'm picturing how on earth I plan on getting clean on drinking water, it eventually runs clear. A line of bottles, identical except for their labels, sits in a shower niche, along with a razor and a fresh washcloth. I peel off my damp clothes, my fingers shaking from more than just cold. Now that I'm alone, the adrenaline crash hits me like a fist.

Tremors wrack my frame as I grip the edge of the bathtub. I'm safe. Safe from my shitty old family. Safe from Gil's bosses. Safe from the FBI. I step under the spray and let it pound against my neck and shoulders until my skin throbs. I scrub harder than needed, trying to wash away the last week and everything that led me here to this creepy old manor on a Godforsaken island.

Lavender fills my nostrils, relaxing my muscles. I finally allow my shoulders to sag.

"Thank God," I say in a breathy exhale. I really got away with murder.

A creak fills the air, making me freeze. Was that just settling? Or footsteps? I hold my breath, listening to water hitting porcelain in sync with my racing pulse.

It could be pipes. Or someone lurking. In a creepy old house like this, it's hard to tell the difference. But I sure as hell can't afford to get it wrong.

The spray turns to ice, making my stomach lurch. With a scream, I leap out and grab a threadbare towel. My pulse hammers so hard I think it'll burst.

What the hell was that?

I turn off the faucet before anything else goes wrong, wrap myself in the towel like it's a safety blanket, and hurry back to the bedroom. I wrestle my way into the nightgown, which pulls tight across my chest. My lungs constrict. Tomorrow, I'll ask for a larger size.

After folding my old clothes and shoving them back in the duffel bag, I turn off the main light and slide into bed. The mattress is unexpectedly soft, a vast improvement from Gil's waterbed. And the sheets smell like lavender and fresh starch. I settle into the pillows, letting my body melt.

My eyes flutter shut, and the permanent knot in my stomach loosens. I've made it. No one will think of finding me on this remote island, let alone this old estate.

But as I reach for the lamp, the balcony door slams.

I bolt upright. Did I forget to lock it?

Sighing, I pad across the wooden floor. Wind blows in through the gaping door, making me think of Lucy from the *Dracula* movie who was turned into a vampire through an open window.

I grab the door, only to see a figure outside in the garden.

It's a man.

He remains perfectly still on the lawn, head tilted up toward where I'm standing. Even from up here on the balcony, I can see he's wearing a mask. Is that the chauffeur? Why the hell is he just lingering there in the dark?

I place a hand over my heart, and he copies the movement. My breath quickens. I drop my hand. He does the same. The pulse between my legs comes to life.

Is he... mirroring me?

No. Whatever he's doing is none of my damn business. And it's not like I have a mask kink. That was Gil's thing. Not mine.

But then he raises a gloved hand and beckons.

Panic bursts across my chest. I scramble back, the nightgown gaping open at the front. When I steal another glance, he's still there. Watching. Waiting. For me?

Fear and arousal twist together until I can't tell where one ends and the other begins.

I pull the balcony doors shut, turn the lock, and check it twice. Once I'm sure it's secure, I yank the curtains closed, blocking out the moon, the gardens, and the creep. With a shiver, I rush back to bed and pull the covers over my head.

My door is locked. The balcony is shut. He's irrelevant.

That's what I tell myself over and over until the words blur into nothing. Until memories of men, manipulation, and murder melt toward oblivion. Until footsteps echo in the hallway outside my door.

Heavy. Slow. Deliberate, they pause outside my room. I swear there's someone breathing on the other side of the wood.

My pulse kicks up several notches, and I try not to think about the masked man. Or the way he called me down. "Please let it be Mrs. Fairfax," I whisper like a prayer.

But the footsteps sound masculine. And whoever's out there is panting like the Hound of the fucking Baskervilles. I ball my hands into fists. The door is locked. Even if he has a skeleton key, he won't get it in.

After what feels like an eternity, the footsteps fade down the hallway.

I squeeze my eyes shut, pull the covers over my head, and tell myself I'm safe.

Goddammit. I have to believe it.

Because if I don't, I'm trapped in a deserted mansion on an island with nowhere left to run.

FOUR
THE KEYHOLE

You crossed the threshold, dripping excitement and rain, pretending you're not afraid.

Now you pace your new cage. You caress the velvet curtains like they're the hairs on my chest, test the locks as if they might offer you protection.

Foolish girl. There will be no barriers between you and I. No escape.

You peel off your clothes, trembling with desire, shivering with need. Don't you know satisfaction is mere inches away?

Crawl beneath the covers, my little pet. They offer no sanctuary. Close your eyes, I'll still be there.

Your fear is exquisite. It lingers in the corners, seeps into the floorboards, rises from your skin in delectable waves.

Pretend you're alone. Pretend you're safe. This is only the beginning.

Sleep, Annalisa. I'll be watching through the keyhole. Always.

FIVE

The thought of being trapped in a cage had my mind spinning the entire night. That, and the man on the lawn and the footsteps outside my room. Paranoia even invaded my sleep.

As I lay flat on my back, an unseen force pushed the key out of the hole, making it fall to the floor with a soft clink. Then the door creaked open, and a large figure stood in the doorway.

In my dream, I was paralyzed, unable to do anything but gasp. He loomed there, backlit by faint moonlight, his broad chest moving up and down like church bellows. Dream man's hips drove back and forth like he was testing how it would feel to split me open.

I blame not having sex for several days after non-stop action with Gil. Scratch that. I blame Gil. And the crime family I refuse to name because they have the murder weapon with my fingerprints.

I tried to move, but the only thing shifting was the sick pulse between my legs. And his powerful thrusts. He kept rocking, like he already owned the rhythm of my body.

Therapists would call it latent sexual aggression. I call it a bad habit of wanting the things that scare me most.

He edged forward, and something loosened in my throat. A scream that had him disappearing into the dark. Before I could even process what happened, the nightmare ended, and I was plunged back into sleep.

A sharp knock has me sitting upright, my head throbbing. Sunlight slices through a gap in the heavy curtains, making me wince. I must have yanked them too hard last night. I clutch my temples and groan. How the hell do I have a hangover when the only thing I swallowed was fear?

Whoever's outside the door knocks again.

"Who is it?" I yell.

No answer. Just more insistent rapping.

I squint, certain this time I'm awake. My gaze darts to the bedside table where I left my phone. With a yawn, I reach across the bed and pick it up. It's 6:30 in the morning, and there's no signal. Maybe service on this part of the island is spotty.

The knocking stops, replaced by the sound of retreating footsteps. I climb out of bed, my bare feet hitting the cold wooden floor. An ache stretches along my back like I've been sleeping on concrete. Maybe it's the stress. Or maybe the mattress is like every rich man I've met. Plush up front, knives in the springs.

There's no time for a shower. Not after oversleeping from such a haunting dream. Not when I imagine eyes at the keyhole, and some man's breath fogging the brass. I stumble to the wardrobe, pull out the black dress, and hold it up against my body. In daylight, it looks even tighter. The heavy wool fabric is unforgiving.

I pull the dress over my head and catch a whiff of

something that isn't detergent. It's sharp, almost metallic. I can't shake off the sense that this once belonged to someone else.

The back of my neck prickles. I glance over my shoulder at the door. The key is still in the lock. It should make me feel better. It doesn't. And I swear I hear the faintest creak in the floorboards like someone is lingering outside.

Shivering, I turn my attention back to the dress and wrestle it down my body. Its buttons strain across my chest, the sleeves dig into my arms, and the stitches threaten to pop. I catch a thread of dark brown hair caught at the collar. With trembling fingers, I pull it free.

Leaving the top three buttons undone, I tug my hair forward to distract from the gaping neckline. It's not elegant, but as close to decent as I can manage.

Still, I can't shake the crawling certainty that someone's watching me fumble through this outfit. A chill shivers down my spine. I force myself to breathe. I can get over myself. I can do this job. I just need to remember I'm safe.

I step outside into a hallway draped in silence and cobwebs I didn't notice the night before. There's no sign of activity, which means the other staff has already left for breakfast. Shit. I'll be the last one to arrive. I square my shoulders, picturing a table full of maids and butlers and busybodies, all wanting to know about the new girl.

Thank God I already wrote out my fake backstory when I replied to the advert on Facebook Marketplace.

The farther down I go, the quieter the house becomes, but it's still crumbling, looking left to rot. My footsteps echo down long hallways lined with oil paintings of faces blurred by time, or maybe just grime. Most of the doors are locked, and the few left open contain furniture draped in cloth. I pass a lounge covered in a faint layer of dust, a library that smells of old paper before giving up.

But I still don't pass any staff. I don't hear any voices or even the clatter of dishes or the dull rhythm of someone sweeping. Shouldn't a house this size be crawling with people?

My stomach tightens as I search the ground floor. The kitchen must be close. I pass a window overlooking the gardens and swear I catch a glimpse of a figure moving toward the forest that borders the grounds. By the time I pause for a better look, he's already gone.

I round a corner to find a view of the gardens where the lawns fall away into cliffs. Suppressing a shiver, I remind myself that no one hunting me would think to look somewhere so isolated.

Eventually, I follow the faint smell of cooking and reach the kitchen, which is surprisingly well kept. It's enormous with an industrial stove, copper pots hanging from hooks, every surface wiped clean. It's like they've concentrated all the maintenance budget in this single room.

I scan for signs of life: an apron slung over a chair, a clipboard on the counter, a dish left out to dry, but there's nothing. Just pristine surfaces and closed drawers, like the room is staged, instead of used.

And still no sign of any staff.

At the far end of the kitchen sits a single place setting of a white plate, silverware, and a napkin folded to a perfect triangle.

What the hell?

Movement at the edge of my vision makes me startle. Mrs. Fairfax emerges from a side door, still masked and in a starched black dress identical to mine. She's even more imposing in the harsh light of day, with her shoulders squared and her black eyes fixing on my chest.

"In Rochester Manor, we have a dress code." The words are flat, but her gaze is sharp enough to slice skin.

I glance down at the gaping buttons. "Then maybe the dress should fit."

Her stare drags over my body, slow, cold, and judgmental. My cheeks heat, and I force myself not to cross my arms over my chest. When her eyes finally return to mine, I resist the urge to step back.

Silence stretches between us like a wire about to snap. She doesn't move. Doesn't blink. Just looms there studying me like I'm a specimen to dissect or discard. My skin crawls under the intensity of her stare. I force myself not to fidget, but the seconds drag on until I'm on the verge of screaming.

Finally, she gestures at the place setting and says, "I'll see what I can do. Now, eat."

She lifts the lid off a platter on the side containing fried eggs, bacon, sausages and tomatoes, and returns with a pot of coffee that smells like heaven. My stomach chooses this moment to rumble, making me flush. The huge woman tilts her head, studying me like she's never experienced a day of hunger. Avoiding her gaze, I scurry over to the counter and load my plate.

"Is everyone else at work?" I ask, spearing a sausage.

"Mr. Rochester has only two employees," she replies.

What? I turn to meet her beady glare. "In a house as big as this?"

Mrs. Fairfax continues staring at me like I'm an exhibit. When she doesn't reply, I shift my weight from one foot to the other, trying to hide my unease. This woman is beyond unnerving. She could strangle someone with her silence. Her gaze follows me as I take the plate to the single place setting on the table and pick up my fork.

"When do I meet the children?" I ask.

Mrs. Fairfax blinks. "There's only one."

I pause, my brow pinching. "I thought the ad said a boy and a girl."

"No. A daughter."

"What's her name?"

"Adele."

"Will I meet her today?"

"No," she replies.

I stare at the huge woman, waiting for her to elaborate. She stares back, waiting for me to crack. I grind my teeth. Does this bitch want me to grovel for answers? After several beats of silence, I purse my lips. Apparently, she does.

"Why can't I meet Adele?" I ask with a sigh.

"She's under quarantine."

The fork drops from my fingers, clattering against my plate. "Quarantine?"

"Typhus fever."

My throat tightens. I stare at the mask covering the lower half of her face. "Wait, how serious is that? I mean, is she okay?"

Instead of replying, Mrs. Fairfax disappears through the door again and pulls it shut.

I glare at the closed door. Seriously?

"Is she contagious? Should I be worried?" I ask with bite, even though I know she's pretending to be busy at work.

No answer. My nostrils flare. What's up with this

freak? If this is some kind of power game, then she's winning.

"What's wrong with Adele?" I ask, trying to mask my exasperation. "Has she had a diagnosis? And what's the point of bringing me here if she's contagious?"

"Mr. Rochester handles such matters," she says from the other room, her voice muffled.

If I had muscles the size of this she-gorilla's, I would rip open that door, slam her to the wall and order her to stop messing with me. But a woman on the run from law enforcement is in no position to make demands. That doesn't mean I'll put my health at risk. Mrs. Fairfax isn't just wearing that mask to hide a square jaw.

"What the hell does that mean?" My voice rises several octaves.

More silence.

I count to ten. Repeat my question. Count to ten again. Shoulders sagging, I continue with my breakfast. What the hell is she doing there? Waiting for me to leave? By the time I finish my plate along with a second croissant, I decide that backing down now would only give her the upper hand. So I ask her again.

A door creaks. My jaw drops. Did she fucking leave? I shoot out of my seat and throw down my fork.

"Mrs. Fairfax, are you still there?" I snap, ready to throw open that door.

"Typhus fever is highly contagious," a deep, velvety voice says from behind me. "But there's no need for concern."

I turn around, my pulse quickening. A man stands in the doorway in a charcoal suit tailored to his athletic frame. He's tall, elegant, with fathomless black eyes that make me forget every lie I rehearsed. Pressure builds up behind my ribs, a tightening that's equal parts fear and desire. The last thing I expected to find in a place like this was someone so lethally handsome.

He crosses the room, extending a hand. "Edward Rochester. A pleasure."

My boss?

He's in his early forties, with jet-black hair starting to gray in the temples, which only accentuate his strong brow, regal nose, and high cheekbones. His features are sharp and defined, perfectly aristocratic, and I'm already picturing what that mouth could do to me in bed.

I accept his hand. His grip is warm, firm and confident in a way that makes my nipples tighten. It's the kind of handshake that says he's used to taking control. I hold his gaze for as long as I can stand before my cheeks turn hot.

"Pleased to meet you," I manage. "I'm Annalisa. Annalisa Burlington."

He raises a brow, a slight smile playing at the corners of his mouth. As if he knows the name I've given him is bullshit. I try not to squirm in my seat.

Still maintaining his unwavering eye contact, he says, "I trust Mrs. Fairfax has helped you settle in."

"She has," I lie, swallowing hard. I had a question about his daughter, but I've already forgotten under that penetrating stare.

"The house can be disorienting at first. If you need anything, just ask," he adds with another disarming smile.

I nod, unable to relax. Just being in the presence of Edward Rochester steals my breath. I can't remember the last time I found a man so attractive. Or so familiar. Maybe I've seen his picture in the business pages? He looks like the type of high roller I would seek out in a club or a casino. Like the kind of man I've always wanted to approach but never dared. His type never comes alone to seek arrangements with girls like me. They're never short of sycophants and dates.

As he turns to leave, something panicked flutters in my chest. "Last night," I blurt. "The man who drove me here. Was that you?"

He pauses, his slight smile returning. The pulse in my throat throbs.

"No. Fairfax handles all our transportation."

My gaze darts to the door where Mrs. Fairfax disappeared, but it's still shut. I want to ask if the chauffeur is her husband, brother, or son. But it doesn't matter because there's still the question about why the hell I was brought into a house to look after a little girl with a contagious disease.

I want to ask, but I can't afford to give him a chance to change his mind. Still, I find myself saying, "If Adele is quarantined, then what exactly am I here to do?"

His smile widens, and for a moment, his eyes flicker with something predatory. "Why, make yourself at home."

Then he's gone, leaving only the faint scent of expensive cologne and the echo of his footsteps in the hallway.

I stare at the door he left through, my heart beating faster than it should. The silence feels weighted, expectant. Like I've just passed some kind of test. I'm not sure if I succeeded as myself, or as whoever Annalisa Burlington is supposed to be.

SIX

THE KEYHOLE

I enjoyed watching you wrestle with the dress this morning. It made me think of how you would writhe beneath me as you took your last breath.

Apologies for the odor, Annalisa, darling. The last girl's scent was particularly stubborn. I promise not to spill a drop of your blood on the dress.

Did you enjoy your breakfast, my little pet? I left a salty treat for you in the butter.

You ate with such vigor, I wonder how you will swallow it from the source.

Enjoy your time at the manor. Make it your home. You may even play at being its new mistress.

Because there is nowhere to run.

SEVEN

Breakfast leaves me feeling unsettled. Maybe it's the contagious fever. Or the rancid butter. But I'm in desperate need of a walk. I exit the house through the kitchen door and step out into a stone patio.

The morning sun cuts through the fog, revealing formal gardens that stretch toward a line of trees. But a distant roar draws me forward, making my chest vibrate. I can't see any signs of the ocean, but it calls like a siren song.

I follow a path through the gardens, past hedges trimmed into perfect geometric shapes that remind me of prison bars. With each step, the air grows saltier, and the roar gets louder until it drowns out my thoughts.

The path leads me through a gap in the hedges, and before I know it, I'm standing at the edge of the world.

I had no idea Rochester Manor had its own cliff. Black rock drops away beneath my feet, plunging down to an impossible drop. At the bottom, white foam crashes against jagged stones, making my insides lurch. The wind whips my hair across my face, carrying the taste of salt and something wilder. It almost reminds me of freedom.

Inhaling the sea breeze, I inch closer to the ledge until my toes hang over empty air. One step. That's all it would take.

The waves below are relentless, smashing against the rocks with a pulse-quickening violence. They pound the stone over and over, never stopping, never giving up. Like they're trying to tear the island apart.

Who would have thought I'd end up on the edge of the world? Who would have thought I'd have to run a second time?

The thought lands with a sting. When I was sixteen, I thought escaping Brother Matthew's house would lead me to true happiness. The kind Mom and Dad said was full of sin. Back then, it didn't matter that I was leaving everyone behind. Or that certain death awaited me if I ever returned. I pictured freedom, adventure, even love.

My first few months in Beaumont City were magical. Sure, I had to entertain a bunch of men, but being a sugar baby was a thousand times better than being a wife. I thought I'd made a fresh start.

But I'm back where I started. Hiding in a stranger's house, jumping at shadows, with yet another identity.

The wind gusts harder, and I wrap my arms around my middle to stave off the chill. Down below, something dark bobs in the foam, getting thrashed back and forth by the waves. It could be driftwood. Could be seaweed.

Could be a body, like the one I left behind.

I lean forward, trying to get a better look. The waves grab the object, slam it into the rocks, then drag it back out to sea before hurling it forward again. After a few rounds, it disappears beneath the water.

My breath hitches. Would it be so bad? To just let the sea take me?

Gil's face flashes through my mind. How he looked at me like I was garbage after his boss threw me out of the mansion. How he chose them over me again and again despite his sweet words.

I take a shaky step forward, almost mesmerized by the ocean. Maybe I'd be better off down there with the rocks and waves. Then I wouldn't have to keep running, keep lying, keep looking over my shoulder.

"What are you doing?"

The voice cuts through my thoughts like a blade. I whirl around, my heart slamming against my sternum.

Edward Rochester stands in the gap between the hedges, his hands clasped behind his back. Sunlight catches the silver at his temples, contrasting with his dark eyes. He stares at me with an intensity that makes my mouth go dry. The man is even more devastating in the daylight—sharp angles and masculine grace wrapped in a tailored suit.

My breath quickens, partly from the shock of seeing him here. Mostly from how his features look carved from marble.

"I was just…" My tongue darts out to wet my lips, and his gaze follows the movement. "Just looking at the view."

"I know what you were doing."

Fear punches me in the gut. My fingers go numb. Has he found out about the cop already?

"What do you mean?" The words tumble out in a panicked rush.

He takes a step closer, and the breeze carries his scent. It's the kind of expensive cologne that once made my knees go weak. "I stood at this very ledge when my wife died, wanting to smash my head on those rocks and end it all."

"No." I shake my head, trying to deny what he's suggesting, but he raises a hand and offers me a gentle smile.

"Grief makes us all consider things we shouldn't. I assure you, there's no judgment."

My shoulders sag with relief. I don't even know why the first thing I thought about was him discovering my secret. "How did you..." I swallow hard, trying to find my voice. "How did you cope with losing your wife?"

Something flickers across his features. It's a shadow deeper than pain. "Celine wouldn't have wanted me to grieve forever. She once told me that time can heal even the most shattered heart."

He places a hand over his chest. My pulse jumps. It's the exact same gesture the masked man made last night in the garden. I stiffen, too frazzled to work out what it means.

Without thinking about it, I also place a palm over my chest. "Does grief ever get better?"

The smile he gives me is wistful, warm, even welcoming. "After all this time, I'm finally ready for love."

My heart skips several beats. The way he's looking at me makes heat pool low in my belly, causes me to forget why I came to this cliff. Surely, he can't be talking about me?

"Come away from that ledge." He offers me the crook of his elbow.

I'm mesmerized. Mesmerized by his authority, the way his muscles strain against his jacket sleeve, the promise in his dark eyes. I step away from the cliff's edge and slip my arm through his.

He's tall enough that I have to tilt my head back to look at his face. When I do, I find the tension melting from his features, giving way to relief.

We walk back toward the gardens in silence, my arm tucked against his side. Heat rolls off his hard body through the fabric, making my head spin. I would bet my last casino chip that beneath the gentlemanly exterior, beneath that strong physique, beats the heart of a man who could ruin me in all the right ways.

As we pass the end of the hedges, he asks, "What brought you to such a remote estate?"

Panic claws up my throat. Shit. I thought we'd moved past this subject. I force myself to breathe, to think. "The job prospects looked good."

He chuckles, a rich sound that vibrates through his chest. "It's rare for a young woman your age to leave the bustle of Beaumont City for Helsing Island."

And he would have a point. Nobody in their prime would leave a vibrant metropolis for a backwater.

"Bad breakup," I mutter, keeping my eyes fixed on the stone path.

When he stops walking, it takes every effort to keep me from tripping over my feet. I gaze up to find his features grave.

"Did the man in question hurt you?"

I squirm, my insides writhing like snakes. Gil never laid a hand on me, but his treachery hurt worse than Brother Matthew's fists.

"It was more like a betrayal," I murmur.

He nods, his dark gaze boring into my soul. "And is he still in the picture?"

"Absolutely not," I say, meaning every word.

Mr. Rochester's eyebrows rise. "Are you still in love with this man?"

"No." The word comes out as a snarl.

Features lightening, his lips quirk into a pleased smile. "And you came here for a second chance?"

"Something like that." I glance away, not trusting myself to speak. I can't exactly tell him I came here because I'm wanted for murder. That would probably make him some kind of accomplice.

"What happened to your wife?" I peer at him through my lashes, desperate to change the subject.

"She died in childbirth." He continues walking.

"I'm so sorry," I say, stumbling to keep up.

He sighs, a sound that comes straight from the heart. "At the time, I felt utterly betrayed. We'd sworn to love and cherish each other forever. Then she left me alone."

The pain in his voice is so raw, so real that my heart aches for his loss. It reminds me so much of Gil's abandonment. And the gut-wrenching betrayal I felt the moment I realized Brother Matthew wanted me for more than just babysitting. We fall silent, walking down the path together in a shared understanding of loss and broken promises. Already like kindred spirits.

But I can't have a man I find attractive associate me with his dead wife. Or with grief. So I scramble for whatever I can say to shake off this somber mood.

"What is Adele like?" I blurt.

When he looks at me again, his whole demeanor brightens. "She's my pride and joy. Beautiful blonde ringlets, crystal blue eyes, and a smile brighter than the sun. You will adore her."

My chest unfurls with warmth, melting away my lingering doubts. It doesn't matter so much that my charge has a contagious disease or the housekeeper is creepy. Even last night's masked man doesn't seem so strange.

"How old is she?" I ask with a smile.

"She just turned five."

"I can't wait to meet her," I reply, already picturing myself with a stepdaughter instead of Brother Matthew's sons.

"Adele is excited to finally have female company," he says.

Something in his tone makes me wonder if he's talking about himself. I peer up at him through my lashes, finding him gazing down at me with an intensity that makes my stomach flip.

"Did you have much of a social life in Beaumont City?" he asks as we reach the house.

I think about the nightclubs and casinos, the cigar bars and hotel rooms. The endless stream of men who paid for my company.

"Not really," I mutter.

He raises his brows. "A beautiful girl like you would have been inundated with dates."

Heat crawls up my neck. "I actually liked the quiet life."

Pausing at the doorway, he places a hand on my shoulder, making me meet his dark eyes. Warmth shines in his handsome face, shadowed with something like longing. "Won't you find Rochester Manor boring?"

It takes every ounce of willpower to tear my gaze away from him and let it survey the house. I drink in its imposing facade, dark windows, and the ivy crawling up the walls. Any other time, I would find it creepy, perhaps even terrifying. But with Mr. Rochester here, it almost feels like my first safe haven since everything went to hell.

"This place is like a sanctuary," I say.

He cocks his head. "Why?"

My gut heaves. Damn it. I said too much. My mind whirs, struggling to reply. How the hell do I explain without giving myself away?

"What are you hiding?" he asks, his brow furrowing.

I shake my head. "Who, me? Nothing?"

"You have secrets."

"No, of course not—"

"Because I have to know for Adele's sake. Will my little girl's heart be safe with you?"

I inhale a sharp breath. The vulnerability in his voice tells me he's worried about his own heart. It's wishful thinking, even though my cheeks bloom with warmth. But I have to say something to hold his interest.

"My last relationship was abusive," I say.

It's not complete bullshit, since my marriage to Brother Matthew was beyond brutal. And Gil might have been perfect until he switched, but the way he discarded me was its own kind of cruelty. "A place like this will be a sanctuary from what I escaped."

His expression lightens with hope. "Could you ever see this place as your home?"

The yearning in his voice makes my pulse quicken.

"God, yes," I say, my voice breathy.

Mr. Rochester's hand on my shoulder tightens. And the look he gives me is pure intensity. I sway on my feet, feeling like we're standing on the precipice of something exhilarating.

"Miss Burlington?"

"Yes?" I whisper.

A muffled thump from inside the house draws his

attention away from our moment. "I must leave on important business. Will you still be here when I return?"

My heart thuds. My throat dries. The pulse between my legs comes to life. "Of course."

"Then please, be at ease here at Rochester Manor. This is your home as much as mine."

"I will," I say, breathless with anticipation.

With a nod, he strides through a set of patio doors and disappears into the house. I stare after him, my skin on fire. My hands tremble so much that I press them against my heart.

It wasn't in my head. He wasn't talking about me as an employee. Heat pools low in my belly at the promise of starting something with Mr. Rochester. I'm already aching for his return.

EIGHT
THE KEYHOLE

I heard the excitement in your voice. Saw the flush in your pretty cheeks that spread down to your glorious breasts.

Did your nipples tingle at the thought of being entombed here forever, my love?

In my domain, you will never age. You will, however, eventually rot.

But not until I've enjoyed every facet of your submission.

Tell me something, my sweet pet. Will your consent be enthusiastic, dubious, or non-existent? It matters little to me since you're already mine.

Sleep well. I will visit you tonight. There's no need to be afraid of me.

Not yet.

NINE

I haven't seen Mrs. Fairfax since that first breakfast, but every morning a meal shows up outside my door before I wake. Pathetic how I miss the woman I couldn't stand days before. Footsteps echo through the hallway in the evening as she retires to bed, but each night when I open the door, she's gone.

She wasn't joking when she said there were only two employees at Rochester Manor. There's her, and a groundskeeper who ignores me like I'm a ghost. Once, I ran across the lawn to introduce myself, but he vanished into the trees.

I'm so lonely I could die.

There's no sign of Mr. Rochester. I keep hoping he'll appear at my door, offer some assignment, or demand my attention. Anything. But he's gone. Like he was never real at all.

By the second week, I've lost track of the days. I eat, I explore, I sleep, I stare. Sometimes I check the same locked doors three times in a row, hoping they'll miraculously open.

I'm sitting in my room by the balcony, eating enough carbs to burst through my uniform, and wondering if I should hitchhike to see the rest of the island. The estate feels like a dream at the edge of the world. Forests at its front, cliffs at its back. Every time I try to leave, I freeze. Not from fear but from an overwhelming sense of dread. I'm not even agoraphobic.

One morning, I find another path leading down to the cliffs and reach a platform lower down on the rock face. Inside is an opening that looks like it's been carved into the stone. Beyond stretches a cave, or some kind of alcove. I almost turn back when I catch a glint of light.

Curiosity powers my feet. Or perhaps stupidity. But by the time I'm halfway in, a giant wave surges up and knocks me off my feet. The spray is cold enough to drive the air from my lungs, and before I can even recover, a wave barrels in, nearly dragging me off the ledge.

I stagger out, drenched, coughing out seawater, my heart beating so hard it rattles my teeth. After that brush with death, I stay the hell away from that side of the estate.

Another day, I explore the paths leading to the gates, finding thickets of trees on either side. The road stretching outside leads to infinity, and I remember the chauffeur driving us for miles. I venture into the estate's wooded area for the hell of it but stop when I find a creepy pet cemetery with crude gravestones.

Most of the names are written in childish script, with some names crossed out. It's like the keeper of this place is some kind of psychopath. My skin crawls, and the para-noia that's kept me alive wonders if the bones really belong to animals. Either way, I'm not about to stick around to investigate.

When boredom around the house becomes unbearable and silence pulls my last nerve taut, I remember how idle hands make the devil's work and find a duster in a supply closet. I wipe down every surface I can find, just to fill the hours. My arms ache from the work, and sweat drips down my spine. When I finally check my phone, it's only been thirty minutes.

Even prison is beginning to sound appealing.

At least in jail, I'd have cellmates. Someone to talk to, even if the guards want to shank me for being a cop killer. Here, I'm going insane from the silence. The only sounds are my own footsteps echoing through empty hallways and the wind rattling windows.

Every night, I still have the same haunting dream. The same man at the door. The same moonlight striping the floor like a stage. His chest rises and falls like he's been running. Or fighting. Or fucking. His hand trembles on the doorframe like he's about to push inside, but he never moves closer. Never speaks. Just breathes and stares and makes my skin crawl with terror and need.

The dream always ends the same way. I try to move, try to scream, but I can't produce anything but a frantic pulse. And in the morning, I wake up with a strange hangover. I tried not drinking the water. Skipping a day of meals. Ditching the soap. But nothing stops them. Something's in the air. I'm sure of it, but there's no one to tell.

My phone is useless. No signal, no Wi-Fi, just the time glowing back at me like a digital middle finger. The battery's on power save mode now, and I only use it as an alarm clock. Sometimes I walk the estate's perimeter with the phone raised toward the sky like some kind of prayer, trying to catch a single bar. Nothing. It's like this corner of the island is a dead zone. I try to tell myself that's a good thing. If I can't reach the outside world, it can't reach me.

Since Mrs. Fairfax never replaced the dress, I've taken to washing it by hand at night and hanging it from the curtain rod. But each morning, it's dry and folded on the foot of the bed, even though I lock the door every night.

After days of someone fucking with the dress, I've had enough. I leave the garment on the bed and stalk through the halls in search of Mrs. Fairfax to demand answers.

But there's no sign of life. No indication anyone's been living here at all. It's ridiculous because who else could be leaving out food every day? Eventually I give up and return to my room, where the dress is gone from the bed and already hanging in the wardrobe.

I don't remember putting it there, which means either I'm losing time... or someone's been in my room.

Most days, I try waking up early to catch Mrs. Fairfax before she delivers the food, but it's always there no matter what time I open the door. Once, I even sat by the door all night with my ear pressed to the wood, hoping to catch her footsteps. But at some point my eyes drifted shut. When I woke, the tray was already outside. Another time, I thought I saw a shadow slide past my keyhole. I yanked the door open, only to find the hall empty. I stay up late to wait for her, but the moment I hear a hint of movement, sleep takes me down like a drug.

I have no idea what the woman does all day, where she goes, or why.

One morning in the third week, I'm returning from one of my walks when I spot a figure in an upper window. She's blonde, pale, and gazing out at me like the princess in the tower. My heart skips. This has to be Adele. I wave, feeling like an idiot desperate for human contact, even from a little kid. But she doesn't wave back or even move away from the window. She just stares, motionless. Like a doll someone forgot to wind up.

I hurry back toward the manor, hoping to get a closer look at the girl. In my haste, I stumble over my feet and splay my hands out for balance. The next time I glance up, she's gone.

Damn it to hell.

At this point, I'd risk typhus fever just for the sound of another voice. Even as I search the interior, calling out her name, she never answers. Just silence.

Close to the end of week three, I catch sight of a shirt-less man in the orchard behind the lawn. He's black-haired, muscular, tan, and wearing faded jeans. His back is turned as he repairs what looks like a section of fence. My pulse stutters. Finally, another human being.

I hurry across the grounds, my heart racing with the prospect of actual connection. But the closer I get, the faster he seems to work, until he's packing up his tools and about to disappear behind a cluster of apple trees. If this is the same groundskeeper who avoided me last time, I'd better not scare him away with my thirst.

But by the time I reach the orchard, he's already taken his bag, leaving no trace he existed apart from the fresh tool marks in the wood.

"Hello?" I call out, cringing at my own desperation. "I just wanted to introduce myself!"

Nothing. Not even rustling leaves.

Determined not to be ignored again, I push deeper into the grounds, past the edge of the orchard bordered by large chestnut trees. My surroundings become overgrown, filled with unpruned shrubs. I continue onward, foliage snagging my uniform until I stumble into a cracked path leading to a gardener's cottage. It's nearly hidden behind a tangle of briar and honeysuckle.

The place looks abandoned to the elements. Moss grows on its roof, and the windows are spider-webbed with cracks. Yellowed curtains hang in the windows like dead skin. As I circle the structure, looking for signs of life, the hair on my body stands on end.

Someone's watching me.

I spin around, scanning the tree line, toward the windows of the manor house, anywhere eyes might be hiding. But there's nothing. No footsteps. No birdsong. Even the wind has stopped.

Or maybe it's the ringing in my ears.

A shudder tears down my spine. If this groundskeeper doesn't want to talk to me, I really shouldn't push. I turn on my heel and walk back to Rochester Manor without daring a backward glance, but I swear those invisible eyes bore into my spine the entire way.

That evening, I take the longest shower possible, letting the hot water pound against my neck until my skin feels blistery. When I step out in a towel to get dressed, I spot a folded piece of paper on the floor by my door.

I pad toward it, my breath quickening, and pick it up. In a neat, slanted script that belongs in a museum is a note that says:

You should have waved back.

The heat from my shower evaporates, and my blood turns to ice. Without thinking, I unlock the door and check the hallway, only to find it empty. Just shadows and the faint scent of medicine. I retreat into the room and examine the note. The writing is elegant, slanted, almost old-fashioned. Definitely male.

I pace my room like a caged animal, turning the note over in my hands. There's only one person who could have written that message: the masked man from the first night. He'd waved, but I ignored him. Now, he's pissed.

A sharp knock interrupts my spiral into paranoia.

I freeze, my heart rattling against my ribs. "Who's there?"

"It's Fairfax," says a familiar voice.

Shoulders sagging, I crack the door open, relieved at the sight of the older woman's massive silhouette. She's in the same black dress, same face mask, and the same hawkish glower.

"Yes?" I rasp.

"Mr. Rochester wishes to see you in his study."

"He does?" I ask.

"Now."

She turns and walks away, leaving me staring at her broad back. Her heavy footsteps echo down the hallway like drumbeats.

My heart flutters. Sensations travel south. Fear and anticipation knot together like barbed wire. Finally, after nearly a month of silence, Mr. Rochester wants my attention.

I don't care what he wants.

As long as he doesn't send me back.

TEN
THE KEYHOLE

You wander the halls like a lost child. You chase shadows across the lawn. I taste your hunger, Annalisa, not for company, not for food, but for my touch.

My dear, sweet girl. I am more than aware you still exist.

You think you're alone here. You think the silence is empty.

It isn't.

You ache to be seen, to be desired, to be fucked. But when I come for you, Annalisa, you will beg to be left alone.

Because, my pet, no one ever leaves Rochester Manor. Not unless I wish it.

Sleep, if you can. I'll be closer tonight.

You. Are. Almost. Ready.

ELEVEN

Ten minutes later, I stand outside the study in the east wing, my palms slick with sweat. My pulse pounds so hard that its reverberations reach my clit. Loneliness has my mind conjuring up a dozen different scenarios: the handsome widower professing his devotion, inviting me to sit on his lap or ordering me to bend over for his pleasure.

Lord knows it's been an eternity since I've had a man's touch. Sometimes, I hate myself for leading with my libido. But sexuality has kept me alive these past years. It's probably too late for me to change.

In a second, my pussy will become slick and urge me to flirt with Mr. Rochester. Shame washes through my veins like acid. Why does my body choose now to wake up?

Clenching hard, I force myself to breathe. This is just a meeting. Nothing more. Or an update on the little girl's typhus fever.

The thirsty bitch inside me keeps circling the timing of Mr. Rochester's summons. It was right after that hand-written note, telling me to wave back. Now I'm picturing him as the man from the lawn. The one who haunts my dreams, panting and thrusting, hidden behind that mask.

Shit. I really need to get laid. Or find something brutal enough to silence the relentless need.

Movement from behind the door snaps me out of those thoughts. I roll my shoulders, raise a hand and knock.

"Come in."

His voice hits low and deep, and my thighs clamp like they're trying to trap the sound. Suppressing a sigh, I step into a wood-paneled study lined with leather-bound books. A huge mahogany desk sits in the center, stacked with writing materials. An old fountain pen lies atop it, still dipped in ink. But the high-backed chair behind it is empty.

I step inside, wiping my palms on the skirt of my dress.

"Hello?" My voice echoes through the elegant space.

Silence. It's the kind that makes me shudder.

I turn, my gaze sweeping the room until I spot an alcove between two bookshelves I hadn't noticed from the door.

Seated behind a smaller desk tucked in shadow is Mr. Rochester. He doesn't look up, just continues writing with an old fountain pen. His dark hair catches the lamplight, accentuating the sharp line of his jaw. The muscles work beneath his skin as he concentrates.

Lamplight brings out the mahogany in his black hair, casting a bronze glow across his brow. It frames cheekbones sharp as blades and a jaw cut from stone. Rugged and brooding, he bends to his writing, lips pressed tight. I sigh. How can one man be so devastatingly beautiful?

I wait for him to look up. To acknowledge my presence. But he gestures toward a small wooden stool in front of his desk without lifting his eyes from his document.

"Sit."

My stomach dips, and I swallow back a surge of disappointment. Was I expecting him to gaze up at me and say something roguish? Maybe. I walk toward the stool, letting my heels click against the hardwood floor.

Most men would look up at this point to check out my footwear. Or at least glance up to see what's making the sound. Mr. Rochester acts as if he's immune to feminine company.

I settle onto the stool, which puts me slightly below his eye level. It's a power move, but I play along. The fabric of my dress pulls tight across my lap as I sit, exposing my thighs. One glance at Mr. Rochester tells me he's either completely disinterested or drawing out the tension.

Irritation has my jaw clenching. If he wanted me on my knees, he could have just said the word. And maybe that's what I find most frightening. Clearing my throat, I adjust my neckline, pull back my shoulders, and arrange my legs to their best advantage.

But he keeps writing.

Silence stretches, along with my last nerves. He remains so preoccupied with his work that my skin prickles. I fidget on the uncomfortable seat, crossing and uncrossing my legs. My molars grind. If he was so busy, why did he summon me to his office? Was it because I chased after that groundskeeper? Or snooped around the cottage? Or ventured back to the cliff? It can't be because I tried talking to that little girl. He would have said something earlier.

"Mr. Rochester—"

"One moment," he says.

I force back a huff, hating myself for speaking first. This time, I wait as if I don't give a damn. The man sitting in front of me is completely different from the one who told me to make myself at home.

Minutes pass, and I clench my fists to stop my fingers from drumming with impatience. Finally, without looking up, he speaks.

"Are you settling in well?" His voice is completely detached. Like he's asking about the weather. "How are you finding your new position?"

I lean forward, letting my voice drop to my bedroom register. "It's lovely, though I have to admit, I've been feeling a bit isolated."

"Mmm." He makes a note in the margin of whatever he's writing.

"Mrs. Fairfax mentioned there were only two of us working in the estate. But I saw a man—"

"How long have you been here? Two weeks?" he asks.

"Three," I reply, hoping he isn't about to say I'm no longer needed. Anxiety flutters in my gut as I imagine what might happen if he decides he no longer wants a nanny. In my most playful voice, I ask, "Edward, is this the part where you decide if I'm worth keeping around?"

He sets down his pen and finally meets my gaze. Those dark eyes sweep over my face with a cold, clinical assessment. A chill skitters down my spine as I wait for his reply.

"You were hired for the child, not for me."

The words hit like a slap. My confidence, already shaky, takes a nosedive. So much for breaking the ice with flirty humor.

I pivot to safer ground. "When do I meet Adele? Is she getting better?"

Mr. Rochester folds his hands, studying me like I'm a specimen under glass. "These things take time."

"I see her at the window," I say, fishing for information. "But she never waves back. Does she know I'm here for her?"

"Difficult to say." His tone is thoughtful, almost philosophical. Like we're discussing the meaning of life instead of his sick child.

I push harder. "Has she been seen by a doctor? I mean, isn't typhus fever serious? It's been nearly a month, and—"

"Mrs. Fairfax takes care of her needs." The dismissal in his voice is absolute.

Silence falls between us like a curtain, broken by the thud of my heartbeat, and the distant tick of a grandfather clock. I would ask why he brought me here when he knew the girl was sick, but if he orders me to leave, I'm beyond screwed.

Still, something about this situation is fishy. Nobody hires a nanny for a child too sick and contagious for company. And I've seen no sign of a doctor, let alone medicine.

Mr. Rochester's gaze drifts down, quick as a snake strike, to my cleavage. It's not salacious, just another cool, clinical observation, like he's cataloging my assets.

Breath hitching, I sit straighter, unable to tell if this is a good or bad sign.

He rises from his seat. "Thank you. That will be all."

My stomach dips. Wait. That's it? I rock forward in my seat. "What about the other staff? Who was that man?

And where does Mrs. Fairfax go during the day? I haven't seen her around since—"

"Miss Burlington." His voice cuts through my questions like a blade. "You are dismissed."

The words sting more than they should. Since leaving home, I've had all kinds of shitty encounters with men: I've been ghosted, dumped, coerced into murder. But never ordered out like a servant.

Mr. Rochester stares down at me, those austere features hawkish and impatient.

He doesn't need to tell me twice.

I rise off the stool on unsteady legs, smooth down my skirt, and meet his cold gaze before walking toward the door. It had been stupid of me to hope he wanted companionship. Men like Mr. Rochester aren't interested in the help. Even if they were, it wouldn't last longer than the time it takes for the cum to cool.

As I leave, he calls out, "Miss Burlington, one more thing."

I turn back, hope fluttering in my chest like a trapped bird.

"Address me as Mr. Rochester or Sir. We are not familiar."

The last of my hope dies a quick, ugly death. "Of course. Mr. Rochester."

I leave the study with whatever dignity I have left, but the house feels colder. Darker. The hallways seem longer, the shadows deeper. Every portrait on the walls seems to be judging me for thinking I had a chance of impressing the master of the house.

By the time I reach the second floor, I'm questioning why the hell he even summoned me to his study. And did I imagine that moment when his gaze lingered on my breasts? I'm probably so desperate for male attention that I'm mistaking indifference for interest.

A plate of food waits on the floor outside my room. I pick it up, lift the metal dome to find two slices of bread, a slab of meat, a pickle, and a blob of pale butter. No cutlery. No tray. No note. Mrs. Fairfax's meals have become progressively more basic. It's like I'm a prisoner being fed through a slot.

Sighing, I take it into my room, close the door, and lean against the wood. I kick off my shoes and try to console myself that tonight wasn't really a disaster. He wasn't even that attractive, but then no one falls in lust faster than a fugitive with nowhere else to stay.

I take the food to the small desk by the window and arrange the meat into a semblance of a sandwich, while I replay every second of our encounter. Mr. Rochester's detachment. His clinical assessment of my body. The way he looked at me like I was something to be cataloged and forgotten.

Maybe murder has made me lose my edge. Maybe I never had much of an appeal. The night I met Gil, I was more interested in his boss. But Gil swooped me up, took me to a storage room, and made me feel like dynamite. Now, it's obvious I was being handled. Powerful men always seem to be immune to whatever I'm selling.

I take one bite of the mystery meat sandwich, finding it overly salted, and follow it with another and another, washing down the dry fare with my refilled water jug. By the time I've finished, my eyes droop, and my stomach feels like lead.

A sharp knock against the window makes me freeze with a glass of liquid halfway to my mouth.

Then there's another knock, sounding like a pebble hitting the pane.

My pulse kicks up again, my system flooding with anticipation. I set down my water and walk to the balcony doors, my bare feet silent on the wooden floor.

Through the glass, I find the masked man standing in exactly the same spot as that first night. Moonlight cuts across the gardens, turning everything to silver and shadow. He stares up at me, unmoving, patient as death.

Then he waves.

This time, I don't hesitate. I raise my hand and wave back.

He rocks forward on his feet, and even through the mask, I can sense his pleasure. He beckons me down with one gloved hand. When I don't move, he mimics turning a key in a lock.

Panic shoots through my chest like electricity. I stumble backward, away from the window, my heart thudding. What the hell am I doing? What the hell is he asking me to do?

I shut the curtains, grab my water and down its contents. What the fuck? After making sure the doors are locked, I undress, retreat to my bed, and pull the covers up to my chin. Not like they can protect me from whatever game he thinks I've just agreed to play, but I'm out.

But even as I squeeze my eyes shut, I can still feel him down on that lawn. Watching. Waiting. Willing me to open that balcony door. And that pulse between my legs tells me I want to go to him more than I want to stay safe.

TWELVE

THE KEYHOLE

Annalisa, here I come.

THIRTEEN

Hours later, a sound jolts me out of sleep. It's the soft scrape of metal against wood. My eyes snap open in the darkness, my heart already racing before my brain catches up.

He's here again.

The masked man stands in my doorway, his silhouette cutting through the moonlight. Cold sweat breaks out across my brow and goosebumps prickle across my skin. My breath hitches in my throat like I've swallowed broken glass. He fills the entire space with his bulky frame, looking inhumanly large.

I lie still, expecting this to be like before. Him standing there, watching me sleep, getting his kicks from scaring me half to death. As usual, my muscles tense, ready to wait out another staring contest until he disappears back into the shadows.

But something's off.

Then a memory hits me like a kick in the gut.

I waved back.

Panic grips me by the throat and squeezes hard. The air thins, and the tips of my fingers go numb.

I hadn't been thinking straight. Not after that bullshit with Mr. Rochester. When the masked man waved at me, I responded. Gave him permission. Said yes to his sick game.

Is he here to collect?

When he steps forward, my pulse explodes. The masked maniac actually enters my room, snapping me out of my dream. Floorboards creak under his weight, the sound making my skin tingle with a confusing mix of anticipation and terror.

This isn't like before. This time, he's not my imagination. This time, he's real and coming for me.

He advances toward me again, and my body flinches.

Shit. What the hell have I done?

His shoulders widen, and his broad chest rises and falls in the semi-darkness, filling the room with his excited breaths. My heart slams against my ribs so hard that I groan. The sound fills my ears like thunder, setting every nerve ending alight.

I waved back. That was pretty much an invitation.

Hands scrambling for the sheets, I bunch them up to my chest like a shield. I want to squeeze my eyes shut, to will him away, but I keep snatching glimpses of that mask. Black fabric stretches tight over his face, obscuring his features. I can't even see his eyes. Can't tell if it's Rochester behind there, the groundskeeper, the chauffeur, or some psycho who swam over from the mainland to gut me like a fish.

He moves forward, each step a nail in my coffin. Maybe this is punishment for killing the cop, for escaping my pedo husband and his spawn, for thinking I could outrun Gil and his mobsters.

The masked man stops at the foot of my four-poster, staring down at me like I'm prey. I freeze, my body going rigid. Silence stretches between us like a wire about to snap, and my skin breaks out in a cold sweat. My chest heaves with shallow breaths that only scrape the top of my lungs.

With an almighty groan, he slams his hips into the footboard, making the bed shudder with the force of his thrust. Every instinct screams at me to run. But where the fuck will I go? Out the balcony? Off the cliff? Into that creepy forest? He'll catch me the moment I so much as twitch. This room is a cage, and his huge body is blocking my only safe exit.

"Who are you?" The words slip out in a whisper.

No answer. Just those hips grinding on the wood.

"Mr. Rochester?" My voice cracks.

Still nothing.

My throat convulses. My bed creaks from the force of his thrusts. His silence is worse than any threat. At least if he spoke, I'd know what kind of monster I'm dealing with. This is like being hunted by a ghost.

Something dark rises up through my fear. The same part of me that didn't hesitate when my husband's hands were around my throat. When I reached for that iron candlestick holder and taught him I wasn't taking any more of his abuse. The part that knows how to survive in a world full of predators.

If he plans on hurting me, I won't go out as a helpless victim.

I lower the sheet, revealing the gaping front of my nightgown. Its fabric is so sheer it might as well be nothing. A cold draft blows across my front, making my nipples stand on end. His hip movements falter for a heartbeat, and the air reverberates with his deep moan. I've never heard anything so animalistic.

Breath quickening, I clench my teeth, ready my fists. This maniac needs to know I'm not a terrified little girl.

"What are you waiting for?" I say, meeting his masked gaze. "Get it over with."

He lunges.

The movement is so sudden that my heart jumps into my throat. Gasping, I scramble toward the headboard, just as he rips off the edge of my bedsheet, exposing my thighs. Instinctively, I curl into myself, but he's faster.

His huge, gloved hand wraps around my ankle like a leather manacle.

"What are you—"

He drags me toward the footboard. I fall backward, my head hitting the pillow, my lips parting with a silent scream.

Then he brings my foot to his face.

What. The. Actual. Fuck?

Head tilting, he studies my sole like it's some kind of artifact. His hot breath fans against my arch through the gap in the mask, making my toes curl. The pulse between my thighs quickens with anticipation of what he'll do next. Then his tongue flickers out, and he gives my skin a quick lick.

I flinch, but a second hand wraps around my ankle, holding my foot in place. My lungs freeze as he takes a second taste, dragging his tongue along my sole from heel to toe.

The sensation shoots straight up my leg and settles in

my pussy. My hips jerk back but his grip tightens, inescapable as a steel trap.

"What are you doing?" I whisper without any force. Even in this befuddled state, I sound too breathy, too excited.

Ignoring me, he runs his mouth over the ball of my foot, his tongue painting wet trails across my skin. Then he takes my big toe between his lips and sucks.

The heat of his mouth sends a burst of sensation that makes me gasp. It's a bolt of unexpected pleasure. I writhe on my back, squeezing my thighs together as he sucks my toe like a popsicle. His deep, pleasured groans hit me in every sensitive spot. I jerk my hips, trying to get a little friction, but he releases my toe with a soft pop. Just as I think he's about to lick a trail up my calf, he moves to the next toe. And to the next. Like each one has a different flavor.

My clit throbs. The pulse between my legs roars back to life. My pussy clenches around nothing, and I can feel myself getting wet.

This is so fucked up. I should be screaming for Mrs. Fairfax. I should be kicking him in the face. Instead, I lie limp on the mattress, like he's already got his mouth between my legs.

His breathing becomes heavier. More ragged. He releases the final toe and presses kisses along the inside of my ankle, his tongue dragging across my skin like he's tasting something sacred. Each touch sends sparks racing up my leg, and each lick makes my pussy quiver.

I sink back against the pillows, my chest rising and falling with quick, shallow breaths. My hands grip the mattress so hard I'm in danger of yanking out the springs.

The rhythm he sets is tongue, breath, suck, stroke.

Like I'm an instrument he's playing and my moans are the music. Between each cycle, he murmurs something against my skin. Words I can't understand, but they sound desperate. Worshipful. Like I'm the goddess of feet.

My hips continue shifting, chasing non-existent friction. My nipples ache under the thin nightgown, and moisture drips into my ass cheeks. I never knew feet could be so sensitive. Like nerve endings wired straight to my clit.

He moves onto the other foot, his tongue swirling around my big toe. A fresh surge of pleasure spreads up my thighs, the sensation making my back arch off the bed.

"Oh fuck," I grind out, the words tearing from my throat.

He slams his hips against the footboard, rocking the four-poster with those powerful thrusts. He takes my toe deeper into his mouth, and I swear I can feel his teeth. The slight pressure sends another jolt straight to my core. All traces of terror give way to urgent need. Need for those strong hands to push open my thighs. Need for that tongue to ravish my pussy.

I drop my free leg open wider in invitation. I don't care if this is the chauffeur, the groundskeeper, or even Mr. Rochester. Not under the strain of this desperate desire. But when he doesn't take the bait, I cry out, exasperated, and he releases another deep, guttural moan. The sound vibrates against my foot, loud enough to wake Mrs. Fairfax. But I'm too far gone to care.

He drags his mouth down my arch again, his tongue following the curve like he's memorizing every inch. His grip on my ankle tightens, possessive and sure.

"Please," I say with a choked gasp. "Please, I need more."

I raise my hips, offering up my pussy. Hoping he'll understand my plea. Hoping he'll put his tongue where I really need it.

But he doesn't move higher. Just brings my foot back to his mouth and starts the worship all over again.

Suddenly, his entire body goes rigid against the bed frame. His breathing turns ragged, desperate. He moans again, longer this time, before I realize what's happening.

He's coming. From worshipping my feet. From boning my bed frame while he sucks my toes like they're the most erotic thing he's ever tasted.

My pussy throbs, empty and aching. Why would he hump a piece of wood when he has me?

His body shudders, then goes still. For several seconds, we both just stare at each other, our frantic breaths in sync. Then he lowers my foot to the mattress, like he's placing it on an altar.

Straightening, he backs away from the bed and walks to the door. Then he disappears into the hallway without a single word.

I'm left sprawled on the mattress, thighs still parted, nightgown rucked up around my hips. My foot tingles with remnants of his mouth and my pussy aches with unfulfilled need.

What the hell just happened?

I press my legs together, hating the wetness, hating myself for being so aroused.

He'll return tomorrow night. I have no doubt. And I don't even know if I'll be able to tell him to stop.

FOURTEEN
THE KEYHOLE

I saw how you writhed on the bed, arching your back, exposing that pretty wet cunt. You were needful. A desperate little thing.

That flush on your cheeks, the way your hips move, the way you ache only for me.

You're not the first I've watched in this room, Annalisa. But you might be the hungriest.

For now, I'll listen. I'll wait. I'll count the beats between your sighs. Until the day you'll beg for my hands. I shall wrap them around your throat. Then I'll gaze into those stormy blue eyes of yours while you beg me to stop.

You lie awake now, twisting in sweaty sheets, wondering if it was a dream. Perhaps it was. You'll find the answer the next time I return.

FIFTEEN

The next morning, I stand in the shower with one foot propped on the white porcelain edge of the tub. Warm water cascades down my body like I'm in a luxury spa instead of a creepy manor. Steam coils around me, and I wait for the usual groggy ache in my skull. But there's nothing. No hangover. No fog. Like someone's flipped a switch.

Last night wasn't a figment of an overactive imagination. The bruise on my ankle is real as hell.

Dark purple marks wrap around my skin like a bracelet. They're finger-shaped impressions that definitely weren't there yesterday morning. I run my thumb over them, pressing until they sting. The pain shoots straight up my leg and settles in my core with a throb that makes me bite my lip.

His hands were on me. He worshipped my feet. And I begged for more.

My pussy clenches at the memory of his tongue dragging along my sole, slow and deliberate. The heat of his mouth when he sucked each toe. The way he moaned against my skin like he was getting the best head of his life while grinding against my bed frame.

Any normal woman would be disgusted. Traumatized. Planning her exit. Instead, I'm standing under a hot spray, getting wet just thinking about it, wishing he'd done more than worship my goddamn feet.

I press harder on the bruise, using the pain to ground myself to reality. This is proof. Proof that I didn't dream the whole thing. Proof that a man was in my room, molesting my extremities.

The question is: who?

My mind keeps going back to Mr. Rochester. Because nothing else makes sense. That summons was a power play. He cataloged my assets like I was room service. But would a classy, aristocratic gentleman sneak into the servants' quarters to suck toes?

Maybe.

Rich men are kinky. Gil liked to fill all my holes with toys when we were fucking. Not to mention the masks. A guy from New Jersey I met at a club draped himself in leather, put a collar around my neck, and walked me around the hotel room like a dog.

Without warning, the water turns ice cold, making my stomach flip. I scramble out of the shower with a shriek. My nipples go rock hard from the shock, and I wrap myself in a towel. Even the plumbing in this place is torturous.

I jog out of the bathroom, dripping, delirious, desperate for a burst of warmth when I spot a folded piece of paper on the floor. Fingers trembling, I hurry across the room to pick it up. The handwriting is different this time, not the elegant script from yesterday's message, but simpler. Scrawled by someone untrained in the art of penmanship.

> *Mr. Rochester requests your presence for breakfast in the dining room. Seven A.M. sharp.*

My breath catches. This is it. Confirmation of my midnight molester. He probably wants the morning-after conversation, and I have no idea what the hell I'm supposed to say. *Thanks for the foot worship, boss. Next time maybe we could try actual penetration?*

Now I'm cracking jokes. This situation is so fucked up.

I get dressed, throwing on the black uniform that still strains across my tits, and run the towel over my hair. My hands won't stop shaking as I try to button the front, and I give up after the third. Let him see my cleavage. It'll remind him where his mouth should have been last night.

Goosebumps prickle up my arms. What is it with me and enigmatic men?

By now, I've memorized the house's layout from days of wandering around the estate. I hurry down to a lavish dining room boasting a long mahogany table large enough for twelve. But only two places are set. Morning sunlight streams through tall windows, casting everything in golden hues.

I marvel at the polished silverware, crystal glasses, fine china covered in metal domes, which match an elegant antique tea service. My mouth waters, and my stomach makes a loud gurgle, welcoming the change from salty sandwiches.

This is like a scene from a period romance where the heroine falls in love with the mysterious lord of the manor. Except I'm a fugitive who now has a foot fetish.

Just what I needed: a new kink when I should be focusing on survival.

I take a seat, my palms slick with sweat. The chair is more comfortable than anything I've sat in since fleeing Gil's penthouse. The napkin is actual linen, not paper. And the aroma coming from under that silver dome makes me groan with hunger.

My fingers twitch toward the plate, but I force myself to wait. Mr. Rochester probably wants to talk about our relationship... Or however you'd describe what happened last night. How the hell do you confront someone about toe sex over breakfast? Thank him? Pretend it never happened? Ask if he's planning an encore?

Before I can even rehearse what I need to say, the door opens with a soft click. Mr. Rochester strides in looking like he stepped off the cover of a romance novel. His navy three-piece suit fits his athletic frame to perfection, showcasing broad shoulders and prominent pecs. Instead of a tie, he wears a cravat, arranged in a wide knot.

He's freshly shaved, with his black hair curling gently around his brow. The man looks well-rested. Satisfied. Like he got exactly what he needed last night.

Which is a pity, because I'm a mess of unfinished business and confused hormones.

My gaze tracks his graceful movements across the dining room. My nostrils fill with the heady scent of cedar. I inhale, pulling his aura deeply into my lungs. Beneath all that tailoring is a man with unbridled lust. Lust a woman like me can satisfy if I can get a chance. I'm already picturing myself a permanent fixture in this manor, safe from my troubles and focused only on his pleasure.

"Good morning, Miss Burlington." He settles into the chair across from me in a fluid movement that screams old money and good breeding. "Did you sleep well?"

I study his handsome features, searching for a sign, a smirk, a sprinkling of knowing. Anything that hints of what he did to me last night. But his expression gives nothing away.

"Not as well as I'd like," I say, trying to hedge.

His lips curve into a tiny smile. "We'll have to see what we can do to help you sleep better, then."

My brain short-circuits. Is he talking about orgasms or melatonin? Because based on the throb between my legs, I could definitely use the former. Hell, I'd settle for him finishing what he started last night.

"Thank you," I squeak, trying to keep my voice steady.

Mr. Rochester lifts the silver dome from his plate, revealing eggs Benedict that looks like it came from a five-star restaurant. My brows rise. Maybe Mrs. Fairfax is good for something other than looming in the shadows.

I follow his lead, uncovering my own plate to find the same. He raises another dome, revealing fresh fruit arranged like artwork. On a third, flaky croissants that smell like butter and heaven rest in a pyramid. When I take one, I find that it's still warm.

"Coffee?" He raises a silver pot.

"Please," I say, my voice breathy.

When he pours it, I drool. The last time I had a cup was on my first morning here, before Mrs. Fairfax disappeared. Since then, it's been tea bags and hot water.

He slips off the jacket, revealing biceps bulging

beneath his cotton shirt. Then he turns his attention to the food, cutting precise bites with the silver cutlery. My gaze drops to the forearms flexing beneath his sleeves. And that mouth, those strong lips I can't help imagining between my thighs instead of around my toes.

Should I say something? I shake my head. Last time I spoke first, he put me in my place. He's the one who issued the invitation. He should start the conversation.

Mr. Rochester eats with controlled hunger, like a man who knows exactly what he wants. Each bite is deliberate, savored. The way he brings the fork to his lips makes my toes turn.

My nipples tighten under the dress, and sensation travels south. Arousal is an unwanted guest at this breakfast, but I can't make it leave. Lord knows I wish I could blame it all on adrenaline.

I've seen men tear through food like hogs, stuffing chunks in their mouths, wiping fingers on shredded napkins, tonguing bites behind their teeth to make room for a swig of beer. It's the first time I've seen a man eat so quickly with so much grace. Mr. Rochester cuts delicate portions with the speed and precision of a surgeon working against the clock. His appetite is bigger than any man's I've ever seen, but he gorges himself with class.

When he swallows, I'm mesmerized by the movement of his throat. How would it feel to pepper that neck with kisses?

He pauses mid-bite, the fork halfway to his mouth, and stares across the table at me with those fathomless black eyes. The sudden attention makes my pulse spike.

"Are you not hungry?" he asks, his voice lilting with amusement.

"Yes," I blurt and cut into my eggs Benedict.

Yolk spills onto the Hollandaise sauce, and I try not to make a mess. The meal is exquisite. I can't help but wonder why Mrs. Fairfax only pulls out all the stops when Mr. Rochester is at home.

"I have a favor to ask you." He sets down his fork and gazes at me like I'm the only woman in the world.

Tension explodes through my chest like a bomb detonating. This is it. He's going to acknowledge last night. Ask if we can make this a more permanent arrangement. I picture myself floating around the manor in beautiful dresses during the day and sleeping with him in the master bedroom at night.

But what if I'm wrong? He's had enough time to check my bogus references. He might even accuse me of something heinous. Or tell me to pack my bags and blame me for being inappropriate.

"What kind of favor?" I rasp.

"Adele's condition worsened overnight," he replies with a frown. "Mrs. Fairfax took her to the mainland for proper medical treatment."

The words hit me like a bucket of ice water. Mrs. Fairfax is gone. So is the little girl. Which means I'm alone in this estate with Mr. Rochester and whoever else might be lurking in the shadows.

And just like that, the fantasy of my perfect hiding place evaporates into steam.

"Are you asking me to leave?" The question tumbles out before I can stop it, my voice cracking with panic. "I mean, if there's no child to care for..."

If they don't need a nanny, they don't need me. And if I have to leave this island, I'm dead. If Gil's people don't find me within hours, the FBI will drag me back in handcuffs. I'll be facing murder charges and a death sentence before I can explain my innocence.

"Quite the opposite," he says, his voice smooth as satin. "With Mrs. Fairfax away, I was hoping you might handle a few household tasks."

Relief floods through my system so fast my head spins. I still have shelter. Still have time to figure out my next move.

"Of course," I blurt. "Whatever you need. I'm happy to help."

He inclines his head. Gives me a wintry smile but doesn't reply. My breath quickens. Why isn't he accepting my offer?

I lean forward, trying not to sound desperate. "I can do everything around the house. I can clean... cook. I know all the basics and can make fancy dishes. Just as long as there's a recipe book."

His eyes flicker with something that might be interest. "Then I look forward to tasting you."

My brain stalls. My pussy clenches. Every nerve ending springs to life. Did he just...

"Excuse me?" I ask, my voice breathy.

"Your cuisine," he says, but there's something in his eyes—a smoldering heat, a touch of humor—that makes me think I didn't imagine the double entendre.

"Right. Cooking." I take a gulp of coffee. "I won't disappoint you."

He stands with that same fluid grace. Then he slides on the jacket with an elegance at odds with how he handled my foot last night. Each gesture is controlled, deliberate, like he's choreographed his entire existence.

"Wonderful," he says, pushing in his chair. "I'll leave you to settle into your new responsibilities."

He strides out of the room, leaving me alone with my throbbing heart and his manly scent.

I sit at the table, stunned, unable to complete this beautiful breakfast. My pulse won't stop racing. One brief conversation has thrown me from hopeful to fearing for my survival, and back to hope. No matter how many times I replay his words, I get stuck on one thing: he wants a taste of me.

Not my food. Not my feet. Me.

I study the chair he vacated, trying to reconcile that calm, controlled man with the desperate beast who came in his pants while humping my bed. The disconnect is staggering. Rochester moves through the world like he owns it, completely self-possessed. But the man in my room was hungry. Feverish. Almost reverent in his need.

Could they really be the same person? Or am I so eager for answers that I'm seeing connections that don't exist?

Maybe the isolation is getting to my head. Maybe I'm losing my mind on this Godforsaken estate, creating elaborate fantasies to cope with the loneliness.

But the bruises on my ankle are real. So is the memory of his tongue on my skin. A man was definitely in my room last night. The same man who left me that note asking me to wave back.

The question is: who?

After eating, I carry the plates to the kitchen, still trying to find answers. A pile of dirty dishes sits in the sink. Mrs. Fairfax must have left this morning with Adele in a hurry.

And there's something new on the counter by the spice rack. A torn piece of paper, ragged along one edge like it was ripped from a notebook. It's set square to the counter, as if someone measured it with a ruler.

I approach it with a frown.

The handwriting is cramped, irregular, like the writer was in a bad temper. At the top is the name I'm using: Annalisa Burlington.

And beneath that, a list:

Gather fresh eggs – beware of the rooster

Prepare stew base with rabbit in cooler (debone completely)

Polish west-facing windows (ladder in garden shed)

Oil all door hinges (start with guest quarters)

Boil linens – use cellar basin

Change guest linens on first floor

Sweep and mop grand foyer

Arrange flowers in main hall

Wipe down portrait frames

Scrub guest room fireplaces (check for nests)

Beat dust from hallway and guest room rugs (use line behind house)

The list keeps going with a string of empty checkboxes next to each item. It's detailed, deliberate, like someone's been planning these tasks for weeks.

My jaw drops. "Didn't know I was being hired as a housemaid."

This isn't the light household help Mr. Rochester made it sound like over breakfast. This is full-scale domestic drudgery. Scrubbing fireplaces? Deboning rabbits? What's next, mucking out stables?

I have no idea how to prepare rabbit. I've never seen a cellar basin in my life. And who warns someone about a rooster like it's a guard dog?

But what choice do I have?

I fold the paper and shove it in my pocket. Looks like I'm getting housebroken.

SIXTEEN
THE KEYHOLE

I saw the hope die in your eyes this morning. You thought breakfast was your chance to become the lady of Rochester Manor.

It was not.

However, my plans for you are proceeding nicely.

I enjoy the way your breasts jiggle when you're on your hands and knees, scrubbing the floors. I can almost taste the sweat seeping through that delightfully restrictive dress.

You're learning humility so you can truly belong to me.

Keep toiling, sweet girl. Teach your body where it belongs. Keep earning your survival lest you end up like the others.

Whether you're good or not, I will claim you. The only choice you have is how much it will hurt.

SEVENTEEN

At sunset, I drag myself up the stairs like a broken-down workhorse, every muscle in my body screaming for mercy. The dust coating my hair is so thick I could pass for a freshly dug corpse. Scratches burn along my forearms, still fresh from tussling with that psychotic rooster. The bastard drew blood over his precious eggs.

My back aches from hunching over cellar stairs I suspect haven't seen bleach since the house was built. The stone steps were slick with God knows what, and I spent an hour on my hands and knees scrubbing grime that multiplied the harder I worked.

All this to stay hidden from the feds. Every blister, every bruise, every bit of backache is the price of not getting dragged back in cuffs or in a body bag.

I only managed a quarter of the list before my body collapsed. And the worst part of it all is that I'm being played. Mr. Rochester said it was a few tasks. Now I'm a full-time servant doing the work of ten. If I refuse, will he replace me with someone else? Probably.

Shit. I need to wash off the day before I lose my mind.

After pushing open my bedroom door, I trudge into the bathroom, which feels like a sanctuary after today's household hell. I peel off my ruined uniform and grimace at the new bruises blooming across my knees and shins. The black dress is torn at the shoulder seam, stained with dirt and what I'm pretty sure is chicken shit.

"Fuck that bastard," I mutter under my breath, although I'm not sure I'm talking about Rochester or the rooster.

I turn on the shower, step under the spray, and grab the soap. The hot water pounds against my sore shoulders, washing away layers of grime and sweat. A groan escapes from deep in my chest, and I let my muscles sag. Steam rises around me like a protective cocoon, and for the first time all day, something feels good.

Tipping back my head, I soak my hair and lather up my aching muscles. The soap's lavender scent fills my nostrils, making me feel almost human. Tomorrow, I'll tell Mr. Rochester the workload is too heavy, but not so much that we need to bring in another employee. New people mean more chances of getting exposed.

Just as I reach for the shampoo, the lights cut out.

Darkness swallows the bathroom whole. My heart slams against my ribs, and my fingers go limp. I fumble for the shower tap, skidding on the dropped soap. The water continues to pound down on my back like torrential rain.

Before I can turn off the spray, a large hand covers mine.

"Relax."

The voice is deep. Commanding. Familiar. I swallow back a scream.

Strong hands settle on my shoulders, thumbs pressing into the knots of tension along my neck. The touch is firm, confident, like he owns my body and knows exactly how to handle it.

"Who—" I start, but he cuts me off with a low growl.

"Hush." His breath heats my ear. "You've had a long day. And I know exactly what you need."

Every survival instinct screams at me to run, to fight. But my muscles go rigid. The hands on my shoulders know exactly where to touch and how much pressure to apply. I melt under his touch like butter in a hot pan.

"Isn't it better for both of us when you're obedient?" he murmurs, working his thumbs deeper into my knots.

Hot water cascades over us both. His hard chest presses into my shoulders, and his hard cock presses into my back.

"Edward?" I groan.

"Rochester," he growls, his voice rough.

Heat pulses through my core at the sound of his name. There's no question of the masked man's identity. It was him. And now, Mr. Rochester is naked in my shower.

He slides his hands down to my shoulder blades, massaging away the tension. Each touch sends sparks racing through my nervous system, and I arch into him like a cat in heat.

"Such a good girl, helping out with the house. You worked so hard today," he murmurs against my neck, his lips ghosting against my skin. "I'm impressed."

The praise hits me like a drug, flooding my heart with warmth. When was the last time someone called me good? When was the last time someone appreciated my efforts instead of just demanding more?

"I tried to do everything on the list," I say, my voice breathy.

His mouth moves to the spot where my neck meets my shoulder, and I shiver despite the hot water. "That's my obedient girl. You're finally learning your place."

My place?

Before I can make sense of that comment, his hands roam around my front, skimming my ribs. The words ring like an alarm bell at the edge of my mind, but the heat building between my legs won't let me search for answers. I grip his wrists, try to guide him to my aching breasts. But he pulls back.

"Good girls wait their turn for pleasure. Are you the good girl who gets her reward or the bad one who gets nothing?"

Heat fills my cheeks—shame mixed with arousal in a way that makes my head spin. I've never had to ask for what I want. Men usually just rush to the good parts.

"Talk to me, pretty pet." He pulls me close, his chest brushing my back, and slides a hand down the curve of my hip. "I can make your thighs quiver. Keep you on edge for eternity. Make you moan your deepest, dirtiest secrets, just for a taste of my pleasure."

I shiver, wanting to cling onto a shred of pride, but his lips graze my ear. "Hold your silence, and I'll have you sobbing for sweet release. Continue being tight-lipped and I'll strip you of everything you hold dear. Or you can promise to be good and let me lavish you with ecstasy."

"I'll be good," I murmur.

He chuckles, low and deep. "Excellent choice. Now, tell me what you need."

"Please," I rasp.

"Please what? Use your words, my beautiful little plaything."

Is this man really going to climb into my shower and

make me beg? The silence stretches between us, filled only by my ragged breath and the spatter of water. The hands skimming my ribs make maddeningly teasing circles, making every nerve ending tingle with need. He's waiting, and I know he won't give me anything until I say the words.

"Please touch me," I manage.

"Where?" His voice is patient, laced with steel. He won't make this easy.

"My breasts. Please touch my breasts."

"Good girl knows what she wants. I like that." The approval in his voice makes my nipples tighten. "Since you asked so nicely, I'll give you exactly what you need."

His fingers slide up my ribcage until he reaches my breasts and cups them with both hands. Tingles skitter across my flesh, and I gasp at the contact. Then he rolls my nipples between his thumbs and forefingers.

I try to turn around, to touch him back, but his arms tighten around my shoulders, holding me in place.

"No moving without permission or the pleasure will stop."

The command sends a jolt straight to my core. No one this sexy ever talked to me like I'm something to be directed, controlled, or owned. It should piss me off. Instead, it floods my pussy with heat. I can't remember ever being so wet.

"These tits," he growls, cupping them tighter. "These beauties have been testing that poor dress since day one. Straining like they're desperate to break free."

A moan escapes my lips. It feels like I've been waiting for him to touch me like this my entire life.

"I can't tell you how much I've been aching for this body, every curve. To claim what's been teasing me for so long. Look at you, writhing beneath my fingers, trying to take charge."

"Oh god."

"Call. Me. Rochester," he growls, his cock nestling between my ass cheeks.

"R-Rochester!"

"Naughty little nymph. Don't you know it's me who controls what you feel?"

"Please," I cry out.

His hands slide down my belly, fingers trailing through the water over my skin. When he reaches the apex of my thighs, I spread my legs wider, wanting more.

"Eager little slut," he says, his voice lilting with a smile. "You moan for me so prettily. Do it again."

I lean against his broad chest, panting hard, not quite believing this refined gentleman wants me to talk dirty. When he slides his fingers away from my sex, threatening to withdraw the pleasure, I blurt, "Touch my pussy."

He chuckles again, deep and rich. "And what do you want me to do with that sweet little cunt? Is she wet? Is she aching?"

"Yes," I moan. "Oh, fuck. Stroke my clit."

"Like this?" He slides his hand lower, over my thatch of pubes to where I need him the most.

The words flow better now. Maybe the darkness makes it easier to be shameless. "Just like that. Please, I need it so bad."

He tilts his hips, his thick cock sliding between my cheeks. I lean against him and moan. Then he ghosts his fingers over my outer lips, giving only the barest hint of sensation.

"How badly?"

"So bad it hurts. I've been thinking about it since last night, since you—"

"Since I what?"

"Since you sucked my toes," I finish, my insides burning with desire.

When he glides a finger over my swollen clit, my knees buckle, but a strong arm around my waist keeps me upright.

"And what did you think about?" he asks.

His finger circles my entrance, collecting the wetness, but he doesn't push inside. The teasing touch makes me squirm against his larger body, desperate for more.

"I thought about your tongue. I couldn't stop thinking about your mouth. I wanted it everywhere. On me. In me."

"Greedy little thing." His finger slips inside me just to the first knuckle, then withdraws. "But you don't get what you want just because you ask for it."

I whimper at the loss of contact, my hips bucking forward on instinct. But the moment I shift, he pulls his hand away.

"What did I say about moving?" he growls.

My mind goes blank. I can't remember anything beyond this aching need. But I've been with enough dominant men to know what he wants. "I'm sorry," I say with a gasp. "I'm sorry. I'll do anything. Just please don't stop."

"I won this body. Every pretty curve. Every delectable inch. You don't get to move. You take what I give you and don't come until I say. Is that understood?"

"Yes... Yes, I understand."

"Yes, what?"

"Yes, Mr. Rochester."

"Better. Now, hold still while I pet your pretty pussy. I'm going to make you purr."

"Yes, sir!"

A growl reverberates against his chest. It's feral, animalistic, and deep. I shiver against him, my legs trembling with anticipation. He slides one finger into my entrance while his thumb finds my clit, circling it with just enough pressure to make my eyes roll to the back of my head.

Fuck. This is everything. I never knew the man in the three-piece suit I met my first morning could be so skilled. I bite down on my bottom lip, panting through his ministrations as he teases me to the brink of madness. But every time I build toward a climax, he changes the rhythm. A moan slips from my lips. This sexy bastard keeps backing off just enough to leave me on edge.

"Please," I whisper, my voice breaking. "Please let me come."

"Not yet." A long, thick finger curls inside my pussy, finding that spot that makes my vision blur. "Beg for my touch all you want, but you don't get that orgasm until you admit you belong to me."

If I wasn't so desperate to climax, I'd keep him waiting. Instead, I play along. "I do."

"Tell me."

My hips jerk again, trying to chase the friction, but he stills his fingers, depriving me of pleasure. A moan reverberates in my throat. This man is driving me insane with the teasing. "You. I belong to you."

"Who?" He curls his digits.

I gasp. "Y-you. Mr. Rochester."

"That's right." His thumb presses hard against my clit, bringing me so close to climaxing that I cry out. The sound echoes off the tile walls, adding to the delicious tension. "You're mine now. My little servant, my good girl."

The words should piss me off after all the shit I've escaped. I'm no one's servant, no one's possession. But something about Rochester makes me want to submit. Maybe it's the sexy voice. Maybe it's the way he plays my clit like a concerto. Instead, his words send me spiraling higher, my body responding to his possessive praise.

He adds a second finger, stretching my walls. He adds a third, and it feels like more than just digits. Like he's trying to own me from the inside. His thumb works my clit in tight circles while those thick fingers pump in and out with a rhythm that drives me insane. I lose track of my history, my troubles, and become nothing but sensation. All I can focus on are his hands on my body, the water streaming over our heads, the filthy words he whispers in my ear.

"You love this, don't you?" he growls. "You love being told what to do in the dark. You love being owned by a man you can't even see."

The thought of giving myself completely to anyone is terrifying, but he's right. I need his protection. I need his pleasure. And damn it, there's a part of me that preens at being his property. Shit. I want to be owned by Rochester.

"Tell me something, little toy." His voice is dark velvet, curling around my spine. "You love being owned by me. Controlled by me. Wrecked by me. Say it. Admit you love being used."

"Yes," I sob. "Yes, I fucking love it."

"And you want this game of ours to continue?"

"Please," I cry, my hips jerking.

"Then you'd better come on my fingers like a

desperate little slut. Show your master who owns this pretty pussy."

"Fuck," I scream.

His digits quicken around my clit, and the thick erection rubs against my back. Rochester continues his filthy tirade until an orgasm hits me like a torrent. Molten ecstasy rips through my body with such devastating force, my legs buckle. He wraps an arm around my waist to keep me from face-planting into the tile.

"Come, little pet. I've got you," he groans as wave after wave crashes over my senses.

I ride the rhythm, my pussy clenching around his fingers. I babble things I won't remember, shuddering against him until my body folds in on itself like it's trying to collapse. Pleasure destroys every coherent thought, drowning out his words of comfort.

When the orgasm finally subsides, I lean back against his chest, boneless and shaking, feeling his heart pounding against my spine, feeling his cock still hard and demanding against my back. Hot water continues to pour over us both, washing away the last of my doubts.

I've never felt so completely and utterly conquered. Or so full of euphoric hope. He's keeping me despite his daughter leaving for the mainland because he needs me as much as I need him. I get it now. This lonely widower yearned for companionship, and I'm the one who can fill his heart.

My eyes flutter shut, and I sigh as he lowers me to the tub, feeling safer than I have since arriving on this cursed island. If he wants to fuck, he's going to have to take me from behind because I'm spent.

But he presses a kiss to the top of my head, so gentle it makes my chest ache. "Rest, now."

Before I can ask what he means, he steps out of the bathtub.

"Wait," I murmur.

Footsteps pad away in the dark, and the door clicks shut. The water turns cold, shocking me back to reality. I'm sitting naked in the tub, my body still humming with aftershocks, and Rochester has left without demanding anything in return.

What did I do wrong?

I struggle to my feet on unsteady legs, grope around the walls with shaking hands and turn off the tap. My mind buzzes, charged with the memory of what the hell just happened. I can still smell him, still feel the ghost of his touch on my skin.

Questions crowd my brain as I fumble around for a towel. How did he get into my room? How did he know I was showering? Has he been watching me this whole time? And more importantly, why on earth isn't he staying the night?

———

The next morning, after the most relaxing sleep I've had since the murder, I wake before dawn. My body still sings with the memory of Rochester's hands. My spirits still soar with ecstasy from last night and my chest warms at the prospect of seeing him again. I know he's my masked admirer, and I know he wants me.

Last night changed things between us and marked the start of something important. He claimed me, called me his property, wants me to stay. It might be foolish to hope this means anything real. But I can't help it. This is exactly what I need.

After dressing, I hurry to the kitchen to make a special breakfast for two. It's a perfect French omelette with herbs I found growing in the kitchen garden. The toast is golden, the butter soft, and I use a fancy Earl Grey blend of tea that smells like heaven.

I set the dining room table with a bouquet of wildflowers from the garden arranged in a crystal vase between our places. My heart flutters. I want this to be the start of something intimate.

But there's no sign of him at 7:05. At 7:15, the omelette cools, but I refuse to start without him. Eating with him yesterday meant the world to me, and last night changed it forever. He didn't promise we'd have breakfast together every morning. But after those words he growled in my ear, I thought we would.

At 7:30, my stomach revolts. I lift the lid off the plate and finally take a bite, but the food tastes like ash. He's not coming. Whatever I thought last night meant, I was mistaken.

Ten minutes later, as I'm finishing my cold eggs, the front door creaks open. My heart leaps, and regret settles into my gut. I should have waited.

Smoothing down my dress, I hurry out of the dining room and down the hallway toward the foyer, my pulse racing with anticipation. I don't know what I'm expecting: an apology? A repeat of last night? At the very least, some acknowledgment that I didn't imagine what we did in the dark.

Mr. Rochester steps inside in a charcoal three-piece suit, but he's not alone.

A woman in a cream cashmere coat glides through the front door like she's walking a red carpet. She's tall and willowy, with glossy black hair pulled back in a perfect chignon and cheekbones sharp enough to cut glass.

She moves with an ease I'll never possess. Polished. Controlled. Nothing like me. She surveys the foyer like she owns it, with the indifference of a lady used to entering grand mansions.

A second man limps behind her, carrying a matching set of Louis Vuitton luggage. A chauffeur's cap sits low on his face, obscuring his features, but I'm too freaked out by this female interloper to care.

"Blanche," Rochester says, his voice rich with affection. "Welcome to Rochester Manor."

Blanche. Of course her name would be something so perfect.

She turns in a slow circle, taking in the grand staircase, the oil paintings, the crystal chandelier. When her gaze lands on me, hovering in the hallway like an unwanted shadow, her lips curve into a smile that doesn't reach her eyes.

"How perfectly charming," she says, her voice carrying the faintest hint of a British accent. "And you must be the help."

The words hit me like a slap. Not Annalisa. Not even who are you? Just the help. Like I'm a piece of furniture.

Mr. Rochester's eyes flick to mine. There's no recognition. No heat. No trace of the man who held me while I shattered around his fingers. Just the cool glance of a man dealing with an employee.

"Miss Burlington, may I present Miss Ingram, my fiancée."

EIGHTEEN
THE KEYHOLE

Spreading your legs in the shower only piqued my interest. It barely makes you safe.

You think I cared how delightful you sounded begging? It's nothing compared to how a woman sounds when I make her choke.

I'm not testing how prettily you moan, my sweet. I'm testing how well you endure.

Crawl for me, little Annalisa.

Be useful. Learn your place.

Or you'll end up rotting underground like the others.

NINETEEN

My fiancée.

The word slices sharper than a knife to the gut. My face freezes into a blank mask, but on the inside, I'm bleeding.

Blanche saunters over to Rochester and leans into him like she's staking a claim. He slips an arm around her waist and pulls her into his side. The pair of them stare back at me—her smirking, him unreadable. I can't tell if they want me to curtsey, grab her Louis Vuitton luggage, or drop dead. Instead, I gape, my breath shallow.

The silence stretches between us until Rochester finally clears his throat. "Breakfast for two, Miss Burlington."

"Of course," I say, my voice distant.

Before either of them can order me to take her bags, I turn toward the hallway. My legs wobble, like they're on the verge of collapse, and the marble floor feels like a chessboard with me as the sacrificial pawn. Dead aristocrats on the walls follow my retreat, their smug faces saying I don't belong.

Fiancée. He has a fucking bride-to-be.

How could I have been so stupid?

The pieces slam into place with sickening clarity. The mask, the darkness—all those strange kinks were plausible deniability, so I could never be sure it was him.

Rich men don't have relationships with the help. They just take what they want, leaving women like me with the bitter taste of feeling used.

Gil did the same thing, didn't he? Made me feel special, wanted. But when he had to choose between his bosses and our relationship, he handed me over like a tithe. I should have seen this coming. Should have known a man like Rochester wouldn't waste precious time on someone like me.

By the time I reach the kitchen doorway, my chest is so tight that I'm barely getting air into my lungs. I stumble inside and cling to the counter's edge, holding tight as the room tilts sideways.

"Get a grip," I say to myself through clenched teeth, but it's futile.

The way he touched me last night, his masterful commands, his declaration of ownership all felt real. The praise when I submitted to him, the gentle way he caught me when my legs collapsed. All of it just another performance. Another wealthy bastard amusing himself while his real life waited in the wings.

Shit.

How the hell am I spiraling? This isn't even new.

I stalk toward the refrigerator and fling open the door, reminding myself I have more to worry about than being used by another rich asshole. Even if he disgusts me now, I can't gather my dignity and leave. He's the only thing keeping the cops off my back.

Hands shaking, I take some eggs and crack them into a bowl. The yolks break and bleed into the whites like wounds seeping into snow. I whisk them harder than necessary, working out my rage on the breakfast ingredients.

Muscle memory is the only thing keeping me functioning. I make the same French omelette I prepared for this morning's romantic breakfast, then add the same fresh herbs and sides.

When I carry the plates into the dining room, Rochester sits buried in his newspaper, and Blanche leans back in her seat, examining her manicure with bored elegance.

She glances up as I approach, her dark eyes raking over my tight uniform with obvious amusement. "Mrs. Fairfax, isn't it?"

Clenching my teeth, I set down her plate. "It's Annalisa Burlington."

Her brows rise as if we weren't just introduced half an hour ago. "Edward mentioned hiring a nanny, but I assumed you were Fairfax."

Heat floods my face. I walk around the table and set down Rochester's plate. He doesn't even look up from his newspaper. He just sits there like I'm invisible, like his fingers weren't in my pussy hours ago, like he wasn't calling me his good girl while I came apart on his hands.

"You know, based on your bulk," Blanche adds, her gaze following me across the dining room.

This bitch is testing my limits. Daring me to say something, to strike back. I grind my teeth, not letting this woman goad me into getting fired.

"Mrs. Fairfax is away," I say, the words clipped. "I'm filling in."

"How versatile of you," she says, her gaze flicking down to my chest.

My throat tightens. I should walk out while I still have my self-respect, let her fester with her two-timing fiancé. But as I turn to leave, Rochester clears his throat.

"Miss Burlington." His tone is cool, distant. "Air out a guest room for Miss Ingram."

I stiffen, my stomach tightening. Then I turn around to find Blanche glaring across the table at Rochester.

"Edward, darling, surely we were going to share."

Rochester finally looks up from his paper, disinterested. "Not before marriage, my dear."

Triumph flares in my chest. Without meaning to, my lips quirk into a smile. I don't know why because he's still a cheating bastard. Blanche leans forward and pouts, trying to capture his attention. When that fails, she reaches across the table to touch his hand.

My eyes narrow. Why is Rochester keeping his distance? Most men would be all over a woman like her, especially if they're engaged.

She catches me looking and hisses, "What are you still doing here?"

I pinch my lips shut and continue to watch her crash and burn.

"Tea," Rochester says without looking up from his paper.

I walk around the table to pour, hyperaware of how close I have to stand to Rochester's chair. His cologne fills my nostrils, different from the scent that was all over me last night. I can't help thinking about how those same hands delicately stirring his drink circled my clit. And those cold lips touching the rim of his cup were telling me how much he loved my tits.

Blanche watches me serve with predatory interest. "How long have you been helping my fiancé?"

"About a month."

"And what exactly are you doing for him?" Her eyes drag over my cleavage like she's checking for bite marks.

My breath hitches. I resist the urge to raise a hand to my throat. She knows. Knows something happened between Rochester and me. Knows there's a reason he doesn't want her in his room. I shake off that thought and focus on her question.

"Cleaning, cooking," I reply. "Picking up the slack for Mrs. Fairfax."

"Are you sure that's not all?" she snips.

I glance at Rochester again, who continues reading like he can't hear the bitch's insinuations. Last night, he was so attentive. Now he won't pay me an ounce of attention.

"Will there be anything else?" I ask through gritted teeth.

"Actually, yes," Rochester says without looking up. "See that the silver is properly polished. We'll be entertaining guests."

I retreat from the dining room, my veins throbbing. Through the doorway, I can hear them talking in low voices, her occasional laughter scraping against my nerves like nails on glass. Guests mean more snobs like Blanche Ingram and more chances of being recognized. And more thankless work. I need to get the hell out of here before anything else goes wrong.

That chauffeur I saw earlier has to be somewhere on the property. Maybe I can convince him to take me into town, or at least find out when he's leaving. I continue down the hallway, round the corner, and slip out the back door.

Fresh air hits my fevered skin, and I take a few deep breaths to calm my thoughts. Leaving the estate is for the best. I circle the mansion, finding the courtyards empty. With a sigh, I continue down the driveway toward a series of outbuildings, but there's no sign of a car.

Days of wandering around already tell me that searching any further will be futile. The grounds stretch endlessly in all directions, with manicured gardens dissolving into wild forest, and rolling lawns that end at the cliffs. I walk toward the gates, but after nearly an hour, I find them already locked.

This estate isn't my sanctuary. It's turning into a trap.

Defeat weighs down my shoulders as I trudge back toward the house with a new plan. If guests are arriving soon, then I can leave in one of their cars. Yesterday's list of tasks sits in my pocket like a blade, reminding me why I'm really here: not as a nanny, not even as a mistress. Just cheap labor.

The rest of the day crawls by like torture. I serve lunch trying not to overhear them plan their wedding. Grit my teeth while she prattles on about guest lists, flower arrangements, honeymoon destinations. Rochester's responses are muted, noncommittal, but he doesn't tell her to shut the hell up.

In the afternoon, I'm spying on them taking a walk through the gardens. She loops her arm through his, yapping about the upgrades she'll make to the mansion and its grounds. When she mentions bringing in her own staff to replace Mrs. Fairfax, I know she's really talking about me.

By evening, they move to the drawing room. I bring

them tea and find wedding magazines spread across every surface. Blanche drapes fabric samples over the furniture, holding swatches up to the light while Rochester sits in his chair looking indifferent.

"Which shades of white do you prefer?" she asks him. "I'm leaning toward ivory. It's more classic, don't you think?"

"Pure white," he mutters.

She rears back. "But I'm hardly a virgin."

I set down the tea service as he says some bullshit waiting to consummate their love. Bastard wasn't so patient with me last night. Or the night before when he molested my feet.

By the time I trudge up the stairs to my room, every muscle aches from a day of being treated like a beast of burden. I lock the door behind me and lean against it, finally allowing my mask to slip.

It's time to plan my next move. Vague plots to leave via the guests' vehicles won't cut it. I need something more concrete. But the moment I try to strategize, my mind goes blank. If my photos have circulated as far as the island, they'll have people checking all the ports. There's truly nowhere for me to go. I change into my nightgown and collapse onto the bed, too drained to think about tomorrow.

Sleep takes over before I can figure out what the hell I'm going to do.

Tonight, I dream about an early encounter with the cop, Callahan, when he cornered me outside my apartment, gripping my arm hard enough to leave bruises. He said my roommate had a warrant out for her arrest, and accused me of concealing her location. I really wasn't, but he shoved his card in my face and ordered me to locate her or he'd investigate why a twenty-five-year-old with no visible means of employment could afford to live in such a fancy building.

Lots of girls have sugar daddies pay their rent. But I didn't want the scrutiny. The last thing I needed was for him to dig up dirt on how I freed myself from being a teen bride.

Hours later, the mattress dips, pulling me out of sleep. Strong arms wrap around my waist from behind, and a familiar chest presses against my back. My heart stops. Shock paralyzes my bones. By the time my brain registers what's happening, I lurch forward, part my lips to scream, but he claps a hand over my mouth.

"Don't move," he whispers, the mask brushing against my neck. "I just needed to see you."

He pauses. Waits for me to relax. Then he releases his hand.

"What do you want from me?" I hiss into the dark. "Why come here when you're engaged to someone else?"

His arms tighten around my waist. "The Rochester estate is bankrupt."

My breath hitches. I go rigid in his arms, my mind scrambling to process his confession. The mansion, the grounds, the limousine. I thought he was old money.

"What do you mean?"

He doesn't elaborate. Just holds me tighter, his breath warm against my neck through the mask.

"Blanche Ingram's money will save us," he mutters. "Her presence here won't change a single thing between you and me."

"What if I don't want to be the other woman?" I ask.

"You won't be."

I swallow hard. "Bullshit."

He nuzzles my neck. Presses his thick cock into my ass crease. "Do you want me to leave?"

I should say yes. Tell him to go fuck himself with Blanche's diamond heels. But the hard length grinding into me from behind is skewering my thoughts.

And despite everything, the lies, the humiliation, the casual indifference, I'm addicted to the way he cocoons me in his arms.

"Stay and explain yourself," I whisper.

"Good girl," he murmurs against my neck, his cock slipping between my thighs. "I'll find a way for us to be together."

TWENTY
THE KEYHOLE

Stay. Good dog.

TWENTY-ONE

The next morning, I walk down the hallway, my heels clicking against the hardwood floor like gunshots. For the first time since arriving at this accursed estate, I feel clear headed. No more confusion. No more romantic delusions. Last night's bankruptcy confession changed everything.

Everything makes sense now: Rochester needs Blanche's money to keep his fancy manor from getting repoed. I need to stay hidden from Gil's people and the feds. And we both want to be together.

He can keep me as his dirty little secret for now, but the next time Blanche Ingram opens that mouth, I'll bite back with teeth.

I reach the study door, finding him sitting behind his mahogany desk. His dark eyes track my movement as I step inside, making my nipples tighten. Shit. My body's still programmed to respond to this bastard.

"Close the door," he says.

I shut it with a click.

"Come here." His voice is commanding, low.

I walk toward the desk but don't sit on that degrading little stool. Instead, I lean against its edge, letting my skirt ride up my thighs.

"You wanted to see me, sir?" I ask, my voice breathy.

His gaze drops to my legs, then snaps back to my face, his expression cool and professional. Like he didn't outline his marriage-for-money scheme last night while fucking between my thighs.

"About the household arrangements—"

The door handle rattles.

"Edward?" Blanche's voice cuts through the wood like a blade dipped in acid. "Are you in there?"

Rochester's jaw tightens. He jerks his head toward the chair in the corner, and I scramble off the desk like a guilty teenager. My ass hits the seat just as the door swings open.

Blanche glides in wearing a cream silk blouse that probably costs more than most people make in a month. Her eyes sweep the room like a security camera, landing on me with naked suspicion.

"There you are. I've been looking everywhere," she says to Rochester, but she's still staring at me like I'm a cockroach that crawled out of the walls.

"Just reviewing household matters with Miss Burlington." The lie rolls off his tongue smoother than expensive whiskey.

Blanche's lips curve in a smile that freezes halfway to her eyes. "How thorough of you. I do hope you're not overworking our little servant."

My fingers curl into fists in my lap, but I keep my expression blank. Let her think I'm the help. She's the one getting scammed.

"Miss Burlington handles her duties admirably," Rochester says.

Blanche moves closer to his desk, trailing her manicured fingers along its edge like she's marking territory. "Edward, darling, I simply must show you the sketches the architect emailed for the east wing renovations. They're in my room."

Rochester glances at me, his expression flickering with something unreadable. He rises off his seat and walks around the desk. "Of course, my dear."

Blanche beams at me like she just won the lottery. "Tidy up here while we're gone. This place is positively disheveled."

She loops her arm through Rochester's and guides him across the study like he's a prize stud she's leading to market. He doesn't resist. Doesn't look back. Just lets her haul him away while I sit there, abandoned.

It's stupid. I know the plan, yet I can't help thinking all I am to him is something to fill his empty nights. Body parts to help him get off. I shiver. So much for shedding my romantic delusions. That woman has a way of making me feel cheap.

The door clicks shut, leaving me alone with the scent of his cologne and the bitter taste of being dismissed.

I wait thirty seconds, listening to the footsteps disappear down the hallway. When I'm sure they're gone, I move to Rochester's desk, scanning the papers scattered across its surface. It's not like I'll find evidence of his bankruptcy among the letters, bills, and legal documents, but something else catches my eye.

It's a manila folder sitting at the corner of the desk with PRENUPTIAL AGREEMENT printed in bold letters.

My heart hammers against my ribs. I glance over my shoulder toward the door. This is dangerous as hell. But I can't stop myself from taking a peek.

I flip through pages of legal bullshit until one clause jumps out:

'In the event of adultery committed by Edward Rochester, Blanche Ingram shall retain all financial assets brought to the marriage, and Edward Rochester shall forfeit any claim to said assets or future inheritances.'

My blood turns to sludge.

No settlement if Rochester cheats. No money. No bailout. No nothing.

But wait. How on earth will he 'find a way for us to be together' if fucking me means he loses everything? The math doesn't add up.

Hands shaking, I place the agreement back into its folder. The papers look exactly as I found them, but my mind spins like a roulette wheel.

Rochester isn't the type to gamble his future on a wet pussy. So what's the angle?

I spend the rest of the morning scrubbing floors and polishing silver, but my thoughts won't stop shuffling. The prenup changes everything. If Rochester cheats, he loses all of Blanche's wealth.

The motherfucker must have a plan. Has to. But what?

My mind won't accept the most obvious explanation.

That he's saying whatever is needed for me to continue letting him into my bed.

The next few days crawl by without answers. Rochester becomes a ghost, appearing only for meals with Blanche glued to his side. She clings to his arm during their morning walks. Drags him to the drawing room to plan wedding details. Monopolizes every second of his time like she's afraid he might stray.

I get no midnight visits. No stolen glances. No opportunities to ask the questions burning holes in my brain.

On Tuesday morning, I dust the same bookshelf three times, hoping he'll come to the study. Nothing. Wednesday, I linger in the hallway outside his bedroom, pretending to polish brass fixtures. He emerges with Blanche chattering about flower arrangements.

Thursday morning finds me mopping the same stretch of floor twice, waiting for a chance to corner him alone. But Blanche's laughter echoes from the drawing room where they're reviewing guest lists for their engagement party.

Suspicions pile up in my head like a stack of unpaid bills. Does he plan to divorce Blanche after the wedding? Get her money some other way? Or is he planning on keeping me as a side piece while he lives happily ever after with his rich wife?

My gut says he's too smart to risk everything for me. But my gut's been wrong before.

By Thursday afternoon, I'm ready to scream. But the rumble of car engines saves my sanity. I drop the egg basket and rush through the grounds, only to find the same black limousine that brought me here, followed by a red sports car and a silver SUV.

Blanche's voice carries across the courtyard as she greets her friends.

"Even more rich assholes," I mutter.

My stomach clenches as the strangers pile out of their cars. New faces. People who might recognize me from news reports or wanted posters. But I force myself to breathe. Gil's boss wouldn't report me to the police. That would be incriminating himself.

Still, my eyes linger on that red sports car. A few days ago, when Blanche showed up, I was planning to steal one of these vehicles if things got too bad. Now I'm conflicted as hell. This estate is still the perfect hiding place, but what's Rochester's plan to get around that prenup? How can we be together if fucking me costs him everything?

Indecision has me rooted to the spot.

"Blanche," cries a woman with pink hair. She's accompanied by a man in a leather coat who's carrying a camera with interchangeable lenses. "Your new mansion is amazing."

I retreat around the corner, not wanting to get captured by the equipment. Four others pile out of the SUV, each holding up their phones, capturing every angle of the house's gothic facade. I can't blame them. Rochester Manor is stunning.

The pink-haired woman is a cooking influencer with a following of three hundred thousand, but she acts like it's three million. She brings a dozen containers of frozen appetizers and barks orders about presentation.

I spend the rest of the day shuttling between kitchen and drawing room, heating pigs in blankets, arranging spinach puffs on silver platters, garnishing sliders while she snaps photos for her social media. Every time I think I'm done, she demands more: different plates, better angles, hotter food. I'm sweating through my uniform, racing back and forth with trays, losing hope of any chance to catch Rochester alone.

By evening, they're on the second crate of wine and have filled the air with the potent stench of weed.

Candles dominate the table, burning bright. My chest tightens as I count the mess I'll be cleaning tomorrow: wine rings on the mahogany, melted wax I'll have to scrape off with my fingernails. Not to mention the pastries ground into the rugs.

The man in the leather coat beckons me forward with an impatient wave. I swallow back a surge of fury, keep my head down, and carry in yet another tray of drinks.

"Poor thing's been running around like a pig in a blanket all day," one of the women says with mock sympathy.

"Still think Edward is fucking her on the side?" another man adds with a chuckle.

Laughter slashes through the room like a whip. My face burns. I keep my eyes down so they don't see me crack. After a deep breath, I glance at Rochester, searching his face for any reaction, but he sips his drink like I'm invisible.

"Burlington, you're dripping sweat all over the crystal," Blanche snaps. "Clean yourself up before you serve another drink."

Their chuckles grate on my nerves. I watch Rochester's expression, waiting for him to twitch, react, show some sign he gives a damn. Is this part of his plan? Does he need them to see me as harmless help?

His face remains blank. Unreadable.

My hackles rise. My skin prickles with irritation. Fuck this. I'm done being their entertainment.

I set down the empty tray and walk toward the door, my spine straight and my jaw clenched tight enough to crack teeth.

"Mrs. Fairfax!" Blanche's voice cuts through the laughter like a whip. "We need champagne. Now."

I stop at the doorway, my hand on the frame. Every instinct screams at me to snap back. Or at least keep walking, but I can't afford to get fired. Not yet.

So, I turn back, grab a champagne bottle from the side table, and return to their circle of cruelty. Hand trembling, I pour into Blanche's flute. The golden liquid rises higher and higher.

Until—

Champagne pools over the rim and splashes across her silk skirt. Blanche flinches and gasps as if she's been electrocuted. Satisfaction surges through my chest like thunder. After hours of her condescending bullshit, I've finally fought back.

"Oops," I say with faux innocence.

She stares down at her ruined skirt, her painted lips trembling. Confusion and disbelief war across her features, and I dare her to speak.

The room goes dead silent. Every pair of eyes spear me with daggers, and the air charges with electricity. They're probably all thinking the help just signed her own dismissal. But I don't give a shit. I made the perfect, untouchable Blanche Ingram look stupid in front of her little friends. And for the first time since that bitch stepped through the front door, I've clawed back an ounce of self-respect.

"You clumsy bitch!" she screams.

I raise my brows, force back a smirk. "Apologies, Miss Ingram, my hand slipped."

Comprehension flashes across her features, followed by rage. She knows it wasn't an accident. She glances at Rochester for backup, but when he doesn't react, she hurls the drink. Liquid hits my cheek but I sidestep, just as the antique crystal shatters on the floor.

He shoots out of his seat, his eyes bouncing from me to the smashed glass. "You dare humiliate my fiancée under my roof? I won't have a servant show her such disrespect. Get out before I throw you out."

I flinch, my breath catching. After everything we've shared, every whispered promise in the dark, he's choosing her. Protecting his investment like I'm expendable. My chest tightens as if he's reached into my lungs and twisted.

Gathering what's left of my self-worth, I flick the champagne dripping from my hair. "With pleasure."

With my head high, I walk toward the door, my feet crunching the broken shards like applause. I tell myself that each step is a victory march, even though my heart wants to hammer through my ribs. Behind me, Blanche's friends rush to comfort her while she rants about ruined clothes and incompetent staff.

But I don't hear Rochester saying a single word in my defense.

Maybe I finally have my answer about the prenup.

The betrayal cuts deeper with every step. He sat there like a statue while his friends hurled insults and his precious fiancée threw champagne in my face. Didn't tell her to calm down, didn't acknowledge that she attacked me first.

He just dismissed me like garbage and meant every single word.

I stride through the hallway, my footsteps echoing off

the marble. Fury propels me past the oil paintings, past ornaments I want to smash into pieces. My mind races with escape plans. I should grab the red sports car keys, take a ferry to the mainland, and disappear into the countryside.

When I push through the front door, cool night air hits my sticky face like salvation. The sudden quiet after all that noise makes my ears ring. I wipe away the champagne and breathe through the burning rage.

I glare at the sports car, my hands shaking as the adrenaline starts to crash, leaving behind the bitter taste of fury and humiliation.

This is a sign that I should grab one of those cars and disappear before dawn. The keys are probably still in the ignition. Rich people never expect their shit to get stolen.

I stare at the car for a long moment, weighing my options. Where would I go? I don't have any safe houses and I sure as shit have no contacts. At least here, I'm hidden from the world that wants me dead.

Freedom versus safety. The unknown versus the devil I know.

A gust of wind blows in from the sea, making me shiver. Lord knows I want to leave. But I'd rather scrub this bitch's toilets than get tossed in a cell or carved up by Gil's people. I turn back toward the house, avoiding the drawing room and their echoing laughter.

Hours later, after a hot shower, I sit up in bed and glare at the door. A chair is wedged beneath the knob, blocking my nighttime intruder. I've also bolted the balcony doors shut.

Let him try to get in now. I've barricaded myself against men like him since the day I grew breasts.

The night drags on and I'm still too wired to sleep.

My mind keeps replaying Rochester's cold dismissal, the way he chose Blanche. Nights ago, he mentioned a plan, but how reassuring are words uttered in the heat of the moment compared to days of coldness and avoidance? It makes every breathy assurance in bed feel like a lie.

When the doorknob creaks, I flinch.

It's him.

He knocks. It's soft at first, almost hesitant. Three gentle raps that could be mistaken for politeness.

I stay silent, my jaw clenching. Where was he when they called me a pig in a blanket?

He knocks louder, each insistent strike making the chair scrape against the floor.

"Fuck off," I call out.

The knocking stops for a heartbeat. I picture him standing in the hallway in that ski mask, his cock straining against his pants. Why doesn't he go worship Blanche's golden cunt? Oh, right. He's depriving her until marriage.

Fists pound against the door like sledgehammers. The chair jolts with each blow, its legs shrieking against the floor. The entire door frame shudders, and the wood groans under the assault.

My stomach drops through the mattress. He's going to break in. Splinter that door and tear through the chair like the Hulk. Sweat breaks out across my forehead. My throat closes up, cutting off my air.

Another thunderous blow rattles the hinges. No one's coming to investigate. He probably waited until they were passed out drunk. I scramble out of bed, my bare feet hitting the cold floor. What the fuck? I retreat to the bathroom and bolt the door.

I wait for him to burst through but he stops.

Minutes crawl by. The sudden quiet is worse than the

pounding. My ears ring in the absence of pounding. I strain to listen, waiting for the next attack, but there's nothing. Only the sound of my own ragged breaths and blood rushing through my ears.

Just as I slide down the wall, deep, guttural sobs echo through the pipes. Is he crying inside the walls? I freeze, heart jackhammering, and suddenly I'm not sure I want to know what happens next.

TWENTY-TWO
THE KEYHOLE

You locked me out of my own domain, while the others shun you.

I'm the one who waits for you in the dark. I'm the one who graces your nightmares. I'm the one who hears you cry yourself to sleep.

You only get to make me beg once.

When it's your turn, I will show no mercy.

TWENTY-THREE

I sit on the bathroom floor, my back against the cold tiles, listening to the broken sobs echoing through the walls. The sound tugs at something deep in my chest, a part of me I don't want to acknowledge.

No man has ever cried for me. Not one. Not even when I left my piece-of-shit husband bleeding on the kitchen floor. Not even when his house caught fire and they thought I'd died.

But Rochester's words from that last night keep creeping back. How he whispered he'd find a way for us to be together. The desperation in his voice when he held me, like I was the only thing keeping him sane.

Bullshit.

He couldn't defend me when it mattered. Too busy playing that basic bitch for her money.

The sobbing becomes louder, more broken. Like he's drowning in his own grief. My chest tightens, and before I can stop myself, I'm on my feet and unlocking the bathroom door.

I creep through the bedroom toward the hallway

entrance, my bare feet silent on the wooden floor. The crying pulls at me like a fishing line hooked through my ribs.

What the hell will I say to him? Stop crying and get into bed? This could be a stupid ploy just for him to jack off. Still, I follow the sound like a moron. Because clearly, I haven't learned a damn thing.

I remove the chair, twist the key, open the door a crack and peer through the gap. There's no sign of Rochester. The hallway stretches empty in both directions, leaving nothing but shadows and the scent of medicine.

But the sobbing continues, even louder now. Coming from everywhere and nowhere, like the house itself is crying.

My throat tightens. I call out, "Edward?"

The broken weeping morphs into laughter. It's unbridled. Feverish, sounding like someone fresh from an asylum.

Terror kicks me in the solar plexus. I slam the door shut and twist the lock, my hands shaking so hard I can barely work the mechanism.

Fucking hell. I'm losing my mind. Too much stress, too much fear, too many nights sleeping with one eye open. My brain is finally cracking under the pressure.

I crawl back into the four-poster and pull the covers over my head like I'm five years old again, hiding from the demons under the bed. Except this time, the monsters aren't imaginary. It takes ages to get back to sleep, and even longer to sort through my confusion.

The next morning drags me back into the routine of playing house servant. As predicted, the drawing room is a mess, but so is the kitchen. The pink-haired woman must have been filming for social media because she left a bunch of equipment.

Movement from outside the kitchen window catches my eye while I'm sorting through what to toss away. A dark figure rushes between the trees at the edge of the lawn. He's too far away to make out any features, but he looks driven.

I blink, and he's gone. Vanished into the orchard like smoke.

A chill runs down my spine. Who the hell was that?

By afternoon, I'm hauling a tray of mint juleps to the terrace where Blanche and her crew are lounging like overfed house cats. There's no sign of Rochester, not that I should care. It's not like he'll defend me, anyway.

I set down the glasses, keeping my head down and my mouth shut. Just invisible help doing invisible work.

"Edward was so desperate to marry me that he signed the prenup without even reading it," Blanche purrs to the blonde at her side. "Poor darling would have agreed to anything. My lawyer says that's how you know a man is smitten."

My body freezes, and I suck in a breath through clenched teeth.

He signed it. Actually put his name on a document that fucks him over if he cheats. Which means every promise he moaned in the dark was a lie. I'm nothing but a hot body for him to use while he plays the perfect fiancé.

"Smart of them to include that adultery clause," the pink-haired woman says with a nod.

Blanche giggles, the sound sharp as a knife to the gut. "I'm not worried about that. Edward says I'm the only woman who makes him forget his grief."

My vision blurs around the edges. The tray trembles in my hands as I back away from the patio. The truth hits me with perfect clarity. If he signed the prenup so easily, then he was playing me for a fool.

It's just like that morning eleven years ago, when Mom shoved me into that wedding dress, telling me it was my time. Dad said I was lucky Brother Matthew wanted a sinner like me. Mom soothed my tears, telling me he was gentle, feeble, a man of God who only needed a wife to help with his kids.

If I'd known the old bastard was a violent rapist, I would have run the moment they left me to get dressed.

After being betrayed by the two people who should have loved me the most, I should have known better than to trust Rochester. Promises don't mean shit with the lure of money and power. Men say whatever they need to get what they want, then show you their true faces when it's too late to run.

Thank God I never allowed him to fuck me raw.

I walk back into the house on autopilot, reach my room and yank my duffel bag from under the bed. Blanche can have him. I'm done being anyone's dirty secret.

By the time I creep downstairs and slip out the front door, there's no sign of the sports car. But the black limousine still sits in the courtyard. I send out a prayer that the keys are still in the ignition. If I can get it started, I can drive to whatever passes for a ferry dock on this Godforsaken island.

But when I try the handle, it's locked.

I yank the next one. Then the other. Then the other. Nothing. Not a single fucking budges. My chest tightens with each failed attempt, panic clawing at my throat. The sob that escapes sounds like last night's broken weeping. I lean against the warm metal and let the tears come, tasting salt and defeat and the sensation of being trapped. I'm completely and utterly fucked.

Later that night, I drag the chair back under the doorknob. I don't want his hands on me. Don't want his whispered lies while he uses my body to drain his balls before going back to his precious fiancée. Rochester can go to hell.

Around midnight, a soft metallic sound scrapes at the door. It's careful. Deliberate.

Scratch. Scratch. Scratch.

What the hell is he doing now?

I slip out of bed, my bare feet silent on the floorboards, and press my ear to the wood. The sound continues. It's metal against metal, like he's working with tools.

A tiny *ping* echoes as something hits the floor on my side. I crouch down, feeling around in the dark until my fingers find a screw. The bastard is trying to break in like a cat burglar.

Rage explodes in my chest like a bomb. This sick freak thinks he can just dismantle my lock while I sleep? Like I'm some helpless victim who won't fight back?

"You motherfucker," I hiss under my breath.

I grab the heavy dresser and drag it across the floor. The wood scrapes against wood, loud enough to wake the dead. I don't give a shit. Let him know I'm onto his sick game.

The scraping from the hallway stops.

I wedge the dresser against the doorway, pressing my full weight against its side. My pulse hammers in my ears, and sweat beads on my forehead despite the cool air.

"Annalisa?" His voice comes through the wood, soft

and broken. Nothing like the commanding tone he uses during the day. "Please. I just want to talk to you."

I clench my teeth. Don't respond. Don't give him an inch.

"What's wrong?" he continues, his voice thick with desperation. "Why won't you let me in? I thought after everything... I thought you wanted this too."

My heart plunges. What the hell is he planning?

"Keep it up and I'll wake Blanche," I call out, my voice sharp. "I'll tell her all about her perfect fiancé."

Silence stretches between us. I press my back against the dresser, every muscle tense, waiting for him to start unscrewing.

Instead, muffled sobbing echoes through the wood. Deep, broken sounds that make my gut clench, and I hate myself for feeling sympathy. Bastard's probably putting on a show, trying to guilt me into opening the door. This is exactly what he wants: for me to crack.

I slide down the dresser until I'm sitting on the floor, knees pulled to my chest. The sobbing continues for what feels like hours, each wail scraping against my resolve.

Still, I refuse to respond. Refuse to give him what he wants.

Eventually, the crying stops. Footsteps retreat down the hallway, leaving me alone with the silence and my racing heart.

Hours later, dawn creeps through the small window, painting everything in shades of gray. My back aches from sleeping against the dresser, and my neck throbs with a painful crick.

When I finally work up the courage to pull the dresser away from the door, I find a piece of paper on the floor. Lips tightening, I bend down and unfold it.

It's the same elegant handwriting as the note ordering me to wave back.

Annalisa,

I know you're confused. I know last night frightened you. But you must trust me when I say there are other solutions, other paths to be together.

We're closer than you think. Every problem has a solution. And every prison has a door if you're brave enough to find it.

Trust me.

Rochester.

My stomach turns. What does he mean by prison? I shake off that question. He doesn't know I'm on the run. It's just word salad. He thinks I'm some girl who melts at a pretty turn of phrase. I read it three times before shaking my head.

What the fuck is Rochester planning?

TWENTY-FOUR
THE KEYHOLE

You will not shut me out again.

TWENTY-FIVE

Later that morning, I'm scrubbing breakfast plates when Blanche's voice cuts through the kitchen like a rusty blade.

"Burlington."

My back stiffens. I don't bother looking up from the sink. She hasn't spoken to me directly since the incident with the champagne. Barbed comments don't count when a bitch is too cowardly to say something to my face.

"Edward sends a message."

I turn around to meet dark eyes glittering with satisfaction.

"Our bathrooms need scrubbing," she says with a smirk.

My jaw clenches. She's enjoying this petty power. Making me clean up her messes while she gets to play lady of the manor. Payback for humiliating her in front of her little friends.

"Break anything, and it's coming out of your wages," she adds.

I roll my eyes. Thanks for giving me ideas, bitch. I'll make sure you won't see the damage coming.

Blanche floats away without another word, leaving me alone with dirty dishes and the bitter taste of defeat.

Twenty minutes later, I'm hauling cleaning supplies into Blanche's room with open windows overlooking the gardens. Laughter floats up from the patio, where she's entertaining her friends. I brace myself for hearing all kinds of slanderous shit about me.

She's left the bathroom in absolute squalor. Towels scattered across the marble floors, makeup smeared on gold fixtures, empty champagne bottles lying like fallen bowling pins. I can't tell if rich assholes live like pigs all the time or if she's staged this mess for my benefit.

I start with the towels, cramming them into a basket. Then I pick up a pair of piss-stained panties with the toilet brush to dump on her pillow. That's when I spot Blanche's Louis Vuitton vanity case sitting on the bed, wide open without a single trace of cosmetics.

My hands freeze. I shouldn't. But the bag sits there practically begging me to dig through her crap.

I creep toward the bed, my pulse trying to burst free from its cage. The bag is stuffed with rolls of cash, credit cards, and baggies of coke. But buried underneath, something catches my eye.

Lots of pills.

Prescription bottles with handwritten labels. I recognize Xanax, OxyContin, Adderall, and Ambien. And enough sedatives to knock out a horse. I pick up one bottle, squinting at a long chemical-sounding name when the hallway echoes with footsteps.

Shit.

I drop the bottles back into the bag and dive under the bed, just as the door creaks open. The space is narrow as a coffin and filled with dust. My heart thrashes like it's trying to claw its way out of my chest.

Heavy footsteps cross the hardwood floor, slow and deliberate, belonging to a man. I hold my breath, repeating the same mantra until one word blurs into the other: *Don't come closer. Don't come closer. Don't come closer.*

Each step makes my vision tunnel until all I can see is the man's shadow moving closer. I crane my neck to catch a glimpse in the full-length mirror across the room.

It's Rochester.

No, no, no, no, no.

His polished shoes stop beside the bed, near enough that I could reach out and touch the leather. The mattress groans as he sits, springs squeaking under his weight. Every part of me wants to bolt, to run, to scream, but there's nowhere to go. He'd drag me out by the ankle. Demand to know why I shut him out of my room.

I freeze in place, my breaths shallowing, but dust tickles my nose. A sneeze builds up in my sinuses, threatening to betray my hiding spot. Squeezing my nostrils between my fingertips, I bite down on my bottom lip until I taste blood, desperate to stop the urge.

The bed dips lower as he leans to the side and reaches for Blanche's case. Every rustle of fabric grates on my nerves, and every clink of pill bottles rattles in my ears. My lungs scream for air, but I don't dare exhale.

What the hell is he doing?

Through the mirror, I watch him picking up each pill bottle, studying the labels. He settles on one container, unscrewing the cap. The contents rattle as he empties them into a white handkerchief. Then he pulls a small plastic baggie from his pocket and pours a different set of pills into the vacant bottle.

Oh my God. Oh my God. He's poisoning Blanche.

Blood roars in my ears. I want to scream at him to stop, to warn her, but I can't even breathe. My vision goes gray at the edges and my eyes sting with tears.

He's going to kill her. And if he discovers where I'm hiding, he'll do the same to me.

The mattress shifts as he leans forward, and I squeeze my eyes shut, certain he's about to peer under the bed. If he sees me, he'll drag me out by the hair. Slit my throat. Bury my corpse in the woods. Every muscle in my body trembles so hard the bed frame might rattle and give me away.

He'll kill me, he'll kill me, he'll kill me.

The springs creak again as he stands. I hear him brushing down his jacket, then arranging the case exactly as he found it. My vision blurs to black spots, and my lungs sear like I'm drowning.

I can't move. Can't breathe. Can't let him know I'm here.

His footsteps move toward the exit with a leisurely pace as if he's accustomed to tampering with people's drugs. Then the door clicks shut, and the sound grows fainter, more distant.

After a slow count to a hundred, I drag myself out from under the bed. I have to crawl to the wall and brace myself as my whole body shudders.

If I think about what just happened, I'll fall apart. My hands move on their own, clawing up towels, but they're too heavy. I keep dropping them. My fingers don't work.

My gaze fixes on the floor. On the mess. I don't look at the bed. Don't think about the vanity case. Don't see his hands opening the bottle.

I'm the maid. That's all. Just the fucking maid. I have to finish the job. Just finish the job.

My feet carry me to the filthy bathroom. I drop to my knees and scrub at the shit smeared on the floor. My hand shakes so much that the sponge slips.

The marble is cold. Like a slab. Like a table in a morgue.

I keep cleaning. Anything to pretend this is normal.

By dinnertime, my hands still shake. I can't wash them clean enough. Sweat. Grease. Guilt. I'm as dirty as Blanche's floor. But if I drop a single plate, he'll know.

Rochester sits at the head of the table like a king holding court, telling stories about the estate's history, charming Blanche's friends like he's campaigning for office. He talks like a politician, but all I see is the man who swapped her pills for poison.

Every time I glance in his direction, I picture those careful fingers doing the devil's work. Every smile he gives Blanche feels like a countdown to her demise. I picture the foam at her mouth, the twitch of her limbs. Her final shudder of death.

I can't look at him. Can't give myself away.

"Darling, you're so knowledgeable in local history. I'm so lucky to have found you," Blanche purrs, reaching across the table to paw at his hand. She beams at him, like a lamb thanking the butcher.

My stomach roils. The poor princess won't be alive long enough to enjoy him. Or her trust fund.

"I'm the lucky one, my dear." He kisses her hand like she's some Renaissance duchess, when he's really kissing a corpse. "I never thought I'd love again after Celine died, but you've made it all possible."

Now he's got me wondering what happened to his dead wife. Did he also tamper with her medication?

Dizziness hits me in a wave so violent, I have to grip the edge of the sideboard to keep from fainting on the Persian rug. The guests clap and make appreciative noises, thinking they're watching true love bloom. I'm the only one watching a murder in progress.

Rochester isn't just going to kill her. He's enjoying her ignorance. Savoring her trust. Rolling it around in his mouth like fine wine.

I set down the last dish with trembling hands, swallowing back a mouthful of acid. Every clink of crystal, every burst of laughter, every word of praise for the happy couple rings in my skull like funeral bells. They're toasting her death and they don't even know it.

As the applause simmers, his gaze meets mine, and my chest caves.

Heart thundering, I flee to the kitchen where I attack the dishes. I scrub until my knuckles turn red, but I can't escape the truth. Every shadow in my peripheral vision could be Rochester. Every sound in the hallway could be him coming to silence the witness. I even flinch at my own reflection in the window.

Does he know I saw? Did he notice the dust disturbed under the bed? Is he watching me right now, calculating when to strike?

I shake off that thought. He can't know. If he did, I'd already be dead.

When every surface gleams like a showroom, I drag my aching body upstairs. The socialites continue drinking in the drawing room, but I know better than to serve them. I don't want to sleep. I don't want to give him the chance to sneak into my room. My shoulders feel like someone's beaten them with hammers, and my hands won't stop shaking.

But as I reach for my doorknob, movement sounds from inside my room.

My heart seizes. My gut clenches. It's Rochester. Maybe he did notice me hiding. Maybe he's in there waiting to finish what he started.

I should run. Find somewhere else to sleep. But where the hell can I go in the middle of the night on an isolated estate on this Godforsaken island?

Without meaning to, I edge closer, my heart pounding hard enough to crack ribs. I push the door open a crack and peer through the gap. But the figure standing in my room isn't Rochester, it's Blanche.

She leans against my dresser holding up my bra with the lace trim. All thoughts of her being a victim evaporate under a burst of rage. I fling open the door and charge inside.

"What the fuck are you doing with my underwear?"

"You think men find udders like this attractive?" she says without turning around.

My mouth opens but nothing comes out. It's absurd to feel so small with a killer downstairs. She has no idea she's one pill away from death, yet she's in my room playing games with my bra.

"Better than bee stings," I say.

"Edward told me everything," she says, her voice cold.

A sharp breath whistles through my teeth. She has to be bluffing. Rochester isn't stupid. He wouldn't jeopardize his golden goose so close to getting his murderous hands on her fortune.

"What the hell are you talking about?" I snap.

She turns around, her painted lips twisting with distaste. "Anyone can get implants. Even a maid with delusions. But a man like Edward could only ever see you as a receptacle for his cum."

My nostrils flare. I still don't know if she's fishing for a confession, but I want to smack that smirk off her face.

"Put that down." My voice sounds weak even to me.

Blanche flashes her teeth. She takes a step closer. My bra swings between her manicured fingers like a noose. "No denial? No protestations of innocence? You really are a pathetic whore."

"And you're insecure," I say.

"Observant."

"I told you to put my bra the fuck down." My voice cracks.

She waves it like a flag of triumph. "You know, someone who gets on their knees for a paycheck ought to—"

"At least Rochester wants me," I hiss, the words tumbling out before I can stop them. As soon as I say it, my blood runs cold.

I can't stop. The rest gushes out with venom. "While you're whining for his cock, he comes to my room every night, begging harder than a starving dog. When I won't let him in, he sobs for me like an orphan."

Her eyes widen. The smile melts off her face, and she suddenly looks young. Fragile. Breakable.

"You're lying," she whispers, her breath catching.

My hands flex. I could shake her. Snap her neck. Part of me wants to grab her shoulders and scream the truth, to yell at her to check her pills and run, but I'm overcome with righteous malice.

I meet those dark eyes. Eyes that glare at me with scorn. Eyes that roamed over my body like it was inferior and hiss, "Ask your precious Edward who he thinks of when he comes."

"Edward loves me."

She steps back, still holding onto my bra. Now, she's pressing it to her chest like a shield. She truly believes in her beloved Mr. Rochester. I almost pity her.

My jaw clenches. Guilt gnaws at my conscience. If I don't warn her, she'll die, and that will make me an accomplice. But if I do, then I'm marking myself for death.

Something flickers in her gaze. It could be uncertainty. Maybe even doubt. But she stamps it out fast, her mouth twisting with spite. Her eyes narrow, the way people's do when they mistake indecision for weakness.

"Once Edward and I are married, he'll have a wife," she says with a sly smirk. "And no more use for a hired hole."

My vision clouds with red. Lurching forward, I reach for my bra, but she dodges.

"Don't be stupid," I snap. "You think it's love because he signed that prenup? He's found another way to take your fortune."

She flashes her teeth, about to say something cutting, then she widens her eyes. "I know where I've seen you before."

Every ounce of blood drains from my face and gathers in my pounding heart. If she recognizes me from Beaumont City, I'm finished.

"Beaumont City." She waves the bra in my face.

"Casino Demartini. You were wrapped around some old man. My friends thought you were an escort. I told them even paid professionals wouldn't dress that badly."

Heat flares across my cheeks. I curl my fingers, wanting to claw at her eyes. It's only a matter of time before she connects the dots and discovers I'm a fugitive. "Never heard of it."

She gasps, her eyes glittering with triumph. "That was you."

"Wake the fuck up, princess," I spit. "You have better things to worry about. Like the man planning to murder you for your money."

My stomach plummets.

Shit. I shouldn't have said that.

She'll run to Rochester. Then he'll know I saw.

Blanche's sneer drops. "What did you say?"

"Nothing."

She grabs my arm. "Tell me."

I clench my teeth. If I keep quiet and she dies, it might as well be me shoving the poison down her pampered throat. "Check your pills before you get high. Or don't. It's your funeral. But the only man who ever wanted a skinny bitch like you is after what's in your trust fund."

She shrieks like I've set her on fire, then pushes past me and stumbles to the door. I watch her disappear into the hallway and hope to God she's checking her meds, but when she screeches for her Edward, I know I'm screwed.

My knees buckle. I rush toward the four-poster, my gut roiling.

Rochester will wring my neck.

I reach beneath the bed and pull out my duffel bag.

Maybe I can escape through the back stairs and figure out how to get off this island before the bodies start piling up.

Footsteps charge up the stairs. I drop the bag, retreat to the bathroom, but it's too late. Rochester charges into my room, his features a rictus of rage.

"What the hell have you been saying to my fiancée?"

TWENTY-SIX

THE KEYHOLE

You agreed to play my game. Now, you're not following the rules.

I will enjoy punishing you most of all.

TWENTY-SEVEN

Rochester fills the doorway like a thunderstorm in a three-piece suit, his black eyes flashing with rage. "Answer me. What the hell did you say to Blanche?"

I stagger back, my ass hitting the window frame. There's no escape. Just a long drop onto stone.

Blanche shoves past him, already a wreck. Mascara streaked down her cheeks in black rivers, her perfect chignon falling apart like her whole world just collapsed. I shake my head. What the hell happened to the ice princess?

"Tell him about the pills!" She jabs a manicured finger toward my face.

My throat seizes. Words stick like glue. I can't force them out.

"She said you were going to murder me for my money!" Blanche's voice splinters on the last word. "That you come to her room every night moaning her name like a dog!"

Rochester's dark gaze fixes on me with surgical precision. I've had men want to hurt me before, but this is different. This is the look of someone calculating exactly how to make me disappear.

"Why would you fabricate such an obvious lie?" His voice carries the kind of quiet that comes before violence.

I work my jaw, but nothing comes out but a dry rasp. When I lick my lips, all I taste is copper. "I... I was just—"

"The poor wretch has thrown herself at me since day one. Haven't you, Miss Burlington?" His voice is smooth, reasonable. The kind of tone that makes lies sound like gospel.

I shake my head, wanting to deny it all, but terror closes my throat.

More footsteps thunder up the stairs. Blanche's friends pour into my room like vultures circling roadkill. Pink hair. Leather coat. All of them staring at me like I'm the evening's entertainment.

"What's happening?" Pink hair demands, reaching for her phone.

Rochester slides his arm around Blanche's waist, pulling her close. "Our little servant's been spreading stories. Some people can't handle being told no."

"Now she's threatening me with tampered pills," Blanche shrieks.

Betrayal curdles in my gut, hitting so hard that my spine bows. I wanted to help the stupid bitch. Do something right for once in my life, and it's backfired. Suddenly I'm back in Gil's penthouse. His hands on my shoulders, steering me toward the door with his boss's gaze like a knife to my throat.

One of the women gasps. "When will these low-level sluts ever learn their place?"

The other friends crowd closer.

My gaze turns back to Rochester, who presses a kiss

against Blanche's temple. "I would never hurt you, my love. You mean everything to me."

I want to scream at Blanche to open her eyes. To see through his manipulations. But she's too desperate to believe in her fantasy to consider the truth.

She gazes up into his dark eyes, melting against him like he's the sun. "You mean that?"

He gives her a wintry smile that looks more like a grimace. "You own my heart. My very soul. If there was any doubt of my devotion, I'd want you to tear it out."

"Edward..." she whispers, swallowing his lies.

He drops to one knee right there on my bedroom floor and grabs her hands. "Marry me tonight. Let's wake up Father Henry. I can't wait another day."

My stomach lurches. The room spins like a carnival ride. This is happening too fast. Surely she can't believe this bullshit?

"Yes! Yes, yes, yes!" Blanche bounces on her toes.

In my head, I'm back in that dingy room staring down at Callahan, my fingers trembling around the syringe. Gil's hot breath fans against my neck as he whispers assurances. It's me or the cop. If I refuse, I'll be the one to die. With a sob, I slide the needle into a vein bulging between his toes.

A slap comes out of nowhere, snapping my head to the side and my mind back to the present. I gape up at Blanche, her features twisted with contempt.

"How dare you poison my pills," she hisses. "How dare you try to kill me so you could have him. This is attempted murder. I'm calling the police."

Alarm kicks me in the chest. She can't. I step back, glancing at Rochester. The mask slips, his eyes flickering with panic. One blink later, he smooths it away and rises back to his feet.

His hand finds her shoulder. His lips brush against her ear. "Forget about her, darling. Tonight should be about us."

She turns to him, her eyes pleading. "She can't get away with threatening my life."

Rochester cups her cheek. "It was probably just a figure of speech."

"If you don't deal with her, I'll drown myself in the pond!" She stamps her foot.

My jaw drops, and I exhale an incredulous breath. The others nod and grumble, seeming to agree with their delusional friend. Every eye turns to me as if I'm the one who threatened to stick Blanche's head underwater.

"Let me deal with this after our wedding." He releases her shoulder and strides toward me with the grace of a predator.

"Wait!" I hold out my palms to protect myself, but he snatches my bicep with a grip like a shackle and squeezes until I gasp.

"Come on. We need to talk."

He drags me to the door like I'm a sack of garbage. The vultures step aside like they're watching trash taken to the curb.

"Don't do this," I say with a whimper. I stare at his handsome profile, wishing I'd kept my mouth shut.

Someone snorts as if they've already found me guilty and deserving of death.

Rochester hauls me down the hallway, down the stairs, past the oil paintings of dead aristocrats who probably also had servants disappear. The entourage follows.

My legs buckle. I fall forward, needing this to stop, but his iron grip keeps me upright.

Numbness falls over my senses for the rest of the journey. It's part disbelief, past trauma. I spent my first two decades being dragged out of buildings by violent men. I didn't escape to suffer the same.

Outside, the cool air hits my fevered skin like a slap. I blink, the back garden coming into focus. Floodlights assault my eyes from all directions, bringing me back to the present. I glance over my shoulder as he marches me across the patio. The others haven't caught up yet, so I take my opportunity to speak.

"I didn't say any of that stuff," I lie. "You've got to believe me. She made it all up."

Silence. The only reaction is his grip tightening until my arm turns numb.

"Don't you want us to be together?" I sob. "Please. I won't say anything. I'll keep my mouth shut. It can be just you and me."

The door behind us opens, and the others step out.

His lip curls with disgust. "Do not think for a minute that I would choose you over my beloved Blanche."

"That's right," she hisses from behind.

My shoulders sag with defeat. This is it. I'm about to die.

He drags me through the manicured gardens, through the orchard. The foliage closes around us like a green tomb. Through the trees, the cottage stands half-hidden by brambles and neglect. Its windows gape black and empty, and the smell of rot drifts from its warped doorframe.

Rochester produces an iron key and turns the lock with the sound of breaking bones.

"Get inside."

I plant my feet, shaking my head like a madwoman. "No. Please. I'll disappear tonight. You'll never have to think about me again."

He shoves me through the entrance. I stumble, catching myself against a wall that feels slimy under my palms. The door slams like a coffin lid, sealing me in silence and rot. The key turns, and his footsteps retreat.

I launch myself at the door and pound on it with my fist. "Let me out!"

Nobody replies. Not even Blanche and her friends to gloat. These bastards have left me here to rot.

I turn in a circle, every fine hair on my body standing to attention. What the hell do I do now?

Water drips somewhere in the shadows like a metronome counting down to my death. How many times in my miserable existence did Dad or Brother Matthew drag me to the barn to await my punishment? I've lost count. Last time, I swore to make sure it would never happen again.

In the dark, I fumble along the walls, my hands finding dust and cobwebs and things I don't want to identify. A fireplace covered in thick cobwebs. Old newspapers that disintegrate at my touch. A wooden crate stuffed with oil-soaked rags. A dented canister of something that reeks of industrial solvent.

I bump into a table, and my fingers close around a box that feels like matches.

Fire. That's my way out.

I should burn this whole place to ashes. Light the shack like a funeral pyre. Won't be the first time. Then I'll take the limousine and drive it off the cliff. If I'm going down, so is this fucking estate.

But they left to get married. The only person I'd be hurting with the fire is myself.

I sink onto the damp floor, my back against the wall.

What's next? Prison? I shake my head. Even if my fingerprints are all over Blanche's bottle, so would Rochester's. He wouldn't dare risk his precious inheritance. Or the insurance payout he's likely to put on his wife's life.

What's left? A shallow grave in these fucking woods?

I spend the night groping through the cottage, looking for weapons. Any means of self-defense. Because when they come for me, I'll be ready.

Hours later, gray light filters through cracked windows when two sets of footsteps crunch across gravel. I scramble back to the fireplace, my heart convulsing.

This is it. Time to fight.

The key scrapes in the lock like fingernails on slate. I tighten my fingers around a lantern in time for the door to swing open.

Rochester strides inside in a fresh suit, his arm around Blanche's waist. She wears a short white dress that barely covers her pussy, her hair pinned up with baby's breath like some beach wedding fantasy. She clings to his arm, her new wedding ring catching the light like a tiny star.

Bitch looks like a bride in a shampoo commercial. All victory and fake purity. Like she's won some game I didn't even know we were playing.

My nostrils flare. They actually did it. Got married in the middle of the night while I rotted in this shit hole.

"Blanche and I will be away for a week," he says, his voice cold. "You have exactly that time to clean up and vacate my home or I will call the police."

My jaw drops. How on earth did he convince her to set me free?

They turn and walk away, leaving me standing in the mouth of my tomb, watching my death sentence disappear into the morning mist.

Seven days to figure out which direction to run next.

But I'm breathing. My heart still beats. Against every expectation, I'm still alive.

For now, that's enough.

TWENTY-EIGHT
THE KEYHOLE

You're about to enter the next phase of our little game.
And so will she.

I will teach you how to gasp, to plead, to whimper when I press silence into your delicate throat. We will repeat the lessons until your voice remembers only the sound of my name.

When I am done, you will convulse at my command.

So wait for me, my disobedient little Annalisa. Let me handle pressing matters.

As soon as she is dead, I will handle you.

I make a slow count to twenty before I can step out of the cottage. Even then, it's like walking into my own execution. Every step feels like it could detonate a mine. Every breath feels stolen.

Even the air feels hostile. Like I've cheated death and the world wants a correction.

This has to be a trap. Killers like Rochester don't hand out mercy. They poison their problems, bury them under rose bushes, or dump them in the ocean. But I can't go back to that cottage.

Legs shaking, I make my way through the orchard, expecting a gunshot between the shoulder blades. Or a knife between my ribs. Something. Anything. Because letting me walk free doesn't make sense unless he's planning something worse.

An apple falls from a nearby tree, making me flinch. Bastard has me so frazzled I can barely function.

At the edge of the formal gardens, I hurry across the lawn, not stopping until I reach the side of the house. I follow the building around to the front, where the black limousine idles like a hearse.

Blanche's little vultures cluster around the vehicle, filling the air with their mindless chatter. I duck behind a rose bush, desperate not to be seen. The thorns catch my dress, but I don't move.

"Three cheers for the happy couple," bellows the man in the leather coat.

On cue, they burst into a chorus of hip-hip-hoorays. Pinky tosses a handful of rice. The blonde and her companion shower them with confetti as if my warning last night meant nothing.

Rochester emerges from the front door with Blanche grafted to his arm. Even from this hiding point, it's hard to miss her grinning like she's won the lottery. The white dress clinging to her skeleton like tissue on a corpse looks even more ridiculous in daylight.

He dips her backward in a romantic movie kiss while her friends squeal and snap photos. My stomach churns at his performance. I never thought I'd be the kind of woman to scorn another for trusting a silver-tongued bastard, but I gave her enough ammunition to cast a thread of doubt.

Instead of investigating her pills, that bitch turned my heads-up into an accusation. She just signed her death certificate with a marriage license.

"What a waste of life," I mutter. "She has the survival instincts of a lemming in heat."

Rochester opens the limo's rear door and helps Blanche across the leather seats like she's made of glass. She waves at her friends through the tinted window, and the limo pulls away in a cloud of dust. I shake my head as they disappear down the driveway, still baffled at how she's ignoring the red flags.

The vultures pile into their vehicles. Leather coat climbs behind the wheel of the red sports car with Pinky. The blonde cranks up the silver SUV. Engines rev like they can't wait to escape this accursed place.

I should run toward them. Beg for a ride. Throw myself at their mercy and hope one of them has a functioning conscience. But terror keeps me glued behind the roses. What if Blanche told them she saw me in Beaumont City? Worse still, maybe she and Rochester poisoned their minds, and now they'll drag me straight to the cops.

The sports car tears down the drive, followed by the SUV. I watch until the engine noise fades into nothing, until I'm alone with the empty house and the sound of my own ragged breathing.

He's gone.

One week. I have seven whole days to find a way to escape.

My relief tastes sour because Blanche is still going to die. Maybe not today, maybe not this week or this year, but Rochester will find his moment. He didn't tamper with her pills for nothing.

I want to dismiss the stupid bitch. Tell myself she deserves whatever's coming for being so vicious and having such blind faith in a man. But I can't shake the image of her melting under his lies, so desperate to be loved that she ignored his every warning sign.

She wouldn't be the first. Been there. Done that. Got the scars to prove it.

But how the hell do I warn the police without getting caught? Anonymous tip? Right. As if they'd listen to my ramblings. Letter? They'd only check for fingerprints.

Maybe last night's scene put her friends on alert. If anything happens to Blanche in the next few months, they'll remember the crazy servant screaming about murder and pills. They'll ask awkward questions, and he won't escape scrutiny with his charm.

It's not much of a plan. But it's something.

I creep toward the back, every instinct screaming that I'm walking into another trap. The kitchen door stands open like a mouth waiting to swallow me whole. He gave me seven days, but I'm giving myself twenty-four hours to figure out my next move.

But not before I gather enough valuables to fund a life on the run.

I try the library first. It's locked. Study. Locked. The drawing room opens, but there's nothing inside except furniture and crystal glasses I can't exactly stuff in my pockets. The dining room silver is conveniently missing. They must have predicted what I'd do next.

Upstairs, Blanche's door gapes like it's been waiting for me. The room is a mess of clothes scattered across the four-poster, makeup spilled across the dresser, and even more empty champagne bottles.

And sitting on the nightstand like a gift from God is her Louis Vuitton case.

I grab it, surprised by the weight. The pills rattle inside like loose teeth in a skull. Since at least one bottle is compromised, I focus on the baggies and syringes, and loose cash. There's enough there to pay for three months of expenses on the run.

Time to disappear before Rochester returns from his honeymoon with a shovel. I run to my room, pack my duffel bag with what little I own and head for the front door.

But the moment I step outside, reality hits like a brick to the face. The driveway stretches endlessly around a forest thick enough to hide a thousand bodies. My stomach rumbles, my joints ache, and I'm already light-headed from sleep deprivation and being worked like a dog. And that's without even reaching the bloody gate.

How am I supposed to make it to civilization with low blood sugar, no car, no plan? It's got to be twenty miles to the nearest town, assuming I don't get lost and end up wandering in circles until I get picked up by a weirdo. Or the cops.

I turn back toward the house, letting exhaustion run over me like a freight train. I still have twenty-four hours to regain my strength. Maybe I'll find something with wheels in the stables. A bicycle. A motorcycle. Hell, at this point, I'd settle for a shopping cart.

For now, I need food and sleep. Can't run on empty.

After gorging on a stack of leftovers, I retreat to my room, pull the curtains shut, and lie in the four-poster bed staring at Blanche's vanity case on the nightstand. All those baggies. All those syringes. Clean needles just waiting to slide into a vein.

Did they leave it here on purpose? A final gift for the servant who knew too much? Make it look like despera-tion drove me to suicide—problem solved, with no messy explanations.

The thought makes my throat thicken. I roll onto my side, press my face into the pillow, and let out the tears. For Callahan dying of that overdose. For Blanche flying toward her death on a cloud of bullshit romance. For my own life spiraling down the drain.

I drift somewhere between sleep and death, half-dreaming of footsteps. When the mattress shifts behind me, I think it's the workings of an overactive mind. But then I feel hot breath. Large hands. Heat. I freeze. Every muscle goes rigid. Strong arms wrap around my waist, pulling me back against a hard chest.

"Don't cry," murmurs a familiar voice. "It's alright. You're safe, now."

My spine jolts. My brain short-circuits. Rochester's supposed to be away, fucking his new wife and planning her funeral. But those are his hands, his voice, his body.

"What..." My throat closes. "What are you doing?"

"I'm here now. I'll keep you safe."

Rage explodes in my chest. This sick bastard thinks he can terrorize me, lock me in that rotting cottage, marry some other woman, then sneak back to get off? Does he think I'm as stupid as his wife?

His erection presses into my ass cheeks, hot and thick and insistent. Dirty bastard. Dirty, selfish wife killer.

Rochester grinds against me, his fingers reaching around to cup my pussy. Heat surges between my legs, and I push back. Moaning, he rolls his hips. My own fingers reach to the nightstand and find one of Blanche's syringes.

"Are you wet for me like a good girl?" he groans, his digits reaching into my panties. He slides a finger over my clit and rubs tight circles.

My pussy, the little traitor, clenches. My blood heats with a mix of fury and shame and hatred. Mostly at myself for responding to his touch. I'm no better than Blanche. I clamp my jaw until it aches, fighting to release myself from his grip.

Ignoring the surge of arousal, I pull off the syringe's cap with my teeth, feeling for the plunger in the dark.

His lips graze the back of my neck, and his thick cock presses between my thighs. "You're soaked."

In one smooth motion, I jam the needle into his arm and press down hard.

He jerks backward with a strangled cry, his hand leaving my crotch. I roll off the bed and spin around, ready to fight for my life. He rises, teeth clenched, dark eyes wide beneath the ski mask. I stagger back, grab the vanity case and swing it like a club.

Instead of lurching forward, he jerks once, twice, three times before falling backward onto the mattress.

"You bastard." I scramble onto the bed, rip off his mask—

And freeze.

The man under the fabric isn't Rochester. He's bearded. Unfamiliar. But the worst part? He's smiling. A twisted, dopey smile like he's dreaming of paradise.

And I've never seen him before in my life.

THIRTY

I glare at the unconscious bastard sprawled across my bed. He's the same build as Rochester. Same broad shoulders stretching his shirt tight. Same height that makes the four-poster look small beneath him. Same black hair. But the thick beard covering half his face makes it impossible to tell what the hell I'm looking at.

Maybe this is the shirtless man I spotted working in the orchard my first week. Maybe he's the chauffeur. I shake off that thought, remembering seeing him driving off with Blanche and Rochester.

He sure as hell isn't any of that bitch's asshole friends.

"What a mess," I mutter under my breath, my gaze drifting to the half-empty syringe. "How many men am I going to kill in one lifetime?"

Is he even alive?

Stomach roiling, I edge toward the bed and shove the curtain to one side. Every limb trembles as I mount the mattress and press my fingers to his neck. His skin is warm, damp with sweat. The steady thump against my fingertips tells me he's still living.

"Thank God," I say with a sigh and back away from this unconscious freak.

Whatever cocktail I shot him up with hasn't killed him.

Yet.

But what the hell do I do now?

I should grab my bag and run while he's down. Scour the grounds for his vehicle and make myself scarce. But I already tried that and failed. Besides, rage keeps my feet planted on the wooden floor. This sick bastard has been sneaking into my room for days, touching my body, giving me false hope, making me think I was losing my mind.

All while pretending to be Rochester.

Shame floods my system as I remember last night's cruel words. Rochester called me a desperate liar. And from his point of view, he's right. The murdering maniac never laid a finger on me. It was this impostor, making me think it was him.

This unconscious man set me up to be humiliated. I wouldn't have gotten so fixated with Rochester if it wasn't for him sneaking into my bed. I owe him pain. After he's explained himself. But first, I need to tie him up.

I yank the curtain ties from the four-poster and wrap them around his wrists. But restraining dead weight is harder than it looks. His arm flops when I try to lift it toward the posts, and I grit my teeth. Sweat beads on my forehead as I struggle to loop the twisted fabric around his thick wrists. The material bites into my fingers as I pull it tight against the wooden bedposts.

Then, I do the same with his ankles, tightening the knots so they're strong enough to secure a stallion. But I'm not sure if I've accounted for the strength of a psychopath. I pad across the room to the dresser, pull out a spare bedsheet, and cut it into strips. After twisting them into four bindings, I lash his limbs to different parts of the head and footboards.

The man's breathing fills the silence with a slow, steady rhythm, making me wonder if this is the calm before the shitstorm. By the time I finish, my shoulders ache and my hands are raw from the makeshift rope. I've left him spread across the bed like a pagan sacrifice, arms stretched wide, ankles bound.

I get dressed, pull out a carving knife pilfered from the kitchen, settle into the chair by the balcony doors and wait. My fingers shake around its hilt. Last time I held a blade just like this, it was to make sure the old bastard I escaped didn't leave the burning house.

Hours crawl by. The sun rises, and dust motes dance in the morning light. All the adrenaline from capturing the masked man dwindles, and my stomach growls. The knife grows slick in my sweaty palm. My eyelids become heavy as lead.

Then a sharp intake of breath jolts me awake.

The man thrashes in his restraints, ropes straining against his ankles and wrists. When his dark eyes find mine, he goes rigid, making no sound but the creak of bed springs and his ragged breaths.

My heart rate kicks up several notches, the shock propelling me out of my seat. On shaky legs, I cross the room and approach the bed. As I grow closer, his chest rises and falls as if he's preparing for an attack. Nostrils flaring, I hold the knife at his throat, making sure to position the blade just below his Adam's apple. One small push and I could open a vein.

"I ought to kill you for molesting me under false pretenses," I hiss.

"But I never lied." His voice is rougher than Rochester's, something I hadn't noticed until now. It's almost like he doesn't use it much.

"Bullshit." I press the knife harder. A bead of blood wells up around the tip. "You told me to call you Rochester."

"I am Rochester. Rowland Rochester." The words tumble out in a rush.

Eyes narrowing, I study his face in the dim light. His eyes are the same deep brown that border on black, like Rochester's, but everything else seems different. I'm not just talking about the unkempt beard hiding his jaw. Or the weathered skin darkened by either dirt or sunlight or years of hard living. His eyes are wild, showing more whites than normal and there's the desperate way he stares at me like I'm his last hope for salvation.

My lips tighten. "Why have you been sneaking around at night, groping innocent women?"

He flinches, making the bindings strain against his wrists. "I... I thought you wanted me. When you waved back."

I grind my teeth. "Who the fuck are you, anyway?"

"A prisoner," he replies, his voice pained. "I've been held captive here since I was a boy. Please believe me. I have proof."

The desperation in his voice has me pulling back the knife an inch, making blood trickle into his collar. I study his features, finding nothing but the truth. Who the hell is this guy? A lunatic? The family bastard?

Throat tightening, I rasp, "I'm listening."

"Edward keeps me locked in the attic between victims."

My stomach dips. "Victims?"

He gives me an eager nod.

"What the hell does that mean?"

He licks his dry lips and glances around the room as if searching for an escape. Something about him is so skittish that I almost believe he might really be a prisoner. And the thought of there being victims strikes an irresistible chord.

I lean forward, my fingers tightening around the hilt of the knife, waiting for him to reply. "Answer me. Which victims?"

"Edward lures women here. It's always the same story. He brings them in as a nanny for a child who doesn't exist. Then he persuades them to carry out domestic duties. And when they're of no use to him anymore..." He shudders.

A chill works down my spine. I shake my head, wanting to dismiss the story as bullshit. "You're lying. I saw Adele from the window."

He gulps. "She's dead."

My throat closes up. "You're wrong."

"She died years ago. Her corpse is in the room that was always locked since you arrived. The key's in my pocket. Check for yourself."

Dread roils in my gut. I should pick up my bag and leave before Rochester returns from his honeymoon with Blanche, but I'm paralyzed by curiosity. I saw what I saw —a little blonde girl with pretty ringlets—and so did Mrs. Fairfax. The woman didn't disappear for no reason. She went to the mainland for Adele's treatment.

But what if the man I'm holding captive is telling the truth, and I really am the next in a line of victims? Rochester is capable of poisoning for money. He may as well kill for cheap labour. Or sport. Ignoring my better judgement, I reach into the pocket of his pants and extract a metal key.

"Down the hall," he says, his voice breathy. "Last door at the end."

Gathering my courage, I back toward the door, still clutching the knife. The floorboards groan under my feet as though warning me not to trust this unkempt man. Leveling him with a glower, I snarl, "If this is a trick, or if you're lying—"

"It's the truth."

With a nod, I hurry down the hallway, which seems to stretch even longer than before. My bare feet slap against marble cold enough to make me shiver. Every instinct screams that there's no dead girl behind the door at the end. The man calling himself Rowland Rochester just needs me out of the way so he can escape.

I reach the door, already breathing hard. Why am I even investigating? Because if there's a chance Rochester has hurt that girl... My throat tightens. I'm sure she's on the mainland with Mrs. Fairfax, but I'm consumed by morbid curiosity.

I knock once. "Adele?"

Silence presses against my eardrums like cotton wool.

"Adele?"

No answer, which means the room is empty or whoever's in there isn't alive. But I don't smell a corpse.

I slide the key into the lock and turn, cringing at the scrape of metal against metal. Part of me thinks this is a trap. The rest of me can't forget how Adele never waved back.

When I push open the door, its hinges shriek, and out rushes a gust of stale air. My insides roil. I gag on the mingled scents of plaster, chemicals, and something cloying. Inside is a child's bedroom with pastel pink walls, complete with an oversized dollhouse. Family pictures fill most of the walls, and on the far left stands a four-poster bed concealing stuffed animals among large cushions. And everything's covered in a layer of dust.

In the corner on the right, sheathed in shadows, sits a little blonde girl in a high-backed chair with her hands folded in her lap. Light streams in through the net curtains, illuminating her white dress with its lace trim, and the blue ribbons in her ringlet curls.

"Adele?" I whisper, my insides roiling.

She doesn't turn when I call her name, doesn't move when I step over the threshold. Silence chokes the atmosphere, save for my own ragged breath.

My pulse pounds so hard its vibrations reach my toenails. Maybe she's a mannequin or an oversized doll, but she's far too lifelike. I creep forward, stretching out my trembling fingers. Floorboards creak underfoot, making every fine hair on the back of my head stand on end.

I finally reach Adele, and memories assault me all at once. Brother Matthew dragging me on his hunting expeditions. The way he laughed when he caught an animal in a trap. How he'd force me to watch him flay his kills. And the preserved animal heads, their skins stretched on wax carcasses.

It lands with sickening clarity. Some bastard taxidermied a child. He stuffed her, dressed her, styled her curls. Replaced her eyes with glass. And then sat her in the corner like she's in a time out.

This isn't typhus fever.

It isn't even quarantine.

Adele is dead.

THIRTY-ONE

I race back to my room, my steps powered by rage. My pulse hammers in my ears like a drum roll, and every inch of my body is covered in sweat. What the fuck. What the actual fuck?

All this time, I've been waving at a little girl's taxidermied corpse.

By now, I expect Rowland to have disappeared into the shadows, leaving behind an empty bed strewn with ropes, but I find him still tied to the bedposts. His head snaps up and he gazes across the room at me, his black eyes glittering with apprehension. The bindings cut red welts into his wrists where he's been testing his bonds, and his shirt rides up to reveal defined abs.

"What the hell did you do to that little girl?" I yell, waving the knife in his face.

He closes his eyes, his body falling limp against the restraints. "Not me," he says with a pained sigh. "Edward. He smothered our sister when we were children."

The words ricochet off my brain like bullets on tile.

My mind struggles to process the fact that Rochester's supposed daughter is his younger sibling. And he's also imprisoned his feral brother who claims there's a long list of victims. Eventually, they sink in, making my gut twist.

I stare at the bound man, finding a resemblance to Rochester. The nose is identical, and beneath all that dirt are the same strong brows. But something about him is off. I can't tell if it's the wild edge or the way he flinches like a whipped dog.

"You're saying he murdered a child." The words are flat, as if they're coming from the other side of the room.

He nods. "Adele was his first victim."

My breathing comes shorter, faster. Each inhale scrapes my lungs raw but never brings enough air. I stare at his face, searching for lies, but all I see is a reflection of myself. His black eyes are empty. Hollow. Like something crawled inside and died years ago. I shake off that thought and focus on the immediate danger.

"Wait. How long ago was this? And how the hell did he get away with killing his own sister?"

Rowland gulps. "He was ten. Father's favorite. The week we were due to go to boarding school, he smothered Adele."

Prickly heat floods my veins. How on earth can he talk about it so matter-of-factly? My free hand clenches into a fist so tight my nails bite into my palm. "And you let him get away with it?"

He shakes his head from side to side, his breath turning shallow. "I didn't know what was happening until the servants found her dead."

"Okay," I whisper, reeling on my feet.

"Father blamed me because Edward told him I put a

cushion over her face the week before. He dragged me to the attic and tied me to a cot, saying no son of his would end up in an asylum. After that, the only kind company I had was Mrs. Fairfax."

Fairfax. The name punches me in the throat. That woman who served me breakfast on my first morning. Who supposedly disappeared to take Adele to a mainland hospital.

I lean closer. "If Adele never had typhus fever, then where the hell did Mrs. Fairfax go?"

Rowland jerks his head to the side, unable to meet my eyes. His throat bobs beneath his bushy beard like he's trying to swallow something too big for his throat.

"Answer me or I'll slice you open." I wave the knife like a baton.

"She died ten years ago in her sleep and has been in the attic ever since," he says, the words a tired rush.

The room tilts sideways. I stumble backward, my hip hitting the dresser hard enough to rattle the mirror. In the reflection is a wild-eyed woman with tangled hair.

"That's impossible. I saw her. I talked to her. She showed me around. She made me breakfast. She was real." I whisper, but even as I say it, doubt gnaws at my stomach like acid.

Rowland squeezes his eyes shut.

My mind races through every interaction with the housekeeper. Mrs. Fairfax filling the doorway with those massive shoulders. The mask covering the lower half of her face. The deep voice that didn't quite sound female. I stare down at Rowland, who still can't meet my eyes.

"What aren't you telling me?" I snap.

Silence stretches between us like a live wire. My heart

hammers against my ribs in double time to the distant ticking clock. It feels like the house is counting down to something terrible.

"Talk to me," I yell.

Rowland squeezes his lips shut. Works his jaw beneath all that unruly hair, and pinches his features like he's tasting something sour.

"What is it?" I say through gritted teeth.

"Between kills, when Edward doesn't have a victim to play the role, he forces me to become Mrs. Fairfax," he mutters.

The knife tumbles from my numb fingers and clatters onto the wooden floor.

Lord have mercy. Don't tell me the person I've been hooking up with this whole time was Mrs. Fairfax.

I stumble backward, my legs giving out as I collapse into the chair by the window. My gaze drops to my trembling hands as I run through every conversation I had with the massive housekeeper. The way she stared at my cleavage with those judgmental black eyes. How she disappeared for days at a time. That mask covering features I should have questioned.

Meanwhile, I've been waving at a corpse. Smiling at a little girl with glass baubles for eyes.

Nausea claws up my throat like a feral animal trying to escape. I press my fist to my mouth, tasting terror and bile. Right now, I can barely look at the man tied to the bed, but I have to know the truth.

"So let me get this straight. Between impersonating the housekeeper, you snuck into my room, sucked my foot, groped me in the bath, and humped my ass at night?" I croak.

Rowland gives me a hesitant nod, still unable to meet my eyes.

"Did you do that with all the... what did you call them? Other victims?"

He shakes his head. "No. You were the only one who waved back."

"I... was the only one who waved back," I say, my voice dripping with disbelief.

But that's not the worst part. The worst part slides into my brain like a knife between ribs, cutting through denial and landing in the soft meat of truth. Because if Rowland was Fairfax only part of the time, then that means...

I stand up so fast the chair tips backward and crashes to the floor. "Now I'm her replacement."

Ever since that breakfast with Edward Rochester, I've been the one cooking. Cleaning. Scrubbing floors, polishing silver, tending to the chickens. Playing the role of the dutiful housekeeper while Rochester entertained his precious fiancée.

I. Am. Mrs. Fairfax.

Terror punches into my stomach and pushes hard. My vision tunnels until all I can see is Rowland's face, grubby and desperate against the white sheets. The room spins like I'm on a carnival ride that's lost its brakes.

"Oh my god, oh my god, oh my god." I pace, round and round the room like a caged animal looking for a non-existent exit, my bare feet slapping against the wooden floor. I can hear him struggling against his restraints, but he's no threat.

"This is a madhouse. A fucking house of horrors." I pause by the window and look out to the lawn, expecting to see another ghost, another stand-in. Is the groundskeeper in on it? "Should've left at the first red flag. I have to get out of here now."

"Annalisa," he yells over my gibbering. "Please listen to me—"

"No! I've been living with dead children. Psychopaths. Peeping Toms in black dresses."

The walls close in. Sweat beads on my forehead and trickles down my spine like ice. Panic pushes my heart past my rib cage. Each beat feels like it might be the last one before it ruptures.

I try to breathe, but my nostrils fill with the smell of dust and decay. It's like the whole house is rotting from the inside. My stomach heaves, but there's nothing left to throw up except the bitter taste of fear.

"Annalisa, listen to me!" Rowland's voice cuts through my spiral like the crack of a whip.

I keep pacing. If I stop, realization might set in and I'll shatter into pieces so small they'll never fit back together. "Listen to what? More lies? More bullshit about your psycho brother?"

"You're in danger!" he yells so loud his voice cracks. "Edward plans to work you to death. When your body gives out and you're too weak to scrub his floors, you'll join the other corpses."

My feet freeze like they're weighted down with concrete blocks. "What?"

Rowland jerks against his restraints, making the bed frame creak under the strain. "He's done it with twelve other nannies. All of them thought they were getting an easy paycheck, but they walked into a trap. They all ended up the same. But I need you to survive."

I sway on my feet, my vision going double as I calculate how much time I have left before he returns from his honeymoon. He'd planned to kill me anyway, before I messed up his plans.

"No one has ever escaped him." His black eyes bore into mine, desperate and pleading. "But I can get you out. I'm the only one left who knows how. You have to trust me."

THIRTY-TWO

I shake my head and back away from the bed, my gaze fixed on the man thrashing against his restraints. This bastard might be telling the truth about his brother's atrocities, but he's still a liar. Even if it's just by omission. This whole house is a death trap, and I'm not sticking around to become the next corpse.

As I reach the door, Rowland rears up and screams, "Annalisa, wait! There's one more thing you must see."

The desperation in his voice stops me cold. My fingers freeze on the handle, every muscle in my body going rigid. His black eyes are wild, like terror might strike him dead if I leave. Sweat beads on his forehead, and his huge chest heaves up and down like he's run a marathon.

"What?" I hiss.

"Take off my shirt. You'll see the scars from years of torture. You'll know I'm not lying. You'll see what he'll do to you next."

My gut clenches. Part of me wants to run, but what if I'm leaving behind the only man who might protect me from Edward Rochester? And the way he said torture sounded like he'd tasted it, lived it, breathed it for years.

Every survival instinct screams at me to get the hell out, but I walk back toward the bed.

Rowland raises his chin. "Do it. Please."

I set down my bag, lift the hem of his shirt, and slice through the cotton with the knife. The fabric parts with a gentle rip, revealing his flesh. Rowland's breathing deepens, and he groans. Then his hips shift against the mattress, drawing my attention to his crotch.

Dirty bastard is getting hard.

I'm stuck in a serial killer's creepy old house with his feral brother, yet all I can concentrate on are the tight abs beneath the torn fabric and dirt.

The shirt finally falls away, revealing a chest crisscrossed with long white scars as if someone used him for fencing practice. Circular burns dot his ribs where cigars or cigarettes were ground into flesh. Some marks are old, faded to silver thread. Others look recent, still pink and raised like angry worms crawling under his skin.

My throat thickens. Tears blur my vision until his torso becomes a watercolor painting of pain. I clap a hand over my mouth, unable to breathe. Or think. Or process what I'm seeing. This body is a roadmap of suffering.

"Oh, Rowland."

He gazes up at me through damp eyes. "I'm telling you the truth. Edward's been hurting me since we were children. It only got worse after he killed Adele when I became his practice dummy."

I stare at the scars, my mind trying to process the horror. "How do you survive years of this? How did you not go completely insane?"

He closes his eyes and exhales a long, tired sigh. "I'm not sure that I did."

"Didn't anyone notice? Teachers? Doctors? Someone had to see." The words scrape out of my throat like sandpaper.

Tears roll down his cheeks, disappearing into his beard. With a shudder, he says, "Father told everyone I died the same year as Adele. Said it was a riding accident, and I had a closed casket funeral. No one questioned the lie, and I've been a ghost for thirty years."

My stomach churns. That's longer than I've even been alive. Those scars tell a story of decades of torture far worse than anything I endured with that old bastard, Brother Matthew.

I sink onto the edge of the bed, my legs collapsing like someone cut the strings holding me upright. It's impossible to imagine three years, let alone thirty of being Edward's personal punching bag while the world thought he was dead.

"You were alone this time?" My voice cracks.

"I had Mrs. Fairfax. She tried to help me when she could, but Father never allowed her to leave the grounds. And when she died and he left, it was just me and Edward."

The room spins around me like a carnival ride that's lost its brakes. I press my palms to my temples, trying to hold my skull together. Every piece of evidence points to the same conclusion—that I should trust Rowland, but my mind keeps screaming at me to save myself and leave.

"Please," he rasps. "Let me protect you. I know this house. I know Edward's patterns. I can get you out alive."

His black eyes bore into mine, desperate and pleading. I stare at his ravaged chest, my thoughts spinning in circles. I shouldn't trust anyone in this house of horrors, but scars don't lie. Nobody could fake decades of torture and abuse.

"I don't know what to believe." The words slip out.

"Let me show you my cell. Then you'll understand everything." His voice is gentle, coaxing. Like he's talking to a frightened animal. "Cut me free and I'll prove I'm not working with Edward."

Hands trembling, I reach for one of Blanche's syringes from the nightstand and hold it against his throat. "Try anything and I'll inject you with enough shit to stop your heart."

He nods, his eyes widening. "I understand."

I grab the kitchen knife. Even as my gut screams that I'm playing the world's dumbest game of Russian roulette, I slice through the rope binding his wrists before moving on to release his ankles. The makeshift bonds fall away, leaving angry red welts. He rubs circulation back into his hands and groans.

"Lead the way." I hold the syringe like a weapon as he rises. "And remember, I'm not afraid to knock you out."

Rowland rolls off the mattress and walks a wide circle around the bed toward the exit. I follow him into the hallway, watching out for sudden movements. My gaze bores into his broad back. It blows my mind how a man this huge managed to fool me into believing he was the housekeeper.

As he reaches the end of the hall, I shake off that thought. Rowland runs his fingers along a panel I've passed countless times, which opens into a narrow staircase. Its wooden steps disappear into the dark, making my breath snag.

"Where are you going?" I ask.

He turns around, his dark eyes meeting mine. "You wanted proof I'm not working with Edward. My cell is up there."

My throat dries. I swallow hard, trying to push back a surge of fear. "This had better not be a trap."

"It isn't," he rasps. "But don't you want to see where I spent the past three decades when he wasn't forcing me into the role of a servant?"

"Okay," I whisper.

Rowland enters the wall opening and ascends, his uneven steps creaking. I follow after him, stepping onto wooden treads that warp under our weight like they're about to collapse.

The air grows thicker with each step and heavier with the smells of mold, dust, and despair. My gut churns, and I try not to think of meat left too long in the sun.

"How much longer?" I whisper, though I'm not sure why I'm being so quiet.

"We're here." Rowland's voice echoes in the narrow space.

At the top, he pushes open another door, which groans on rusted hinges. The sound makes every hair on my arms stand on end. I follow him into an attic that resembles something out of a nightmare. Low ceiling beams cast shadows that move in the dim light filtering through grimy windows. I hold my breath, trying not to gag.

Rowland steps aside and sweeps his arm toward a narrow cot sitting against the far wall, its frame bearing iron shackles. The mattress is thin and dark. Beside it sits a chamber pot filled with human waste.

My insides heave. I press my free hand to my mouth and fight back a surge of bile.

But that's not the worst part.

Implements hang from the crossbeams—knives, chains, pliers with jagged teeth, leather whips with multiple tails. Some of the tools are rusted and old, others clean.

"Oh god," I groan from behind my hand. "You were stuck here this entire time?"

Rowland's dark gaze turns solemn. "Both of us."

I follow his gaze to the corner where something sits in a wooden rocking chair. In the dark, it looks like a pile of forgotten clothes, until I draw closer and light catches a skeleton sitting propped in the seat. Its bones are held together by dried sinew and scraps of flesh. Wisps of gray hair still cling to the skull in patches, and the jaw hangs open in a permanent scream.

But it's what the skeleton is wearing that makes my blood freeze.

It's the same kind of black dress I've been wearing since my first day here, with the same high collar, buttoned front, and the same long sleeves. The same white apron is tied around what used to be a waist. Its fabric is faded and moth-eaten, but it's identical to my uniform.

My throat closes. Terror punches into my stomach with both fists, making me double over.

"What the fuck?" I cry, my eyes stinging.

"That's the real Mrs. Fairfax." Rowland's voice is gentle, like he's breaking news to a child.

I can't speak. Can't breathe. Can't do anything but stare at the corpse wearing my uniform. I've scrubbed floors in it. Served meals in it. Picked foreign hairs off it. It's a mark. A claim. A promise of what's waiting for me if I don't escape.

But I'm not just wearing the uniform of one dead woman. This is probably the style of clothes worn by a dozen other women like me, forced to serve a psychopath.

My vision tunnels until all I can see is that corpse in my clothes. Then the room spins like I'm on an out-of-control merry-go-round.

"Your brother killed her?" I rasp.

"She died in her sleep," Rowland replies, his voice pained. "Edward couldn't stand the thought of losing his perfect housekeeper, so he…"

Rowland bows his head. He doesn't need to complete the sentence because the evidence speaks for itself. Edward kept her. Like a trophy. Like a fucking souvenir.

Tears stream down my face, hot and bitter as arsenic. I want to slide down the wall and sink through the dusty floor.

"How many?" I ask.

Rowland gazes down at me, his eyes wide.

"How many other women died because of Edward Rochester?"

A sound cuts through my spiral. Low and distant at first, then growing louder, followed by the rumble of engines. It's vehicles.

Rowland's head snaps toward the window. "Shit."

Red and blue lights slice through the grimy glass like neon knives, painting the attic in alternating colors. I rush to the window, finding police cars filling the courtyard, their headlights cutting through the morning light.

I stagger backward, my insides twisting into agonizing knots. The cops have finally discovered my hiding place.

THIRTY-THREE

I'm no longer thinking. Because staying in this house is certain death. I don't care if the police have tracked me here. At least with them I might have a chance of survival. Or at worst, a clean death.

Pulse quickening, I race down the hallway, past the portraits of dead aristocrats who may or may not be killers. Past the room housing the taxidermied child and past the room where Rochester tampered with Blanche's pills. Rowland shouts my name, but I don't stop. Can't stop. Can't block out the image of that skeleton in my dress.

By the time I reach the main staircase, I don't know whether I'm running to salvation or condemnation. I grip the banister and descend on legs that feel like noodles.

The doorbell rings.

I freeze at the bottom of the stairs, my heart slamming so hard against my ribs that I feel it in my throat. The bell rings again, long and insistent, echoing through the empty house like a death knell.

This could be my way out. But what if they ask for my

name? My fingerprints are still all over that syringe I shoved into Callahan's foot. One wrong word and I'll be trading this nightmare for a cell on death row.

The bell rings a third time, followed by heavy knocking that rattles the door in its frame.

Fuck it. Anything's better than staying here with those corpses.

I reach the entrance hall and fling open the heavy door to find two cops on the front steps. The older one has gray hair and tired eyes. His partner is younger, clean-shaven, with blue eyes that scrutinize my face.

Behind them, the courtyard swarms with police cars, their red and blue lights fracturing the pale morning. Officers stream across the grounds leading German shepherds straining against their leashes, with noses to the ground like they're hunting something specific.

My stomach drops through the floor. This isn't a routine visit. This is a full-scale search operation.

The older cop flashes his badge. "Good morning, ma'am. I'm Detective Hayes. This is Detective Morrison. We're looking for Mrs. Rochester. Have you seen her?"

This isn't about me? But why are they looking for Blanche? And why so many?

"Blanche? No. They left yesterday morning for their honeymoon."

Hayes pulls out a notebook. "What time? How did she seem?"

"Around ten AM. They both seemed happy. What's this about?"

Morrison steps close enough for me to smell the coffee on his breath, his gaze dropping down the gaping front of my dress. My hackles rise. What the hell did Blanche say about me to the cops?

"And you are?" the younger detective asks.

"Annalisa." I glance from the first cop to the other. "Annalisa Burlington. Just the maid."

"Mrs. Rochester is missing," Hayes says. "She left her hotel last night and returned here alone. Any idea why?"

My jaw drops, and my mind goes blank. This is unexpected. I gaze up into the older man's eyes and say, "I haven't seen her. The house has been empty since they left."

Hayes gives me an absent nod and flips open his notebook. "We understand there was an incident between you and Mrs. Rochester."

I glance at Morrison, whose gaze bores down at me like an X-ray. Someone talked. Probably one of Blanche's little friends. My mind scrambles for answers. What the hell do I tell them without incriminating myself?

"She got upset over nothing. Rich women like to create drama," I reply with a shrug.

"What kind of drama?"

"She grabbed one of my bras and accused me of trying to seduce her fiancé. Then she threatened to hurt herself if he didn't fire me on the spot."

A voice shouts from behind the house. "Detective! We found something!"

I stiffen. Hayes and Morrison exchange glances that make my skin crawl.

The older one turns to me and says, "Ma'am, we need you to stay right here. Don't go anywhere."

Before I can ask what the hell is happening, they hurry down the steps and across the courtyard. My legs quiver. My heart thrashes loud enough to drown thought. I lean against the doorframe, watching them disappear around the corner of the house.

What did they find? My mind races through the possibilities and comes up blank. There's a corpse in the attic, another in Adele's room. According to Rowland, there are others. Women like me, who came here under the false pretense of a nanny job.

I shuffle my feet, wishing I'd left at the first sign of suspicion. It's too late to run now that the cops have seen my face. Dogs bark in the distance, and the morning air carries jumbled voices. Whatever they've found has to be big.

Acid churns in my gut when an ambulance enters the courtyard. I duck behind the door as paramedics rush past with a stretcher. What the hell is happening?

Minutes crawl by like hours. I wrap my arms around myself, shivering in my woolen dress. I'm almost certain this isn't about me, but everything feels wrong. Like the world has skewed sideways and I'm about to slide off.

Finally, Hayes appears from around the corner, his face grim. Morrison trails behind him, speaking into his phone in urgent, clipped tones.

"Ms. Burlington, we need you to come with us for an identification," says the older man.

My throat closes up. Identification means a body. "What did you find?"

"We'd rather show you. This way."

On trembling legs, I follow them around the house. Gravel crunches underfoot as we pass the rose bushes where I hid yesterday morning when Rochester released me from captivity. Once again, I regret staying, as each step brings me closer to something I don't want to see.

We reach the back gardens where the paramedics wait at the pond's edge with the cops and canines. Officers in waders stand waist-deep in the water, floating something between them that's shaped like a body.

My blood curdles. It's a woman in a white dress floating face-down on the surface. Her black hair fans out around her head like spilled ink. Her arms drift at her sides, pale and lifeless. The fabric of her dress billows around her body, melding into the water.

I recognize that dress.

I recognize that body.

It's Blanche.

As we reach the edge of the water, darkness closes in around my vision like a tunnel. My gaze skips from her pale skin to the white fabric moving with the gentle current because anything is better than facing the truth. Blanche is dead. Like she finally followed through on that threat to drown herself.

Or did she?

"Oh god." The words slip out as a whisper. I press a hand to my mouth to stop myself from saying anything else.

"Is that Mrs. Rochester?" Hayes asks, his voice gentle.

By now, they've turned around the body. Her face is slack and pale, lips parted, eyes clouded. Her fingers hang limp, wrinkled and white from the water. An officer crouches at the pond's edge, scooping small baggies of white powder into an evidence pouch.

Terror seizes my throat. I can't speak. Can't breathe. Can't process what I'm seeing. My pulse thuds in my ears, drowning out all sound.

Hayes grips my shoulder and gives me a hard shake, snapping me out of my fugue. "Ms. Burlington?"

"I... yes. That's Blanche."

But my mind is already racing ahead. Rochester

brought her back. Used the threat to drown herself to make it look like she got high and went under. Set up the perfect cover for murder.

The bastard actually did it.

Hayes leans in, his voice low. "You sure you didn't see her come back?"

I blink, startled. "No."

He studies my face like he's taking notes. "You didn't hear any vehicles approaching?"

When I was busy holding an unconscious man hostage? "No."

Morrison pulls out his phone. "We need to contact the husband."

I hold my breath, my skin crawling at the man's evil ingenuity. At how quickly he pivoted from swapping out her pills to killing her in the very pond where she threatened to drown herself. I imagine him sitting in a hotel, surrounded by witnesses, while he frets about his missing wife.

"Mr. Rochester?" The younger cop pauses. "This is Detective Morrison. I'm afraid I have bad news about your wife."

The conversation is brief. Even from where I stand, I can hear that bastard's voice through the speaker, asking if there's been some terrible mistake. He sounds baffled, shocked. Heartbroken. But it's all part of a performance.

I tune out the rest of the conversation, watching the officers fish Blanche's body out of the water and zip her into a black bag. Morrison gives me his card and allows me to return to the house, where I stand by the door, watching them load her into the ambulance and disappear down the winding drive.

Rochester got away with murder. And now he's about

to inherit millions. He'll be rich enough to make problems disappear without a trace. Rich enough to hunt me down no matter where I run.

I'm the only person alive who knows the truth about the pill-swapping. The only witness who can connect him to Blanche's death. Which makes me the biggest loose end in his perfect crime.

Maybe I should call Morrison. Tell him and Hayes about the murders, the corpses in the attic. But I'm also a killer, wanted for another set of crimes.

Making that call means trading one death sentence for another. Besides, I misplaced my phone weeks ago.

With Blanche's money, Rochester will have resources beyond imagination. There's nowhere I could hide. And when he finds me, I'll end up like Blanche. Like Adele. Like Mrs. Fairfax. Like the other servants.

There's only one person capable of protecting me. A man who's survived Rochester's cruelty for decades. Who knows every secret of this house. A man who hates that murdering psychopath even more than me.

I close the door, cross the entrance hall and climb the stairs. Rowland crouches in the opening of the wood-paneled wall, his arms wrapped around his knees. He stares up at me, his eyes wild.

"What happened?" he whispers.

"They're gone," I reply, my voice flat. "The cops found Blanche's body in the pond."

He gulps. "Edward killed her already?"

I nod. "He made it look like suicide."

"Do you believe me now?" he rasps.

"Yeah."

Rowland's face crumples with relief. His tears come fast, his body trembling with the force of his emotion.

"Thank you for being the only person who ever took my side."

I stare down at this broken man who's survived decades of hell. The only person who knows Rochester's weaknesses.

Rowland is my only chance of surviving that monster.

But even he might not be enough.

THIRTY-FOUR

I take Rowland down to the kitchen and guide him to a chair. It's messy from the recent visitors, scattered with crumbs, shattered glass, and half-eaten pastries, but I clear space on the table, place my hands on his shoulders and order him to sit.

My mind still churns from recent revelations. Three dead bodies in a single day. All women. All connected to this house. And soon, Edward Rochester will return home to tie up loose ends.

"You need to explain your plan to protect me from your psycho brother."

Rowland rubs the back of his head and stares at his lap. Sunlight streams through the windows, illuminating his scraggly beard and eyes that dart around like he's expecting punishment.

"Talk to me," I say.

"I'll overpower him before he gets the chance to hurt you."

"Just like that?" I ask.

He sits straighter. "What does that mean?"

Lips tightening, I switch on the kettle and reach for the tea bags, pull cups from the cupboard and set them on the counter. What I say next has to be worded carefully, since I need Rowland's courage.

I grew up with younger brothers, along with boys who were technically my stepsons. One thing men have in common is bravado. They talk tough, overestimate their abilities, and never grow out of that bullshit. Men always make promises they never keep, but I'll hold that observation to myself. Right now, I can't afford to discourage Rowland.

The kettle rumbles, building toward a boil. I lean against the counter, studying his scarred chest through the torn shirt. Some of the marks are so precise, they could only have come from being tied down and tortured.

"Annalisa?" he asks, his thick brows knitting together. "Please tell me what's on your mind."

Those scars mark decades of torture. Decades of subjugation. No one suffers that long and comes out able to protect others from their abuser. I hesitate. Gather my thoughts. Search for the most tactful way to voice it.

"If you can defeat Edward, why were you his prisoner for so long?" I ask.

"My mind was imprisoned," he replies, his voice pained. "Father and Edward treated me like an animal. They made me believe I was too dangerous to exist and had to be controlled with punishment."

I swallow hard, my chest aching. Family has a way of brainwashing a person until they can't tell wrong from right. The only reason I didn't end up like Rowland was because I took such drastic steps to leave.

The kettle erupts in a sharp whistle that makes me

flinch. I pour hot water over the tea bags, add milk, and set a cup in front of Rowland.

"You're telling me your mind is free now?" I ask.

He gives me an eager nod.

"What's made the difference?" I take the seat opposite and blow on my hot drink.

"I finally have something to fight for." He gazes up at me, his eyes softening.

"What does that mean?"

He reaches across the table, places his hand over mine, and brushes his thumb over my knuckles. The touch is gentle, reverent, like I'm something precious instead of a fugitive hiding from the law.

"The night you waved back made me so happy," he replies, the words choked with emotion. "No woman ever invited me in before. No woman ever begged for me."

My throat closes, and I lower my lashes, unable to withstand his hopeful smile. He thinks I chose *him* over his brother, when I didn't even realize there were two of them. The truth sits heavy in my chest like a stone, but I can't shatter whatever hope is keeping him functional when I need him to survive.

I bring the cup to my lips. "How exactly will you protect me?"

"I can take Edward's place. Become him."

My stomach dips. "Switch identities?"

"Why not? Everyone thinks I died the same year as Adele. Edward is a recluse. We're the same height, same build, same features."

"What will you do about your brother?" But even as I ask, I already know the answer. Can see it in the way his jaw sets, the hardening of his black eyes.

"He joins our sister."

The words settle in my gut like stones. This is the line I swore I wouldn't cross again. Except now it doesn't feel like a choice. I fall still, letting the silence stretch until all I hear are my heartbeat and the soft hiss of the cooling kettle.

Rowland breathes hard, his dark eyes penetrating my soul. What is he looking for—my permission or my approval?

"You want to kill him," I say.

"Yes," he growls, his eyes flashing, his chest heaving with excitement.

My heart shrivels. I picture Callahan, lying on the floor, held down by mobsters. And the syringe they forced into my hand. Even though Rowland seems excited at the thought of us killing Edward together, I shake my head, unable to get involved in another murder.

Rowland sets down his cup and stands. "Edward is too dangerous to let live. He'll kill you just like he killed the others. Come with me. I'll show you something that'll change your mind."

He strides out of the kitchen, leaving me so spooked I have no choice but to follow. We continue through the hallways, passing locked doors, until we reach Edward's study. Rowland slides his fingers behind a wooden panel and opens another doorway.

Inside, he walks toward the mahogany desk and opens its bottom drawer. I enter, swallowing hard as he pulls out a leather notebook.

"Look at this." He sets it on the desk.

"What is it?" I hover by the door, wringing my hands, my feet ready to bolt.

Rowland doesn't reply. Something in his dark eyes tells me I need to see for myself.

Throat tightening, I edge forward until I reach the other side of the desk and pick up the notebook. It's heavier than expected, with expensive, cream-colored paper. I open it to the first page, finding elegant handwriting flowing across it in dark ink. The first entry reads:

> Grace Poole. Age 36. Dark brown hair, stout build, escaping drunk-driving conviction. Arrived via evening ferry. Performed well during the transport interview. Eager to please. Shows promise for extended service.

I flip the page, finding more details about Sarah. How she cleaned. How she cooked. How she cried when she realized there was no child to care for. Then a jagged tear where a page was ripped out.

The final entry in the same writing says:

> Subject strangled with stockings after six months of service. Disposed of in cottage basement. Next candidate scheduled for following month.

Bile rises in my throat. I flip to the next entry, then the next. Each woman gets the same treatment. Detailed observations of their performance as servants, followed by a ripped-out page. Then a cold, clinical accounting of their death.

My hands won't stop shaking as I read their names, their ages, their desperate circumstances and their cause of death:

Bertha Mason. Age 32. Black hair, average build, fleeing abusive husband. Asphyxiated with bedsheets.

Helen Burns. Age 26. Light brown hair, petite, recently evicted. Garroted with piano wire.

Louisa Eshton. Age 20. Blonde hair, pregnant, abandoned by family. Choked with leather belt.

The list goes on and on. Each name is a person. Each person had the same thing in common: they were either on the run or cast out, only to be murdered by Rochester. Throttled by curtain cord. Ligatured with shoelaces. Strangled with bicycle chain, clothesline, leather belt, rosary beads, silk scarf, telephone wire.

I blink away tears, imagining hordes of clueless women, lured here by desperate circumstances, only to be manipulated then murdered. Every one of them suffered and died for the amusement of that maniac.

Then I reach the last entry and the words close in like a trap.

Annalisa Burlington. Age 24. Blonde hair, large breasts, fleeing law enforcement. Highly motivated by fear. Performed adequately during transport interview. Shows promise for extended domestic service.

My heart slows. My body goes so cold I can barely

feel my fingers. The wretched bastard cataloged me like livestock. Like I was a product on trial. A disposable appliance to be replaced when I broke.

I turn the page, finding another ripped-out section, followed by an insultingly detailed graphic description of how I looked cleaning the fireplaces on my hands and knees. Then there's a blank page with a single word written at the top in the same elegant script: *DEMISE*.

"You see," Rowland says from the other side of the desk. "He plans on killing you next."

My hands shake so much that I drop the notebook onto the polished mahogany. I reach into my pocket and pull out the crumpled piece of paper containing the task list left for me in the kitchen that morning after our breakfast. The one that seemed outlandish, but not a red flag.

When I smooth it out against the desk and hold it up to the torn space in the notebook, it's a perfect fit.

I breathe hard, my pulse pounding with painful realization. Every task he gave me. Every floor I scrubbed, every meal I cooked, every humiliation I endured. It was all planned. All part of his evaluation process to see how long I'd last before he added my death to the final page.

"You saw him do this over and over and didn't lift a finger to stop him?" I ask, the words choked.

"Edward's control over me was absolute until you," he replies.

A shudder runs down my frame, igniting every nerve ending until I'm coming apart at the seams. All those nights I lay in bed wondering if I was losing my mind with Rochester blowing hot and cold. All those times I questioned my own sanity for playing along with this charade while he studied me like a bug under glass.

"I don't believe this," I say through clenched teeth.

"Do you want to see the corpses he keeps in the cottage basement?" Rowland asks.

"No." The word comes out strangled. I can't handle returning to the place where he locked me up that night. Can't handle seeing another body. Can't handle knowing that I was trapped mere feet above a graveyard.

Rowland rounds the desk and pauses at a distance. "I meant it when I said I'd find a way for us to be together. Every word. But I have to know, do you still want to be with me?"

I stare up at this broken man who's survived hell. Who still has enough humanity left to want to protect someone else instead of just saving himself. Who knows exactly what kind of monster his brother is because he's lived it.

His black eyes burn with something fierce and desperate. Like the next word from me could condemn him to a lifetime of captivity or set him free.

"We're not so different," I murmur. "Just trying to survive in a world that wants us dead."

His breath quickens. "Then you agree? That Edward must die?"

I glance down at the notebook. At my name written in the elegant handwriting marking me for death. At the page titled DEMISE waiting for him to fill it with details of how he killed me.

Rochester isn't going to stop. Even if I run, even if I disappear, he'll hunt me down. And when he catches me, I'll end up in that cottage basement with all the others.

"Yeah." The word tastes like blood. "Edward dies."

Relief transforms Rowland's features, smoothing away the lines etched with pain. Seconds pass, and he doesn't move. Just gazes down at me with those fathomless black eyes like I'm the keys to his salvation. Then he takes a slow step toward me, his fingertips skimming the desk.

At the second step, I straighten, finding him more imposing than he was in the kitchen. Taller. Thicker in the shoulders. The quiet confidence in his next step makes him feel heavier somehow—more rugged, more masculine, more real. How on earth did I not notice this before?

Has he always been like this? Or did something inside him shift when I said the words? Or maybe I've been so focused on survival that the only viable men to me have been those with resources. High rollers, sugar daddies, gangsters like Gil. For a moment of insanity, even Edward Rochester. And the entire time, I'd been looking in the wrong places.

Rowland's rawness and blunt edges are the polar opposite of Rochester's refined manipulation. Nothing about him is calculated. Everything about him is unvarnished and direct.

He stops close enough that I can smell the attic on his skin. Feel the heat radiating from his scarred chest. My pulse quickens, and shivers run down my spine as he lifts his fingers toward my face, hesitating just an inch from my skin. His features flicker with uncertainty as if needing my permission.

I raise my chin, and he trails them along my jaw, making my skin tingle.

Breathing hard, I place a hand on my chest, only relaxing when he breaks eye contact to let his gaze roam across my face as if he's memorizing every contour. No one's ever looked at me like this before. It's like I'm the answer to every prayer he's been afraid to ask.

Then he leans closer until our faces nearly touch. His breath warms my heated skin. The air thickens, the walls grow closer, the study ceases to exist. It's just me and him and this unspoken need.

"Annalisa?" he asks, his voice wavering and unsure.

"Yes?" I whisper.

"Kiss me," he says.

THIRTY-FIVE

The request hangs between us, thick as smoke. I stare into Rowland's black eyes, finding the kind of naked hunger that makes my insides seize. Oh, God. When did anyone ever need me this much?

But I have to know.

"Why do you want to kiss me?" I whisper.

A flush floods his cheeks, disappearing into his unkempt beard, and he drops his gaze to the Persian rug. "Annalisa." The tremor in his voice catches me off guard. "I've never..."

He trails off, his massive frame somehow looking fragile. My brows crease as he struggles with the words, stirring something protective in my chest. This broken man is trying to give me something precious: his truth.

"I've never been kissed," he finally mutters.

My breath catches. I study this mountain of a man, all scars and untamed hair, and something inside me shifts. "Never?"

"I've never been with a woman, either," he adds, the confession tumbling out in a rush.

My mind goes quiet. All those nights in the dark, those gentle hands, that reverent touch. It was him. This broken man who's never known tenderness was the one who made me come apart.

"What about the others?" I ask.

"I used to hear the first few from up in the attic, but I only broke through my restraints after Father left." He rubs his wrists, and I notice the permanent red welts circling them like bracelets. "After that, security became lax."

The timeline hits me hard. He was just a child when they locked him away. Ten years old when his family decided he was too dangerous to exist. My throat tightens imagining him growing up in that cage while his killer brother lived free.

"What happened to your father?"

Shoulders sagging, Rowland crosses the study and settles on a leather sofa. Pain flickers across his features like he's reliving old wounds.

"What is it?" I ask.

He struggles with the memory, his jaw working beneath that thick beard. Something about his anguish makes me want to reach out to offer comfort, but I wrap my arms around my middle.

Finally, he says, "Father and Edward fell out over Mrs. Fairfax. It was terrible."

"What happened?"

"Mrs. Fairfax was the glue that kept the family together. When she died, they turned on each other like wolves." He runs a hand through his hair and sighs. "Father wanted her buried. Edward wanted her preserved."

The word hangs in the air like poison. I step toward the sofa, my insides churning. "Preserved how?"

"Like the taxidermy Father did to Adele and—" He shakes his head and sags.

My breath hitches. It makes sense in a sick sort of way. Edward was ten when he murdered his sister, too young to create that monstrosity. I lower myself on the seat beside him and place my hand over his. "So he loved Mrs. Fairfax?"

He nods. "Edward begged Father to do the same to her, but he refused. Said she was fat and old and unworthy of preservation. That's when Edward turned on him and threw him down the stairs."

I reel forward, my jaw dropping. I'd assumed Edward was a misogynist. Apparently, he's an equal opportunity monster.

"Where is your father now?"

Rowland raises his shoulders toward his ears. "Edward never told me. All I heard from the attic was Father yelling for help, saying he'd broken his hip."

"Shit," I whisper.

"Father's gone. So is Edward." He turns in his seat, his gaze dropping to my lips. "But you're here."

Heat crawls up my neck, bringing me back to his request for that kiss. His black eyes burn with an intensity that should be terrifying, but my body finds it thrilling. I draw back, wondering why the hell I'm so skittish with a man who's already given me orgasms. Maybe it's because I need to know what really happened in this house.

"Rowland," I say, trying to be tactful. "Did your dad know Edward was killing women?"

He glances at his lap, taking away all his warmth. "Father could be willfully blind. Admitting that Edward was the violent one would mean admitting he'd made a terrible mistake with me."

"So he ignored it?"

He nods.

"But you said security got lax after your father left. You must have spoken to some of those women."

"Disguised as Mrs. Fairfax," he says with a shrug. "Edward was always close by, making sure I followed the script."

I nod, remembering how quickly Rochester showed his face that first morning. It was exactly when I was trying to get the truth from what I thought was the housekeeper.

"And the night visits?"

Pain flickers across his features like lightning. "I tried warning the first woman. Edward made sure I didn't warn the second."

He lifts his beard, exposing a thick white scar on the base of his neck. I hiss through my teeth. Rochester slit his throat. That bastard could have killed his own brother.

"Oh, God... That's..." I shake my head, unable to muster up words to describe the pain, the helplessness, the guilt. It makes what I suffered with Brother Matthew look like a spat. "Rowland, I'm so sorry."

He hangs his head and nods, every line of his body radiating shame. It's like he can barely admit to enduring so much torture. "I never gave up, though," he says, sounding so earnest that my heart aches. "I put on the ski mask, tried to frighten them at night, but it only drove them into Edward's arms."

"Weren't you afraid he would punish you again?"

Rowland raises a massive shoulder. "Edward learned after the first time not to be so vicious."

I wince at the implication that Rowland ensured even more torture trying to do the right thing. "You even tried to frighten me."

"But it didn't work." He gives me a sidelong look.

"No, it didn't."

"You didn't scream like the others. You didn't run to him for protection. You seemed to like it when I took hold of your foot."

Heat floods my cheeks, traveling down my chest. It tightens my nipples and seeps low in my belly. I squirm in my seat and gaze up at him through my lashes. "Put it this way," I murmur. "I didn't know my feet were so sensitive."

A shy smile breaks across his features, making him look less feral. "I became addicted to you."

My breath catches. "Why?"

"No woman ever showed me kindness except Mrs. Fairfax."

Warmth fills my chest. In a world full of darkness and pain, the thought that I could mean anything to him steals my breath. "Oh, Rowland."

His face crumples, and he bows his head. Tears roll down his cheeks, and his massive shoulders heave with sobs. Seeing this huge man cry cracks something open in my chest. I place a hand on his bicep.

"Rowland, what is it?"

"Mrs. Fairfax told me something before she died." His voice cracks.

"Do you want to talk about it?"

"She was our mother."

I reel back, my mind conjuring up the corpse rotting in the attic. "She said that?"

His features pinch with agony. "Father used her as a

servant. Never acknowledged her as a wife and mother. He worked that poor woman to death."

My mind races from the attic, to the notebook of victims. All those women. Used up and thrown away like broken appliances. All this time, Mrs. Fairfax was the original. Was Edward trying to replicate his mother's trauma?

"Was she also a prisoner?" I ask.

"She couldn't leave with me chained up in the attic. Even though she knew Edward was dangerous, she couldn't bear the thought of him in an asylum."

"That wasn't fair," I whisper, pulling him into a hug.

"Father forced her to be his accomplice in caging me up like an animal."

I rest my head on his shoulder as he continues to cry. This might be the first time he's told anyone about his trauma. But how can a person ever process decades of that kind of betrayal?

"Rowland, I'm so sorry. You should never have experienced a day of captivity. You were innocent."

"And so was Mrs. Fairfax."

"Right," I say.

"I watched her take her last breath. My own mother. Treated like a slave until the day she died."

"That was terrible."

He lifts his head to meet my eyes, and the anguish in his features makes me splinter. "We never knew the truth until it was too late."

"I just don't have the words," I say, feeling inadequate.

He shoots off the sofa. His chest heaving, his hands opening and closing into fists. I scramble off, my palms raised, not knowing whether he needs another hug.

"Rowland?"

He turns to me, his eyes wild, his face etched with raw anguish. "I've never known love. Never known tenderness."

Heat radiates off his body like a furnace. I step back, my pulse quickening to a drumroll. His dark eyes seize mine and bore deep into my soul. My stomach dips. What on earth is he about to confess next?

I take another step backward, then another, but he continues advancing on me until my ass hits the desk. He reaches out and cups my cheek with surprising gentleness.

"My life was nothing until you waved back."

A lump forms in my throat. I only waved back because of the note, yet that small gesture changed the trajectory of a prisoner's life. I swallow hard, trying to withstand the intensity of his gaze. My lips part, but I produce no words.

"It was meaningless until you chose me instead of him," he murmurs.

Every instinct screams to run, but I can't move. The ache in his voice batters at what's left of my defenses, and my heart cracks open. Rising on my toes, I press my lips to his, and hope to Almighty God I'm not making a terrible mistake.

THIRTY-SIX

Rowland's mouth goes still under mine. Like he's forgotten how to breathe. How to move. How to be human instead of a caged animal waiting for the next beating.

Then something inside him breaks open.

His arms crush me against his chest, all those scars and burns pressing into my body through his torn shirt. His mouth moves against mine like he's drowning and I'm his last breath of air.

The kiss is urgent. Hungry. Desperate. Desire coils low in my belly, arousal already pooling at the thought of what he'll do with those hands.

He pulls back, his black eyes stunned and feral. Like he doesn't quite believe I'm real, let alone choosing him.

"Annalisa... I've said your name a thousand times in the dark, but it's never sounded real until now."

I cup his bearded face, feeling the rough hair against my palms. "I'm here."

He exhales a ragged breath. "I've wanted this since

the night you looked at me from that balcony. Every night, I prayed you'd see me. That you'd choose me instead of him."

The words hit deep in my chest. I was an idiot for even thinking Edward Rochester could be an option.

"I'm choosing you now," I say, meaning every word.

His mouth finds my neck, lips trailing over my pulse point. His tongue darts out, tasting my flesh. I arch against his broad chest with a gasp.

"You smell like salvation," he groans against my throat.

His beard scratches my skin, making my nipples tighten under my dress. Every inch of me aches for more.

"Touch me," I say, my voice breathy.

With trembling fingers, he skims the neckline of my dress. The first button slips free, then the second. Cool air hits my skin as the fabric parts, revealing the valley between my breasts. Rowland kisses every inch of exposed cleavage like it's precious, making my nerve endings sing.

"I dreamt of you when I was in chains and shadows. And now you're here, in the light, in my arms," he says as more buttons pop free.

His breathing gets heavier, his lips more insistent as my dress falls open completely. He pushes it off my shoulders, letting the fabric pool at my feet. I stand before him in just my bra and panties, my nipples aching for his touch.

His hands hover over my skin, just shy of claiming. "You're more beautiful than anything I ever let myself imagine."

Heat blooms across my cheeks. Nobody has ever

looked at me with such naked hunger or unbridled reverence. His gaze burns away every dismissal, every cruel word still haunting my psyche, and every time a man ever made me feel like garbage.

"But you already know what I look like," I say with a smile.

He shakes his head. "Not like this. Not when you're giving yourself to me."

He traces the curve of my waist, thumbs brushing the underside of my breasts. I shiver, all sensation racing south.

"I thought about this every night," he murmurs. "About having you. Tasting you. Making you mine."

His hands slide up to cup my breasts through the lace. I moan as his thumbs brush over my nipples.

"Please, Annalisa. Let me worship those perfect breasts. Give this poor bastard a taste of heaven."

I reach behind me, unhooking my bra. It falls away, and his breath catches. My nipples tighten with need, and I arch my back. He drinks in every detail with his dark eyes like he's storing it for later.

"Fuck," he groans. "Even prettier than in the dark."

He cups my breasts, lifting and weighing them, thumbs circling my nipples until I'm panting. When his mouth finds a peak, his tongue flicks over it and I cry out, tangling fingers in his hair. He sucks harder, his teeth grazing tender flesh.

"God, yes," I say with a gasp. "Just like that."

He moves to the other breast, giving it the same attention. My pussy throbs, soaking my panties. I need him inside me, but I don't want this to end. I want this man to worship me forever.

"Rowland," I moan.

He drags his mouth from my nipple like it hurts to stop. "Tell me what you need, Annalisa. I need to hear it."

"You. All of you."

Something fierce flashes in his eyes. He straightens, his hands dropping to his waist. I lick my lips, my gaze locked on the massive bulge straining his pants. I slide my hands beneath his shirt, peeling off the torn fabric to reveal broad shoulders and thick biceps. My gaze roves over his chiseled chest, tight abs, and the huge cock standing to attention. It's thick, veiny, with a bulbous head already glistening with precum.

"Fuck," I whisper.

Rowland claims my lips again, kissing me deep and sliding his hands down to my ass. He lifts me onto the edge of the mahogany table, where that psychopath cataloged me for death. Now it's ours.

"I want to ruin you right here on Edward's desk," he says against my lips.

The symbolism isn't lost on me. Claiming this space. Taking back power from the man who destroyed his life and would have ended mine.

"Then fuck me," I say.

After hooking his fingers in my panties, he slides them down my legs and places the soaked cotton to his nose with a groan. "Fuck, I could live on your scent for a hundred years. You have no idea how much power you hold over my soul." He slides my underwear into his back pocket and ghosts his fingers over my folds. "You're drenched. It's like your body's begging just as hard as mine."

"Only for you," I murmur.

Rowland positions himself between my spread thighs,

the head of his cock nudging my entrance. We're both breathing hard, our hearts pounding in sync.

"I've waited an eternity for this moment," he says, his voice raw with emotion. "For someone who would accept me into her heart and into her beautiful body. For someone to give me the courage to fight back. For someone that makes me want to live."

My chest tightens. The way he looks at me, like I'm everything he's ever wanted, reaches a part of me no man has ever touched. All my life, I've only ever been useful to men. Useful for sex, useful for cleaning, useful for taking blame when things go wrong. But with Rowland, this is different.

I give him meaning.

The thought hits me like a revelation. I'm no longer a workhorse, a whore, a convenience, or a scapegoat. Rowland looks at me like I'm his salvation. Like my presence alone gives him a reason to keep breathing.

My throat tightens. I don't know what to do with this feeling, this weight of being someone's lifeline instead of their plaything. It's both terrifying and thrilling. What if I let him down? What if I'm not strong enough to be what he needs?

But the desperate hope in his eyes makes me want to try.

"Let me be your everything," I whisper.

He moves over me with trembling hands, his breath shaky against my neck. I can feel his nervousness in every touch, the way he hesitates like he's afraid I might disappear.

"I don't want to hurt you," he whispers, his voice thick with emotion.

My heart clenches at the tenderness in his voice.

After everything he's endured, he's still thinking of my comfort. I reach up and cup his face, my fingers sinking into his coarse beard.

"You won't," I reply, my voice breathy with need.

When he lines his cock at my entrance, it's with a reverence that makes my chest ache. He pushes inside slowly, and I gasp at the sensation. He's bigger than I expected, and my body needs time to adjust. But there's no urgency in his movements, no selfish taking. Just careful exploration, like he's memorizing every sensation.

"Oh god," he groans, his entire body shuddering. "You're so tight. Exquisite. My Annalisa."

He says my name like a prayer, like I'm something sacred and worthy of worship. I slip my arms beneath his shirt and over his shoulders, feeling raised scars. Each mark tells a story of survival, of enduring hell.

Drawing back, he looks me full in the face. "Am I doing this right?"

His vulnerability breaks my heart. I pull him down for a kiss that tastes of salt and redemption. "Don't stop. I'm not fragile. I want all of it. All of you."

He sinks deeper, until he's buried to the hilt. The connection between us becomes so incredible, my muscles tighten around his impossibly thick shaft. He presses his forehead into mine and moans, "You feel divine. Like you were made for me."

Maybe I was. Maybe all the shit I've endured led me to this moment, to a man like Rowland whose suffering far eclipses mine. I dig my fingers into his muscled back, wrap my legs around his thighs and rock my hips.

"I could stay inside you like this for a thousand years and it wouldn't be enough. You're my sun, my moon, my salvation. The star guiding me out of this eternal darkness."

My pussy spasms. "Oh, Rowland."

"Fuck. If you keep squeezing me like this, I'll implode. Is that what you want from me? To see me come undone?"

"Move... Please."

He pulls back, stretching me as he withdraws. His bulbous cock head drags along every nerve ending, only for him to enter me again with a hard thrust. Sensation overloads my core, and my eyes roll to the back of my head. He continues fucking me with long, rhythmic strokes that make my toes curl.

"I love you, Annalisa, to the very marrow of my bones," he says, the words raw, wrecked.

Throat closing, I turn my head. It's the one word I can't hear without flinching, flung so casually by manipulative men and used as bait. I swallow, not believing it even though a secret part of me hopes he means every word. I cling to his shoulders and moan into his skin. His hand finds my cheek, forcing me to meet his burning gaze.

"When I save you, you'll say it back," he murmurs.

"O-okay," I rasp. "I will."

And I mean it. Every other man I've been with was about maintaining a lifestyle. What I have with Rowland isn't just survival. It's something deeper. A partner, a protector, a kindred spirit. Someone just as broken as me.

He quickens his strokes, pounding into me harder, the desk creaking under our weight. His mouth finds mine, swallowing my cries as he drives me higher and higher. I lose myself in his touch, in his motions, in his thrusts.

"Come for me," he growls against my lips. "Let me feel you fall apart."

His thumb finds my swollen clit and rubs tight circles. Sensation builds and builds until I can barely breathe. My vision whites out, the world narrowing to the pulse between us, then vanishing until an orgasm erupts like wildfire.

"Rowland," I scream as ecstasy slams through my senses.

"You're mine. All mine," he groans, his rhythm faltering.

My pussy clamps down on his cock, milking him until he stiffens.

"Fuck, Annalisa," he groans, his rhythm faltering. "I can't hold back. I'm... I'm coming."

"Fill me up," I say with a gasp. "Make me yours."

With one last thrust, he breaks apart, spilling into me with a groan like he's been starving for this. For me. His larger body collapses against mine, his arms pulling me into his chest.

We cling to each other, both shaking from the intensity of our joining. His heart pounds hard enough for us both.

"I love you, Annalisa, down to my last breath. You've filled my heart, mended my soul, and I will never let you go. If I have to raze the world to ashes to keep you safe, so be it. It's you and me, forever."

But I still can't say the words. I don't let go, either. I hold tight to this broken man who's willing to fight for me. I finally have the one who will choose me above all others.

When he pulls out, he hovers over me, wild-eyed and untamed. His chest heaves, every ridge of his stomach tightening and releasing with each ragged breath. I've never seen him look so feral. And still he's hard, his cock slick with my juices, bobbing back and forth like he's ready for another round.

"Annalisa," he says with a wicked grin.

My heart skips a beat. "What?"

His grin turns savage, teeth flashing like he's seconds from sinking them into my throat. "Run."

THIRTY-SEVEN

Run?

My heart flatlines. Then it bucks.

I stare into his eyes, searching for the man who told me he loved me five minutes ago. He's gone, replaced by something wild. Ravenous. Full of bloodlust.

He rolls his shoulders, making the muscles ripple like a predator about to pounce.

Shivers skitter down my spine. This is just a game, right?

The hunger in his gaze says he's not joking. I feel it in my gut, in the slick heat still dripping down my thighs. In the way my nervous system is screaming danger.

Rowland shifts forward, looming over me like a threat. His pupils dilate, swallowing the brown until there's nothing left but raw hunger. It's the same feral look from earlier, only now it's got teeth. His breaths turn ragged, his lips curling back in something that isn't quite a smile. It's like a mask has slipped, and he's no longer holding back.

Every instinct yells at me to escape.

"Wait." I slide off the desk, my hands twitching toward his heaving chest. "What are you doing?"

"You have a count of ten to run, little pet." His voice drops to a low growl. "When I catch you, I'll split you into pieces."

I back toward the door, every nerve in my body tingling. My skin prickles with goosebumps. "Oh, god."

"God won't save that sweet pussy," he snarls, his words rolling through my senses like thunder. "But I will make you beg for salvation."

Rowland advances toward me, his huge cock swinging like a broad sword. He moves like a hunter preparing for the kill. My stomach drops. My thighs clench. Something deep in my gut whispers that I've just made a terrible mistake.

What the hell do I really know about Rowland Rochester, apart from him being a wounded beast? I got so caught up in his story, I didn't fully challenge his role in helping Edward trap the murdered women. Now, he's turning that lethal attention on me.

I should run.

I should scream.

I should disappear.

Instead, I skitter backward, trembling and slick, caught between fear and desperate need.

"Ten," he growls. Something in his voice tells me he isn't playing.

Fuck.

I turn around and bolt out of Edward's office.

My feet slap against the cold marble floor, breath tearing from my throat. I race through the hallway, past oil paintings of dead aristocrats who stare down like they know exactly what I've just unleashed.

"Nine."

His voice follows me, and there's something wrong with the tone. It's far too calm, like he's done this before.

I round the corner, my feet skidding on a pile of dust I must have missed while cleaning. My lungs burn. My legs scream with each step. The hallway stretches endlessly ahead, lined with locked doors that hide god knows what horrors.

"Eight."

Shit. I sprint past the dining room, past the drawing room door and into the kitchen, my breasts bouncing with every stride. The back door crashes open under my hands, along with a gust of wind. Gritting my teeth, I burst out into the cold morning.

"Seven."

I knock over a discarded wine bottle, but I don't stop. Can't stop. Gravel crunches underfoot. I'm panting harder than a racehorse. Every instinct warns that if I slow down, it'll mean something terrible. Sweat beads on my forehead despite the chill. Blood tinges the back of my throat from breathing so hard.

"Six."

My heart somersaults. I push harder, legs pumping. Each breath burns hot and raw. I glance over my shoulder. The garden blurs past. The house grows smaller, but I can feel him watching in the windows. Tracking my movement with deadly precision.

"Five."

The orchard looms ahead, its trees heavy with red apples. I crash through tangled limbs, branches clawing at my skin. Rotting fruit litters the ground, sticky and sweet. The air reeks of decay and something older.

Cool wind blows in from the sea, chilling the outer

layer of my skin. My body becomes slick with sweat and fear and the cum still leaking from my pussy. The trees close in behind me, swallowing the path. Everything smells overripe. Like things left to rot in the sun.

"Four."

Oh shit.

What the hell?

I trip over a root, scrape my palm on rough bark, but I don't stop. Not with a potential maniac at my back. Not when he's threatening to tear me to shreds. I push harder, my lungs gasping for air. The orchard seems to stretch forever, its branches reaching like skeletal fingers trying to drag me back.

My legs shake from the sprint. Every muscle burns with each step. Copper floods my mouth, and my pulse roars at me to go faster. I can't hear him. Can't see him. But I feel him on every hair on my body standing on end. My skin buzzes with electricity, like he's already here. The silence is worse than his voice. But then most predators hunt without sound.

I sprint toward a row of tall trees looming at the orchard's edge. My chest heaves and the blood pounding in my ears drowns out all sound. Every vein feels ready to rupture, and my heart beats like it might burst free.

"One," says a cool voice from deep within the forest.

My heart stutters. What the hell happened to two and three? I whirl around, scanning the trees for movement. For a glimpse of his scarred flesh or wild hair. Everything's so tightly packed that all I see are crawling shadows.

"Rowland?" I whisper.

No answer. Just rustling wind through the leaves and

my own ragged gasps. Is he toying with me? Or am I going crazy?

The wind hisses through the branches, teasing the edges of my hair. I crouch low, listening for footsteps. For breath. For anything. But the woods are silent. Maybe he's gone the other direction. Maybe I ran hard enough. Maybe I actually got away.

A hand slams over my mouth. An arm yanks me back against a wall of scarred muscle and heat. We fall hard to the ground, grass and dirt scraping my knees as his weight drives the air from my lungs.

"Caught you," he growls into my ear and pushes me face-down into the dirt.

His breath is hot. Heavy. He smells like sweat and sex and a darkness that makes my stomach lurch. What happened to the man who needed me for courage? The man who declared his love?

I bite down on his fingers hard enough to draw blood.

He doesn't flinch. Doesn't yank away his hand. He groans, guttural and low, the sound vibrating through my spine like a tuning fork set to chaos.

"I knew you'd bite," he growls, his voice ragged.

My cry gets swallowed in the meat of his palm.

"Fuck, I love that sound," he rasps against my neck. "You're always the sweetest when you're scared."

I want to fight, but my body wants to stay. My mind shouts this isn't right, but my traitorous pussy clenches around nothing. It's hungry, obscene. I can't believe my body's response.

Rowland trails his fingers over my slit and growls, "Your greedy little cunt is dripping down my hand, begging me to fill it again and again. This is what you were made for. For me."

Oh, fuck.

Before I can crawl away, his cock slams into my pussy. Hard. Brutal. With no easing in. Pleasure shoots up my spine, sparking along every nerve ending. I shriek once again into his hand.

"That's it. Scream for me. Take every inch."

The crazy bastard drives into me like a man possessed. My body jerks along the ground with the force of his thrusts, stretching around his impossible girth. His thrusts go harder, deeper, like he's marking territory.

"You feel that? It's your body recognizing its master. Taking me like any way I demand."

"Rowland," I say with a choked gasp.

"You're. Mine." He punctuates each word with a brutal snap of his hips. "Who. Do. You. Belong. To. Little. Pet?"

"Why?"

"You ran like prey," he says, his teeth clamping down on my ear. "Now, I get to fuck you like a dog."

He pounds into me from behind with punishing force, his larger body overpowering mine. I scream my throat raw, a deadly cocktail of ecstasy and terror. What made me think Rowland was noble? His imprisonment, his suffering? I've never met anyone so unhinged.

The moment I try to crawl away, he threads his fingers through my hair. "Did you think you could escape me, little prey?"

I thrash within the cage of his limbs, buck against his hard chest, but the power he has over me is absolute. "You're insane."

He growls. "And you're about to discover what I do with my pets."

Alarm crackles on the edge of my consciousness.

What the hell happened to my Rowland? Where is the man who declared his love? Did I imagine him based on what I wanted to see?

"You're so fucking tight. So wet," he says through manic thrusts. "Tell me how much you need this cock."

"Oh, shit... Fuck... Rowland."

"Say it, or you don't get to come."

"I need. It. I need it. Give it to me, please!"

Just as I think he'll play with my clit, he flips me onto my back and pins my arms over my head.

Rowland no longer looks human. He's a mess of tangled hair, an unkempt beard, and eyes flashing with insanity. Sunlight shines through the trees, backlighting him like a halo. I blink away the glare, remembering something about Lucifer being a fallen angel. What the hell have I gotten myself into?

"You have such a beautiful neck. Such delicate veins. I've dreamed of possessing you like this."

This isn't love. This is hunger that's lost its leash.

He wraps his free hand around my throat, fingers digging into the soft flesh of my neck until all I can feel is my pulse hammering against his palm.

"Rowland," I say, my voice choked.

His grip tightens, cutting off my air.

My lungs spasm. I claw at his hands, dig my nails into his wrists hard enough to draw blood. I kick my heels into the ground and raise my hips, trying to get leverage. But he doesn't move. Doesn't let up. His gaze bores into mine, determined to snuff out my life.

Spots dance on the edge of my vision. My throat fills with acid.

The grip around my neck tightens as he drives into me, each stroke relentless and deep. Each powerful snap of his hips makes my limbs twitch from the force of his movements. My pulse roars between my ears, blotting out the slick, obscene sounds of fucking.

He bares his teeth. "You're mine. You belonged to me the moment you invited me in."

My life flashes past like lightning. The old bedroom where Dad locked me up for being a sinner. The church where Brother Matthew made me a child bride. Him ordering Mom to inspect me for signs of pregnancy. His house in flames. A blur of penthouses and hotel suites filled with worthless sugar daddies. Then the abandoned brothel where I was forced to kill a cop.

I open my mouth to breathe again, but it sticks in my throat. I buck, kick, try to twist free, but he keeps me pinned to the ground. Leaf litter flies in all directions. My fingers spasm, tingling like they're falling asleep. My tongue goes numb. My lungs scream for mercy, while he fucks me like a demon dragging my soul straight to hell.

"Mine," he growls, voice distorted into something dark. "Say it."

I try. Can't force out the words. Just rasp like I'm dying.

Panic blooms under my skin. I jerk my head back against the ground. He tightens his grip around my wrists and slams them back to the dirt. His other hand continues squeezing my neck until the world fades to a pinpoint of light.

Pressure in my head builds until my skull is about to crack. Blood rushes through my ears with a desperate ring. Darkness creeps in from the edges of my consciousness like spilled ink.

My pussy pulses and clenches around his cock with ravenous need. He groans, the sound rippling through every pleasure center. It's horrifying, it's sick. I can't think past the need for air, but my body won't stop convulsing.

Rowland is going to kill me. Maybe he's the one who murdered all the others. Maybe both brothers are equally as corrupt. I made the same fucking error as always: thinking I could tell predator from protector.

His face hovers above mine, both beautiful and terrible. Eyes black with insanity. Mouth curved in a grin sharp enough to slit my throat.

And it will be the last thing I see.

This is it.

I'm dying.

And I made the mistake of inviting him in.

THIRTY-EIGHT

White light explodes across my vision, wiping out everything except a mind-blowing climax. Pleasure rips through my body, and my pussy clamps down on his cock so hard I swear I'll break him in half.

I can't breathe. Can't think. Can't do anything except feel the orgasm ripping me to shreds. Ecstasy tears through every inch until I'm a vessel of ruin.

My back arches off the ground like I'm electrocuted. The scream that rips from my soul is inhuman. Hell, I don't even know if it's coming from my throat. I drift above the wreckage of my body, too broken to scream again, too empty to care.

Just when I think I'm about to expire, Rowland's grip on my throat loosens.

Air rushes into my lungs so fast it burns. I return to reality with a noisy gasp, my chest heaving like I've been stuck underwater. The black spots crowding my vision fade as oxygen reaches my brain.

I try to swallow but my throat is scraped raw. It's like forcing down shards of glass.

What the hell?

What the actual fuck?

My body goes limp beneath Rowland's, every muscle turning to liquid. I can't lift my arms to shove him off. Can't move my legs to kick free. All I can do is lie within the prison of his limbs, panting through the aftershocks. My pussy twitches around his softening cock, making me realize he's also come.

"Annalisa?" Rowland's voice sounds like it's coming from the treetops.

I sink into the leaf litter, not completely knowing if I'm alive or dead.

"Are you alright?" he asks, sounding closer.

My lips move, but my tongue is thick and useless. I try to answer but only manage a weak whimper.

"I've got you," he murmurs.

Strong arms slide under my thighs and back, lifting me off the grass like I'm weightless. My head lolls against his shoulder as he pulls me into his chest. I groan against his skin, which is slick with sweat, inhaling a heady mix of salt and sex.

He carries me through the orchard, his heart beating just as fast as mine. Branches rustle overhead, and I stare up into the treetops. Each step jolts my frame, triggering pulses of muted pleasure.

As he steps out past the last line of apple trees and into the lawn, a breeze cools my fevered skin, raising goosebumps. If I wasn't so lethargic from being choked to orgasm, I'd demand to know what the hell he's doing.

My head flops forward, and my gaze settles on the pond. Water stretches out like a black mirror, reflecting the stormy sky. My insides seize at the memory of

Blanche's pale face frozen in death, her dark hair fanned out like a shroud.

"No," I whisper, finding my voice. "Not there."

Rowland stops walking, his arms pulling me into his warmth. "What's wrong?"

"Don't take me to that pond. That's where..." I can't finish. Can't say the words out loud. Can't tell him I don't want to die like Blanche.

Rowland follows my gaze to the pond and shivers. "We're going inside."

Relief trickles through my system like warm honey as he continues past the water toward the manor's back entrance. When he opens the door and steps into the kitchen, I finally allow myself to relax.

He carries me up to my room, lays me on the bed, and walks into the bathroom. My survival instincts urge me to run, but it feels like the muscles have melted from my bones. I just had the most intense pleasure of my life at the very edge of death.

The pipes groan and shudder as he turns on the water. I gaze through the bed curtains with heavy-lidded eyes, wondering what the hell just happened. If he hadn't loosened his grip, I would have died. Did he mean to kill me? Why did he spare my life?

Rowland steps out of the bathroom, still naked. Light from the balcony windows carves across his scarred chest. He looks powerful, monstrous, his torture marks reading more like war wounds. After what he just did, it's impossible to ever see him as a victim.

"Can you stand?" he asks, his voice soft as velvet.

I can't even shake my head.

When he approaches the bed with his arms

outstretched, I flinch, making him pause. "Annalisa, love, it's just me."

That's exactly what I find so frightening. That switch from prisoner to predator. How much my body reveled in his madness, while my mind recoiled with horror.

He pulls off my shoes, scoops me up into his arms and carries me across the room. "You never need to fear me, love. I'd bleed for you, break for you, rip out my own heart if it made you smile. Whatever you want is yours. Your happiness is the only thing that keeps me breathing."

The words glide off my consciousness like oil. I rest my head against his shoulder, my body too depleted to protest. Rowland enters the bathroom, cradling me like I'm fragile, lowers me into the tub, and places a kiss on my temple.

Hot water stings the slashes on my skin, making me hiss through my teeth. But as I sink into the heat, steam curls up from the surface, surrounding me in a warm cocoon, and the knots in my muscles unfurl.

Rowland climbs into the tub behind me and wraps his arms around my waist. He pulls me against his chest and murmurs, "Come here."

We sit together in silence, his chest rising and falling against my back. Water laps at the sides of the tub in a relaxing rhythm. After several minutes, my pulse finally starts to slow.

"Are you scared of me?" he murmurs.

The question hangs in the air then dissolves into the steam. Fear doesn't begin to describe what happened in the woods, and terror is too weak. I've never come so close to the edge of mortality, not even when Brother Matthew beat me unconscious. Not even when Gil and the gangsters pressed that syringe into my hands and turned me into a cop killer.

What Rowland did was savage, raw, and a primal part of me enjoyed being taken to the brink of death, even though inside, I was screaming for escape. I think about lying, about playing it safe. But after what just happened, I can't afford to say the wrong thing.

"What the hell was that about?" I ask instead.

He sighs, his breath warm on my neck. "I used to watch Edward with women through peepholes in the ceilings. They always liked it dirty and rough, and I thought that was what you wanted."

Chest tightening, I picture him locked in that attic, forced to witness his brother's sick games. Forced to learn about sex from a psychopath.

"Did I hurt you?" His voice is small, uncertain.

My throat thickens then convulses as I figure out the right words. "I was terrified. I thought you were going to kill me."

He stiffens, every muscle going rigid. "I... I just wanted to give you pleasure. Edward always called it la petite mort. And Mrs. Fairfax used to enjoy that with Father."

My stomach plummets at the mention of his biological mother, the original housekeeper. Of course the woman was fucked and choked. She birthed that man's children while being relegated to domestic servitude. This whole house is built on twisted relationships. At least now I know where he learned his techniques.

"You can't just grab a woman's throat without getting her permission in advance," I say.

"You didn't like it?" he asks.

My pussy clenches, and sensation floods my clit. I

shift uncomfortably in his embrace. "That's not the point. We need safe words."

"Safe words?" His voice lilts with confusion.

I twist in his arms to meet his dark eyes. They're shadowed beneath thick brows, his beard unkempt and wild. But it's the look in them that stops me cold. Stricken. Shaken. Like he's scared of himself. My heart clenches.

"It's a word we can use if things go too far," I murmur. "If I say it, you stop."

He cocks his head. "But why would you want me to stop if you're enjoying it?"

My shoulders sag. Shit. He really doesn't understand, and who can blame him, being locked up his entire adult life under the control of an unhinged father and a serial killing brother? Of course his views on sex will be warped.

"Rowland, sometimes fear and pleasure get mixed up. What feels good in the moment can be dangerous."

His eyes fill with something that looks like shame. "You think I'm a monster."

"No." The word comes out fierce. "You learned about sex from two abusers. It's only natural you'd be rough."

He searches my face as if he's looking for lies. "Have you done this before?"

I almost laugh. "Are you asking if I'm a virgin?"

"No, I mean..." He swallows hard, his gaze dropping. "I've never made love before. What we did today was my first time. With anyone."

My breath catches at the thought that he believed that animalistic, terrifying fuck in the dirt was love. The worst thing is that some part of me wants to fold this madness into something tender. Something real.

Rowland isn't just a broken man but a shattered soul

raised on pain. And he's trying to build love out of the scraps of someone else's violence.

"That explains a lot," I murmur. "You did fine."

He pauses, his lips turning downward. "Will you think badly of me for killing Edward?"

I rear back, the change of subject catching me off guard. I place a hand on his cheek, my chest aching at his vulnerability. He's asking for permission to be a killer. Like I'm some kind of moral authority.

"Why would you think I'll judge you for murder?"

"Because you hate my brother, and he's a killer."

I settle back against his chest, feeling the steady thrum of his heartbeat. "When I was fourteen, my parents married me off to an elder in the church."

"You're married?"

"Not anymore," I rasp. "He was mean. Violent. Abusive. When I wasn't cooking and cleaning after him and his kids, he was trying to put another one in me so I wouldn't leave."

Rowland growls. "Where is he? Tell me where he lives?"

"Utah. Last time I saw him, he was dying from a knife wound, trapped in a burning house. From a fire I started." I tilt my head to gaze at his profile. "So how could I ever judge you for killing in self-defense?"

Rowland's arms tighten around me. "You did it because he hurt you."

"Every day for years." My throat thickens, and my eyes sting. "One day, his punishment got so bad, I hit him with an iron candlestick holder. He went down hard and swore to have me exorcised in front of the congregation. That's when you get beaten by a bunch of members while they're screaming prayers. He said it would be different this time because I'd be branded. I couldn't let that happen."

He breathes hard, his chest rising and falling against my back. "Did they... Did they do this to you before?"

"Multiple times, but they never left permanent marks."

"So you killed him before he could hand you over to them."

"It was the only way I knew to survive."

We sit together in silence. I wait for judgment, for horror. For him to realize I'm just as fucked up as his brother.

Instead, Rowland presses his lips to my temple in a kiss so soft, so reverent, that it takes everything in me not to cry.

"How did your parents even allow this to happen?" he asks.

I sigh. "My dad was just as brutal as that old bastard."

"And your mother?"

"She was even younger than me when she married my dad. That life was all she ever knew."

"But she must have guessed you'd be miserable with that elder?"

My heart sinks, because he's right. Mom knew exactly what was in store for me when she persuaded me to marry Brother Matthew. "The congregation has a way of punishing mothers whose daughters don't comply."

"I'm so sorry." He strokes my hair. Slides his fingers down the side of my neck. "We're so similar. Both survivors, brought together by fate."

He's right. We're two broken people who've escaped hell and found each other in the wreckage.

"Red," I say.

"What?"

"Our safe word. If either of us says 'red,' everything stops immediately."

He nods. "Red to stop."

"And Rowland?" I turn to face him again, making the water slosh. "Next time you want to try something new, tell me first. Communication is important."

His lips curve in a small smile. "There'll be a next time?"

I smile back, my heart fluttering. "You can bet on that."

Should I be terrified that I'm aching for this man?

THIRTY-NINE

Hours later, after being cradled in Rowland's arms, I wake to the scent of wildflowers.

My eyes flutter open, still heavy from sleep. Moonlight streams through the balcony doors, creating pretty patterns on the walls. The bath drained me more than I realized. Or maybe it was that chase through the grounds, followed by the extreme breath play. Either way, my body hasn't felt so relaxed since before the evening Gil woke me up for that murderous encounter.

A bouquet sits on my dresser, bursting with color. Wild poppies and cornflowers, field scabious and red campion. They look like they were just picked from the estate grounds, still damp with dew. The arrangement is artful. Careful. Like someone took time creating a thing of beauty.

Beside the flowers rests a note with my name written across the front in a familiar script. I pad across the room on bare feet and pick it up to read:

Dinner is at eight. I hope you like what I've made for you.

- R

The neat script fills my chest with a ripple of warmth. I glance around the room, searching for something new. That's when I spot a dress hanging from the wardrobe door.

It's a cornflower blue that matches my eyes, made of soft cotton that makes my woolen uniform feel like a Brillo pad. It looks exactly my size, with a curved neckline and a nipped-in waist to accentuate my figure.

I cross the room, lift the dress from its hanger, and hold it against my body. The fabric slides through my fingers like water. I turn it inside out to find neatly hemmed stitches that remind me of Mom's home sewing.

Shit. I shouldn't be so touched. Or feel so at ease in the home of a killer, but I do. This is perfect. I can't remember the last time anyone gave me something so beautiful and thoughtful.

I slip it over my head, and for the first time since arriving here, I don't have to fight with buttons or crush my boobs into something too tight. The dress flows over my curves, resting above my knees. This must have been tailored specially for me.

The woman staring back at me in the mirror looks fresh and carefree. Like she's a guest at Rochester Manor instead of confined to scrubbing its floors.

A soft knock interrupts my thoughts.

"Come in," I call out.

The door opens, and Rowland steps inside.

His hair is still damp, combed back from his face. His beard is still full, but shaped to accentuate his strong cheekbones. My stomach does a little flip. In his black pants and white shirt, he looks almost civilized.

"You're beautiful," he says, his voice breathy with awe.

Cheeks heating, I squirm under his admiring gaze. "Thank you. I love the dress. Where did you get it?"

"I made it," he replies with a tiny smile.

My jaw drops. "You? How?"

"Mrs. Fairfax said sewing would keep my mind sharp. She taught me when I was locked in the attic." He ducks his head, suddenly bashful. "I've been working on it since you waved back. I had to guess your measurements from... from watching you."

"Just watching?" I ask with a smile.

He grins. "And by feel."

Picturing him crafting this dress while trapped in the attic makes my heart ache. Rowland still thought of creating this gorgeous gift for me while being tortured by a psychopath.

"It's perfect," I whisper.

"Come. I have something else to show you."

He holds out his arm, and I take it, feeling like a lady. He escorts me out into the hallway, and we descend the main staircase.

Instead of heading to the dining room, Rowland leads me outside. By now, the sun has set, casting shadows across the lawn. We pass the pond where Blanche died and the orchard where he chased me down like prey. At the very edge of the trees stands a gazebo illuminated by candles.

A table sits in the center, set with china and crystal, and rose petals scattered across the white tablecloth.

"Rowland," I say, my voice breathy. "This is..."

"For you," he replies.

We step inside, and he pulls out my chair with a courtly bow. Did he learn that move from Rochester or his father? The dress fabric pools around my thighs as I sit, making me feel as elegant as Blanche. I study the dome-covered plates, wondering what he prepared.

Rowland lifts the metal covering, releasing a swirl of fragrant steam. Inside waits roasted chicken speckled with herbs, surrounded by colorful steamed vegetables and buttery new potatoes.

"How did you make all this?" I ask as he fills my glass with white wine.

"Have you forgotten already?" he asks back.

I gaze up into his dark eyes. "What do you mean?"

"Edward forced me to take on the role of Mrs. Fairfax."

In between victims. Rowland leaves that unsaid. My insides roil at the reminder.

"I've had decades to learn to cook," he adds as he settles into his seat. "Sometimes, when Father was away on business, Mrs. Fairfax would let me out to use the kitchen."

"Why didn't she set you free?"

He lowers his gaze. "I already told you. In the end, she was just as much of a prisoner as me."

I drop the subject, not wanting to ruin this beautiful moment with talk of his captivity. We eat in comfortable silence. Rowland fumbles with the silverware, his fingers clumsy, like he's been forced into a lifetime of eating with his hands. Apart from his strange table manners, this feels like a real date. Like a normal man courting a normal woman.

But we're not normal. And neither is this situation.

"Do you really think it will work?" I blurt.

His gaze snaps up to meet mine. "What?"

"You plan to impersonate your brother," I reply. "Do you think you can make it work?"

He shifts his expression, straightens his posture, and smooths his features into a slight sneer. "Of course I can, Miss Burlington," he says, his voice cultured. Clipped. Cruel. "I've observed Edward Rochester my entire life."

My spine stiffens. Every nerve in my body screams danger. Even knowing it's Rowland, that superior expression still triggers my urge to run.

Rowland's smirk drops, his eyes widening with alarm. He reaches across the table and takes my hand. "I'm sorry." When he speaks again, his voice is familiar. Warm. Safe. "I won't use that tone unless it's necessary."

I shudder. "That was terrifying."

He nods. "But I'm convincing enough to fool Edward's associates, especially his lawyer and the local priest."

"Right. Of course." I settle back into my chair, trying to shake off the chill.

We keep eating, but the mood dulls. The air feels heavier somehow, like a shadow has fallen over our perfect evening. Maybe it's the impending reality that this moment was never going to last. Maybe it's the reminder that Rochester will soon return.

"Can I ask you something?" I say during a lull in conversation.

He nods.

"What made your brother so evil?"

Rowland sets down his fork and bows his head to think. "I can't even remember when it began. He's always been twisted."

"But why does he do it?"

He tilts his head, chews his lower lip. "Edward used to trap animals when we were boys. It wasn't enough for him to kill them. He liked giving them the hope of freedom then watching them break."

"What does that mean?" I lean forward, my breath quickening.

"Edward isn't just a hunter. He's more like a keeper. The kind of sick person who puts people through psychological experiments just to watch them die inside." Rowland falls quiet for several heartbeats, candlelight flickering across the scars peeking out from his collar. "Sometimes I wonder if he left you here as bait."

My jaw drops. "What?"

"Think about it. He left us alone together. He had to know I'd sneak out of the attic, either to warn you or let us fall in love. Maybe he planned the whole thing. There's no telling if he's watching us right now, waiting to see how we'll react."

The food settles in my stomach like a stone. "Why would he do that?"

"Because I've been getting better at escaping my bonds. And more resilient to his punishments. Maybe he fears I'll become a real threat." Rowland's jaw clenches. "But if he has you, he can control me. Use you as leverage."

Panic claws through my chest. I try not to think about Rochester observing us from afar, playing us both like chess pieces. But it's so plausible, I can't help glancing from side to side into the darkness.

"Are you sure?" I whisper.

Rowland rises from his seat and pulls me to my feet. "I don't know. But if this is all some elaborate game,

Edward will die before he involves you in his sick fantasies. I promise you that."

I place a hand on his chest, feeling the steady beat of his heart. These words should be comforting, but why do I feel like prey caught between two predators? I gaze into Rowland's eyes. Eyes that burn with defiance, determination, and devotion. He despises his brother as much as he admires me. That resolve is what will keep us both alive.

It no longer matters that Rowland is damaged, or that he couldn't tell the difference between lovemaking and rough sex. It doesn't matter that parts of him are monstrous. Because he's mine.

"Enough talk about Edward," Rowland says, his voice turning low and rough. "It's time for dessert."

"What are we having?" I whisper.

"You." He lifts me onto the table, sweeping aside plates and glasses. China scatters to the edges, smashing as he kneels between my parted thighs and pushes up my dress.

My breath catches. The air thickens, heavy with heat and anticipation. My heart slams behind my ribs, caught in that place between panic and hunger.

"Spread those pretty thighs for me. I'm going to eat this pussy like it's my last meal."

"Rowland, what are you—"

His lips descend between my legs, his tongue finding my clit through the cotton of my panties. I gasp, my muscles twitching. Rowland slides the fabric to one side, exposing my heated flesh to the elements. The cool air hits my pussy, making me jerk like I've been shocked.

"What a pretty little cunt. You're already soaked. Is that all for me?" he growls, his hot breath making me tingle.

"Yes," I murmur.

"Tell me what you need?"

I roll my hips. "You. Your mouth."

He swipes his tongue up the length of my slit, working me with the same careful attention he put into making my dress. My breath quickens. My thighs quiver around his head. Just as I'm about to moan, he suddenly stops.

"I want to hear you beg. Tell me how much you want my mouth."

I fall backward, gripping the edge of the table with one hand and grabbing his hair with the other.

"Please," I say with a gasp.

"Good girl. Lying back for me with your legs spread. Tell me something, little pet. How much does that pretty pussy ache for my tongue?"

"Fuck," I moan. "Give it to me, Rowland. I'm begging."

He builds me up with slow and steady strokes. His beard tickles my inner thighs, triggering little bursts of electricity that ripple to my core. I whimper, trying to stay still, but my hips keep chasing his mouth. My body doesn't know how to resist him.

"You taste so good. And you're mine. Say it, little pet, if you want to come."

"I'm yours!"

"Louder. Don't hold back. I want everyone to know whose pussy this is," he rasps before sucking hard on my clit.

I throw my head back and moan. The pleasure is so intense, I can barely breathe.

"You like that?" he snarls. "You like me ruining you on the table?"

My mouth opens and closes, but I make no sound. My toes curl, my eyes roll to the back of my head. I grip his hair so tight I swear I hear him groan.

"That's right, my pretty little pet. I want to feast on you all night. Drink every sound. Savor every tremble. Make you come until dawn. But first, I need you to make a mess all over my face."

He doesn't ease off. His mouth stays relentless, keeping me pinned. Every lick, every suck, every flick of his tongue makes me writhe beneath him. When I come, it's gentle. Safe. Warm. Nothing like that brutal explosion. His hands tighten around my hips as I tremble, and he keeps licking until I've given him everything.

When the pleasure fades, and my breathing slows, I loosen my grip on Rowland's hair. He lifts his head from between my legs, his beard glistening with my arousal. His eyes catch mine, still shining with reverence and hunger. Then he licks his lips as if he's just enjoyed a feast.

"Look at you. Utter perfection."

"R-Rowland," I say with a gasp.

"Do you like baked Alaska?" he asks with a playful grin.

I blink at him, still fuzzy from the orgasm, wondering what he's talking about. "What?"

"I made you a dessert. Are you ready for it?"

When I give him an eager nod, he helps me down from the table, straightens my skirt, and settles me back into my chair. My breath shallows. No man ever made me dinner, let alone dessert.

"I'll be right back." he says with a kiss to my temple and strides toward the house.

I sit back in my seat, marveling at his confident strut. The man who was terrified of being called a monster just hours ago now moves like he owns the world. As he disappears into the house, I release a happy sigh. Everything looks hopeful. Rowland is determined to get rid of Rochester, and his impersonation was impeccable.

If we stick together, we can make this work.

Chuckling, I rise off the seat and pick up the plates, glasses, and silverware that fell on the floor. Some of them smashed on the way down, and I'm careful not to cut my fingers. I set right a bottle of wine that's lost half its contents and drink the dregs.

After several minutes, a breeze blows through the gazebo making the candles flicker. I twist around in my seat and look across the lawn toward the lit kitchen. What's taking him so long?

Worry gnaws at my stomach. Maybe the dessert is more complicated than he thought. Maybe he's having trouble finding something in the kitchen. Maybe he's just searching for a tray.

But the silence feels wrong.

My survival instincts are pinging. After everything that's happened, I can't just sit here and wait.

I rise off my seat, cross the lawn, and head toward the house. Even from this distance, I can't see movement from behind the kitchen window. The back door stands open, spilling light onto the gravel. I quicken my pace, squaring my shoulders, readying myself for the worst. Then I step through the doorway into chaos.

The kitchen chairs are overturned. Pots and pans litter the counters. A knife glints on the floor, its blade smeared with something wet and dark.

"Rowland?" I call out, my voice echoing in the empty kitchen.

No answer.

Just silence.

And the metallic tang of blood.

FORTY

Edward Rochester is back.

There's no other explanation. Rowland is missing and there's blood all over the floor. I race through the manor, clutching a kitchen knife. That sick fuck must have returned early and taken him.

Moving as quietly as possible, I strain to hear a sound: footsteps, voices, anything that might betray their location. The dining room is empty. As is the study. All the other doors are locked.

I need to find Rochester before he finds me.

Nausea roils in my gut as I creep up the main staircase, taking the steps two at a time. My chest burns, each breath coming in ragged gasps. I thought we had more time. That Rochester would be more concerned with covering up Blanche's murder. It was supposed to be two against one.

Now it's just me with a kitchen knife versus a man who's been torturing and killing people for decades.

The first-floor doors are locked. I creep up to the second, testing each step to avoid creaks. The hallway stretches ahead in darkness. Rochester could be inside any of these rooms, but entering them would give away my position.

Instead, I press my ear to the first door and hear nothing but silence. The next room is the same: no sounds of struggle, no muffled voices. Outside, the clouds part, and moonlight streams through the hallway window and hits the panel leading to the attic.

It's open.

My blood freezes. Rochester must have dragged Rowland back to that torture chamber. Back to the shackles and chains where he spent thirty years of hell.

I climb those narrow stairs, my heart thrashing so hard I taste copper. Rowland said his brother liked to set traps. He could be waiting upstairs for me with a garrote. I could be playing into his hands.

Every instinct screams at me to run. Grab what I can and get the hell out. Rochester's probably left a car somewhere on the grounds. I can escape while he's busy with Rowland.

My hands tremble around the knife, and my feet don't want to move toward the stairs. They want to turn around and race out into the night. Just as I did with Brother Matthew. And with Gil. And every other time my life ever turned to shit. I've never walked into danger. Always knew how to survive.

But Rowland is up there, maybe bleeding. Maybe dying. Maybe already dead while I stand here like a coward, calculating escape routes. He made me a dress while in captivity, prepared a beautiful meal, worshipped me like a goddess and gave me meaning.

I am the only thing that inspires him to fight back. How the hell can I abandon him now?

"Fuck it," I snarl, my feet finally moving. I can't leave the only man to ever give a damn about me in the grip of a psychopath.

Holding my weapon, I reach the top and freeze at the entrance. With my free hand, I grip the door frame, not wanting to get trapped.

On the right, Mrs. Fairfax's skeleton sits in her rocking chair, still wearing that black dress, her gray wisps of hair reflecting the faint moonlight. On the left, the narrow cot with its iron shackles sits empty beneath the instruments of torture.

But there's no Rowland. No Edward Rochester.

Where the hell did they go?

My mind spins through possibilities. The cottage basement where Rochester dumped the other bodies? The cliffs? Some other torture chamber on the grounds? Rowland could be anywhere on this godforsaken estate, and I'm wasting time searching empty rooms.

I race back down to the kitchen, desperate for more clues. Maybe there's something I missed. Some sign of where Rochester took his poor brother.

But as I scan the overturned chairs and scattered pots, movement across the lawn catches my eye through the window. A dark figure slips between the apple trees, moving deeper into the orchard. My stomach drops. Is that Rowland trying to escape, or Rochester dragging his body?

Either way, I need to get down there.

Gripping the knife, I slip out the back door onto the patio. Fresh air hits my face as I step outside, tasting like fear. I cross the lawn, my feet silent on the grass. The orchard looms ahead, dark and full of places to hide a body.

Or to stage an ambush.

I head toward the trees, ignoring the branches catching at my dress. My feet make no sound on the soft earth, but my heart thuds so loud it might as well be a drum.

Footsteps sound up ahead. I freeze, straining to hear over my own frantic breaths. I weave between the apple trees, through the shrubs toward the snap of twigs breaking underfoot, but then it stops.

A large figure steps out from behind a tree. He's clean shaven, wearing a black suit and a chilling smile.

My heart plummets to my feet.

It's Edward Rochester.

"Miss Burlington. You're still here. What a delightful surprise."

"You gave me a week to leave," I stammer, backing away.

"And you chose to spend that time with the family pet." He advances like a panther closing in on its prey.

My back hits a tree trunk. Rough bark digs into my shoulders through the dress's delicate fabric. Rochester's dark eyes drop to my throat. When his lips curve in a sadistic smile, my breath slows to a stutter.

I'm trapped.

"Interesting marks around your neck. Care to explain?"

My free hand flies to cover the bruises. I tighten my grip on the knife with the other. "I don't know what you're talking about."

Rochester throws back his head and laughs. It's a cruel, vicious sound that sets my teeth on edge. "Oh, this is priceless. Did my simple-minded brother finally get laid?"

I bristle. He's talking about Rowland like he's defective. Like what we shared was a pity fuck.

"What do you mean?" I snap.

He flashes his teeth. "Rowland was unusually spirited. He fought me like a man protecting something precious."

My breath stills. My eyes sting with tears. This monster has my Rowland. Before I can stop myself, I blurt, "Where is he?"

"You'll be reunited soon enough."

He shoots out a hand, grabs my throat with an iron grip, and slams me back into the tree trunk. Pain explodes across the base of my skull, making my vision go white. I clench my teeth, forcing myself to fight back. My hand shoots up with the knife, but he's faster. His hand clamps around my wrist and twists hard, jerking my arm off course.

"Are you flirting with me, Miss Burlington? Bad girls who play with toys without my permission get punished."

He squeezes my fingers, grinding the bones until the knife falls loose and hits the ground with a thud. I cry out as he drags me through the orchard toward that cottage.

"Let go of me, you psycho—"

"I know what you did in my study. Did you really think I wouldn't notice the stench of your little tryst? Did you think I'd leave an insult like that unpunished?"

We reach the cottage, its windows gaping like dead eyes. With a roar, he kicks open the door and shoves me inside. I stumble into the dark room, my hands flying for balance, and crash into the table. A lantern I noticed days ago knocks to the side, spilling oil across the wood.

Rochester closes the door, encasing us in the semi-darkness. Moonlight streams in through the filthy windows, illuminating his monstrous silhouette. After securing the lock, he turns toward me, and bares his teeth.

Terror kicks me in the gut. He's walking over the graves of all those women he lured to this accursed house, worked half to death and then murdered. Did he add Rowland to the list of corpses?

He takes a slow step forward, his feet creaking on the rotted floorboards. I stagger backward, using the table as a barrier.

"Tell me something, Miss Burlington. What was it like to fuck an animal? How did it feel to take pleasure from a man who spent years writhing in his own filth?"

Rage explodes in my chest, white-hot and consuming. I snatch the nearest thing off the table. It's cool and round, like a snow globe. I don't dare drop my gaze to check.

"I thought even you would have better taste after all that salivating you did over me," he says, his voice lilting with amusement. "Or did my rejection drive you into the arms of my drooling brother?"

"Rowland is twice the man you could ever be," I yell.

His eyes flash with something inhuman. "That whimpering stray I kept alive out of boredom?"

"At least he's not a child-killing psychopath."

Rochester's mask slips, his features twisting with contempt. He glares at me from across the shack like I'm filth. "Careful, Miss Burlington. You're in no position to make accusations."

But I'm beyond caring. This sadistic bastard has done something to Rowland, and I won't give into fear. Not when the only man who ever treated me like I was precious is locked away, suffering.

Rochester crosses the room, stopping close enough

that I can smell his expensive cologne. I cringe into the wall, wishing I could sink through the bricks.

"You really think that sniveling creature can satisfy a woman? He can barely look me in the eye without pissing on the floor."

I lunge forward and slam the snow globe into his balls.

He doubles over with a strangled scream. "You fucking bitch!"

I smash the globe over his exposed head. His hands fly up in self-defense, reminding me of how Brother Matthew cowered after I'd hit him with that poker. Violence is the only language monsters like him understand.

It was the moment I stopped being a victim and became a killer.

But Rochester doesn't go down. He staggers, just like Brother Matthew did. I bring the globe down again, harder, and he groans. On the third blow, the glass cracks, spilling water over his head. On the fourth, it collapses. I drop the broken pieces and bolt for the door. The handle turns but it won't budge.

Shit.

Shit.

SHIT.

"You'll pay for that, you worthless whore," snarls a voice from the shadows.

I spin around. Rochester straightens, his face twisting with rage.

Terror reaches into my ribcage and seizes my heart. My knees buckle and I stumble against the door. My hand lands on a chunk of broken timber.

"When I finish with you, you'll be praying for death," he roars.

He says that like every controlling bastard who tried to put a collar around my neck. Like Dad, who used scripture to keep me under his thumb. Like Brother Matthew, who subdued me with rape, fists, and the threat of keeping me barefoot and pregnant. Like Gil, who let them put a murder weapon into my hands and make me a killer.

Fuck that. I'd rather die than become another prisoner.

I straighten, my heart jackhammering, my fingers closing around the wood.

Rochester charges at me with a roar. I step forward and bring the timber down on his skull. It hits with a sickening crack, and he jerks, eyes going wide. The sound is beautiful. Wet and final.

He drops to his knees, blood streaming down his temple. I raise the wood, waiting for his next move. But his eyes go unfocused, and he reaches for his head wound like he can't believe what's happening.

I hit him again. For Rowland. For Adele. For the original Mrs. Fairfax. For every woman who died at his hands.

Rochester crashes face-first into the moldy boards and goes limp.

I rush to the door and yank the handle again. It's jammed. Of course, it is. I watched the bastard lock it and pocket the key. Chest heaving, I whirl around, finding Rochester still sprawled face-down on the floor.

My heart thrashes against my ribs like a caged bird. He's motionless as roadkill. Now's the time to search him for the key, but what if this is a trap? But I don't have any choice, unless I want to crawl through broken glass. I edge toward him on trembling legs, my pulse hammering loud enough to drown out all sound.

Floorboards creak underfoot. Each step toward him feels like walking toward my own grave. But as I reach striking distance, his arm lashes out like a cobra.

Panic punches into my chest, stealing my breath. With a scream, I stumble back, and crash onto my ass. Pain shoots up my tailbone, making me hiss through my teeth. Then a hand wraps around my ankle like a steel shackle.

He drags me toward him. My stomach lurches. I kick back with my free leg, my heel connecting with his face in a satisfying crunch.

"You fucking bitch!" he roars, his grip loosening to grab his nose.

I scramble away on my hands and knees toward the table. My dress tears as I claw across the floor powered by desperation. Splinters dig into my palms, but I barely feel the sting.

Just as I reach the shelter, a metallic clink has me whirling around.

"I'm going to strangle you with this belt." He snaps it between his hands. "Watch you fight for air. Keep you on the edge. Make you beg for death."

He raises the belt and lashes it down like a whip. I stagger backward, my hand landing on something metallic and cold. The floor drops inward. I tumble backward into darkness with a silent scream.

FORTY-ONE

A heartbeat later, I land hard on my side. The impact drives the air from my lungs, sending agony through my hip and shoulder. I stumble to my feet in the dark. What the hell was that? A trap door?

I stretch out my arms, feeling around for something—anything. Above me, Rochester's silhouette fills a square opening, backlit by moonlight. Even from down here, his grin is all teeth and malice.

"Eager to die, Miss Burlington?" he calls down, his voice echoing off the walls.

"You sick bastard!" I scream back, my voice cracking.

I can't stop thinking about that movie where the psycho kept a woman in a pit, feeding her with items he lowered down in a bucket. My skin crawls, and my throat fills with bile. What the hell is this place?

"Isn't this the time you scream at me to let you out?" he says, his voice lilting with amusement.

My teeth clamp shut. I'm not playing his sick games.

"I'll even give you the key." He tosses something small at me, which hits the floor with a metallic clink.

Disgust ripples through my insides, making me want to scream. What use is the bloody key when the door is twenty feet above, completely out of reach? Despite thinking this, I bend down to pick it up. Maybe it will be useful.

"Make yourself at home," he says.

Something falls on my head with a gentle clunk and drops to the floor. Sparks fly from its tip. I draw back and pick up what looks like a lighter. My gaze flicks back up to the opening, where he gazes down at me, his pale features sharpening. Straightening, I flick the metal lever, and a small flame springs to life.

"What is this place?" I ask. "Where you keep your victims before they die?"

His lips quirk. "Not quite."

It's probably a trap. Didn't Rowland say Rochester liked to watch animals struggle for freedom before their deaths?

I hold the flame out like a torch, searching for a weapon, an escape route, anything that might keep me alive. But as I move deeper into what feels like a cellar, my foot bumps into something soft. It feels like a sack of grain.

"Take your time," Rochester says, his voice breathy with arousal.

I shouldn't play a game he's rigged, but if there's a chance I can turn this around on him, I need to take it. Shivering, I lower the flame. The light reveals hollow eye sockets staring back at me from a skull.

Shock punches me in the gut, drawing out a scream. I lurch backward so fast the lighter switches off. Cold sweat erupts across my skin. My stomach convulses, threatening to bring up my dinner. Oh, God. That was a corpse. One of his victims.

My back hits something solid. It's a warm, breathing body.

"I see you've met Celine," Rochester's voice fills my ear.

I skitter away, my mind reeling. How the hell did he get down here without a sound? I spin around, flicking the lighter, its flame casting his face in hellish shadows. The twisted bastard grins down at me like a wolf who's cornered his prey.

"She was a spicy one," he croons. "Rowland used to watch me fuck that woman on her hands and knees. Worthless bastard used to come in his pants."

Edging backward, I hold up the lighter like I'm fending off evil. "Stay the hell away from me."

Rochester takes a step closer, his dark eyes reflecting the firelight. "Rowland always envied me. I'm the one who got the women while that simpleton could only drool and touch himself. But he finally got his dick wet."

My lip curls.

"I suspect he made a mess of his first time. Did he cry in your arms? Did you have to reassure him that ten seconds was normal for a big boy?" He laughs, the sound grating on my nerves.

"You seem awfully obsessed with your brother's sex life," I say from between clenched teeth.

His smile turns predatory. "I plan on showing Rowland exactly how to please a woman."

My heart leaps. "He's alive?"

"Clinging onto survival as always. He's looking forward to taking his front-row seat when I fuck you to death."

"Shut up!" I yell, backing away until my shoulders hit cold stone.

"Don't tell me you've actually fallen for that moron." Rochester laughs, the sound mocking.

"Better than a sadist who has to rape to feel superior," I spit.

"How precious. I'll pluck out your heart and serve it to him on a platter."

He lurches forward. I dash to the side, crashing into another pile of bones. They scatter across the floor with sickening thuds. My knee hits something hard. It's a skull that rolls away into the darkness.

"Ah, you've found Bertha. She stopped being fun after she went mad."

Rage flashes through my chest. Everything Rowland said about his brother was right. Rochester wasn't satisfied with working women to death—he also had to break their minds. My fingers close around what feels like a large bone. It might be a femur. I tell myself it's a club.

"You pathetic psychopath," I say through clenched teeth. "I'll fucking kill you."

"Sticks and stones, Miss Burlington. Now, crawl to your master."

"Go to hell," I snap.

Grinning, he unzips his fly. "I'll take you there myself. On your knees. Mouth open."

Nausea jerks my stomach tight. My gaze darts away from his exposed cock to a sliver of light from above, casting faint illumination on stone steps leading up to another door. An escape plan forms in my head, desperate. Stupid, but it's all I've got.

"Why don't you come here and make me," I say, mustering every ounce of defiance.

He chuckles, low and deep. "With pleasure."

Stroking his cock, he stalks forward, his hand reaching for my hair. Before he can so much as grab me, I swing the bone like a baseball bat. It connects with his temple and snaps. Sending a silent apology to Bertha, I lance the jagged edge into his throat.

Rochester staggers backward with a roar, "You wretched cunt!"

I don't wait to see if the wound is fatal. I charge across the cellar and up the stairs. Rochester bellows like a wounded beast as I reach the door. It's a heavy wood, reinforced with iron bands. I throw my weight against it, stagger through, and slam it shut.

On the other side, my fingers find a bolt. I slide it home just as Rochester slams into it from below.

"Open this fucking door!" he shouts, the wood shuddering with each impact.

I scan the space for inspiration. Another way out. Windows, floorboards—anything. There's nothing. Just the same rotting walls and broken furniture as when he first dragged me here. The windows sit too high, glass caked in grime. They might as well be painted black.

Wait a minute.

Rochester gave me the fucking key!

"I'm going to make you wish for death. Your humiliation will make Rowland's suffering look like a picnic!"

The door bangs again as he throws himself against it, the wood groaning under the impact.

I rush to the door, slide the key in the lock and pray that it's not another one of his sick games. It opens with a creak, letting out a gust of apple-scented air. Just as I'm about to escape into the night, he screams loud enough to shake the shack.

"Let me out," he yells, desperation creeping into his rage.

No. I can't leave. Leaving will only continue this twisted charade. There's only one way to make sure he never hurts Rowland, or another woman. And that means putting an end to his tyranny.

I need to silence this monster forever.

Turning back, I find a canister of kerosene glinting in the corner. I rush to pick it up and splash liquid around the rotted walls. I douse the door for good measure and pour the rest down the trap door.

Back at the overturned table, I search through the debris until I find a box of matches. Fingers trembling, I extract a matchstick and strike it against the rough wood. Its head flares to life, casting dancing shadows on the walls.

"I'll make you wallow in your own filth until you forget you were ever human," he screams. "You won't die like the others. Your prison will keep you at my mercy until the end of your days."

"Say hello to Brother Matthew in hell."

I drop the match.

Flames catch the kerosene and race across the floorboards, sending waves of heat licking at my skin. I rush outside into the cool night with the key and lock the door. Inside, fire spreads up the walls, eating through decades of rot and decay. Orange light flickers through the windows as smoke pours from the doorway.

Some monsters deserve to burn.

But as the fire roars behind me, one thought cuts through everything:

Where the hell is Rowland?

FORTY-TWO

I try to forget about the night I left Brother Matthew, but the flames tearing through the cottage drag me back. It's the same molten glow licking at broken windows. The same roar of wood surrendering to fire. The same smell of smoke that means something's finally dead and burning.

But this time, there isn't an ounce of guilt.

I move between the apple trees, checking every shadow wide enough to hide a body. My feet slip on rotting fruit, and I splay my arms to stay upright. Branches catch at my dress as I push deeper into the rows of trees, looking behind every trunk thick enough to conceal a man.

"Rowland!" I call out, my voice carrying across the grounds toward the dark outline of the manor.

What did Rochester do with him? He could be anywhere.

My gaze flicks toward the outbuildings. The stables stand about fifty yards from the orchard, their doors hanging open. I jog across the lawn and enter an enclosure stinking of horse piss and old hay. Empty stalls stretch into the darkness, each one possibly hiding Rowland.

I search through the enclosures, kicking piles of moldy straw that reach my knees. Dust clouds rise with each movement, making me cough. But there's no sign of an unconscious man.

"Rowland?" I call again, my voice hoarse and hollow, like the trees might answer back.

I move to the greenhouse, the garages, the storage sheds, tearing through the grounds like a madwoman. By the time I've searched all the outbuildings, the cottage fire reaches the sky. Every muscle in my body aches. My chest heaves like I've run a marathon, and my voice is nearly gone from calling his name.

What if Rochester dumped Rowland beneath that cottage? What if Rowland is lying among the corpses, unconscious, and trapped in the flames?

I can't think like that. I can't give up hope.

The night wears on, and Rowland isn't in the tool shed or the chicken coop. Each empty building brings me closer to a truth I don't want to face. Each search leaves me more exhausted, more desperate, more certain that I'm looking for a dead man.

Legs trembling, I stumble back toward the manor. My chest heaves as I try to catch my breath, but every inhale feels like sandpaper. My muscles no longer throb. Nothing compares to the pain of losing Rowland. Tears blur my vision, mixing with the sweat and grime covering my face.

Up ahead, in the highest point of the manor, a light flickers. I blink away the dirt and saltwater to look again.

My pulse stutters, then kicks into overdrive.

The attic.

I hurry to the kitchen and rifle through the drawers until I find a heavy cleaver. My legs shake so badly I cling to the banister to keep from falling as I rush upstairs. Hope flutters in my chest, but by the second floor my vision grays and every breath burns.

Upstairs, the wall panel that leads to the attic is shut. I claw at the edges with my fingernails, searching for the hidden lever. When I find nothing, I throw my body against the wood. It refuses to budge. I press harder, using what little strength I have left, but the thing's sealed tighter than a vault.

Rowland has to be inside. There's no other explanation. I raise the cleaver, aiming its blade at the panel.

The first blow sends jolts up my arms like lightning. Pain shoots through my shoulders, and splinters fly into my eyes. I raise the blade again and strike once more, opening a small crack in the wood.

By the tenth blow, I've carved a hole big enough to see the dark staircase beyond. I'm drenched in sweat and my arms shake so badly I can barely hold the weapon.

I squeeze through the opening, not caring about the wood that tears my beautiful dress. It's ruined anyway from searching through the grounds. The stairs groan under my weight as I climb into the dark, gripping that cleaver like a lifeline.

At the top of the stairs, I lean my head against the door to catch my breath and gather my strength to raise the cleaver. My arms scream in protest, but I bring the blade down, channeling every ounce of rage, every ounce of hope, everything I have left.

The impact jolts through both arms. The door doesn't even show a scratch.

I raise the cleaver again, putting my whole body

behind the blow. The blade bites into the wood, leaving the barest of marks.

"Come on," I growl, raising the blade again. "Break, you bastard."

Rowland groans again, weaker this time. Like he's fading.

"Don't you dare give up on me!" I scream, bringing the cleaver down again and again.

Chips of wood fly with each blow, but the door holds. My arms feel like they're tearing apart at the joints. Sweat pours down from my brow, stinging my eyes. I'm half blind, half mad, but driven by determination. I keep swinging, keep fighting, because the alternative is losing the only person who ever gave a damn about me.

After what feels like hours, I've carved a groove in the wood deep enough to fit my fist. Not much, but it's progress.

It takes another eternity to make an opening big enough to crawl through. By the time I drop the cleaver, my whole body trembles and I can barely stay upright. But I squeeze past the splintered wood into the attic.

The space stretches before me, lit by a single candle that flickers in the draft from my entrance. And there, chained to the far wall, is Rowland.

He hangs from shackles binding his wrists, his head drooping forward so I can't see his face. Blood covers his chest and arms, and his shirt hangs in tatters around his shoulders.

He looks dead, but his chest rises and falls in shallow breaths.

"Rowland." I stumble toward him on legs that barely work.

He lifts his head, slow and trembling, like his neck is

held together by thread. His black eyes struggle to focus, but when they find mine, something breaks across his battered face.

"Annalisa?"

I rush to him, my knees nearly buckling from the climb. With trembling hands, I assess the damage. Through the blood and bruises and dirt, there's a gash near his hairline deep enough to make my throat convulse.

He's conscious. But barely.

"Where else are you hurt?" I ask.

He blinks, trying to focus. "Annalisa, you need to run."

"I'm not leaving you." I grab at his chains. The iron is solid and cold, built to hold a man for decades.

"Edward will come for you next," he wails. "I failed to protect you. He can't be stopped."

"I killed him." The words tumble out between gasps for air. "I locked him in the basement cottage and set it alight. The bastard's finally dead."

Rowland's eyes snap into sharp focus, suddenly alert despite his injuries. "Did you kill him before the fire?"

Something settles in my stomach, colder than dread, heavier than exhaustion. "No, but the door was locked. The fire would have—"

"Edward has survived worse. I've seen him crawl out of things that should've left him in pieces. He'll find a way out. And when he does, we're both dead."

FORTY-THREE

Apprehension coils through my insides like a venomous snake. If Rowland is right about Rochester surviving, then he's already out there. Watching. Hunting. Planning his next move while I've been hacking through doors like a madwoman.

I grab the chains securing Rowland's wrists. The iron shackles won't budge. There has to be a lock mechanism somewhere, but my hands shake too much to find it in the poor light.

"They won't open without a key," he says, his voice stronger now that I'm here. "It's in Mrs. Fairfax's pocket."

My belly churns. I glance toward the corner where that skeleton sits in its rocking chair, its yellowed bones visible through gaps in the rotted fabric. Of course the key's with that corpse. Even in death, she's still Rochester's housekeeper.

"Are you sure?" I rasp.

He shudders. "Last thing I saw before I blacked out was Edward rifling through her dress. Leaving the key there is the kind of twisted game he'd play."

Bile rises in my throat, but I force my legs to carry me across the attic. Each step feels like walking through quicksand. Up close, the skeleton is gruesome. What's left of her face clings to the bone like jerky. What I thought were wisps of gray hair are actually thick cobwebs.

I reach toward the yellowed apron with trembling fingers. The fabric is stiff but intact enough to hold its shape. I feel around where pockets would be, trying not to think about what I'm touching. There's nothing on the first side apart from a bone jutting through the cloth, and I have to swallow back a surge of vomit to continue.

Suppressing a shiver, I search the other side. My fingers close around something small and metal.

"Got it," I yank my hand back like I've touched fire.

By the time I turn around, Rowland's head is bowed, as if he's lost consciousness. I rush back to him and fumble with the shackles until I find the lock mechanism. I free his wrists, and he collapses forward with a groan, his weight nearly sending us both to the floor.

"Annalisa," he groans, pulling me into a hug. He's damp with blood and sweat, but all the tension that's squeezed my chest since finding that blood in the kitchen fades.

"I thought you were dead," I whisper into his neck, breathing in his masculine scent. "I searched everywhere. Every building on the grounds, terrified I'd never see you again."

His arms tighten around me until I can feel his heartbeat. "I heard you calling my name. That was the only thing keeping me conscious. Knowing you were out there, still alive."

I pull back to look at his battered face, and cup his

cheek with my palm. Fresh cuts mark his forehead, and his left eye is swollen nearly shut. But at least he's alive.

"I'm sorry." His voice cracks.

"What for?"

He dips his head, his gaze dropping to his lap. "I promised to protect you, and I failed—"

"Don't say that. You survived. That's how we win." I lift his chin, forcing our eyes to meet. "What happened to us isn't anyone's fault but his."

We gaze at each other in silence, our breaths synchronizing, taking this moment to reconnect. Seeing Rowland safe and well is everything. I never realized how deeply I cared for him until he was gone.

Having him here fills my heart to bursting, and I can see myself spending the rest of my days basking in his love. But I don't linger, not if Rochester is out there, waiting for the right moment to strike.

I run my thumb over a cut on Rowland's lip. "Can you walk? How badly are you hurt?"

He flexes his hands, testing his wrists where the shackles left angry red marks. "A few burns, some cuts. Nothing permanent. He didn't have time to do any real damage. His dark eyes search my features, taking in every detail like he's memorizing my face. "Did he touch you?"

"No," I say. "That bastard never got the chance. I smashed him over the head before he even tried."

"My brave girl," he says, his voice thick with emotion. "I can't tell you how much it means to me that you're safe."

"Come on. We need to find out if your brother is actually dead."

Jaw tightening, Rowland's eyes harden. "Let's make sure Edward doesn't survive the night."

We both groan as I help him off the cot. His weight settles on my shoulder, making my knees sag. Whatever Rochester did to Rowland has him disoriented and swaying on his feet.

After securing the cleaver, we make our way down the narrow stairs, Rowland's hand gripping my shoulder for balance. He's heavy against my side, but his weight is reassuring proof that he's alive. I squeeze back through the splintered hole in the panel first, then help pull him through. His shirt catches on the jagged wood, tearing fresh holes in the fabric.

We continue through the hallways and down the stairs in silence. Rowland breathes hard at my side, dripping blood on the floor. My heart aches. There isn't a single thing I can do to help him until we find a first-aid kit.

When we reach the kitchen, he pulls open the drawer to select a carving blade with a wicked edge, then lowers himself into the chair with a groan.

I fetch the first aid kit and tend to his wounds. There are bruises, shallow cuts, and burns. Rowland looks like he barely survived Rochester's frenzied attack.

"What the hell did he do to you?" I ask.

"He's done worse," he replies, the words gruff. "But we can't delay. Let me tend to your wounds then we'll find my brother before he finds us."

Rowland eases me onto a kitchen chair, fumbles through the kit, and dabs antiseptic on my wounds with trembling hands. I close my eyes, my body melting under his touch. After surviving Rochester and scouring the grounds, I have to look ghastly, but he touches me like I'm precious.

Afterward, we step outside into the predawn air. The sky lightens in the east, painting everything in shades of gray and pale gold. Smoke hangs over the grounds like fog, and the breeze carries the stench of burned wood. It mixes with the scent of dew on grass and the distant salt smell of the ocean.

As we head toward the orchard in silence, I can't help noticing how everything looks different beside Rowland. The estate is smaller, less ominous. Less like the nightmare it felt when I was alone in the dark.

The cottage crouches like a blackened skeleton beneath the apple trees. Most of the roof has collapsed inward, and we walk around its perimeter to find the soot-covered windows all shut. Embers still glow deep in the ruins, pulsing red against the charred wood. Steam rises from the wreckage where morning dew meets hot ash. The wooden door hangs crooked on its hinges, warped by heat but still closed.

"He has to be dead," I say. "No one can survive a fire like that. If the flames didn't reach him, then he would have suffocated on the smoke."

Rowland stares at the smoldering shell, his face grim. Lines of worry crease his forehead as he studies every angle of the destruction. "There's a tunnel connecting the cottage's basement to the house's cellar."

My breath stalls. Of course there's a secret passage. Of course this nightmare has layers. But I still blurt, "What? Where? Why?"

"Our great-grandparents were smugglers," he mutters. "And there's a trap door beneath the basement. If Edward had a key and made it down there before the fire spread to the floor..."

Rowland doesn't finish the thought, but I can see it in his eyes. Rochester could be in the house right now. Could be watching us from the windows, biding his time.

"Where does it come out?" I ask.

"Wine cellar. Behind the racks." Rowland grips the knife so hard his knuckles turn white.

"Let's go."

We head back toward the house, but as we reach the lawn, Rowland's steps falter, and he grabs my arm. I glance up to find him scanning the windows, seeming to look for any sign of Rochester.

"What is it?" I whisper.

"You need to be somewhere safe while I handle my brother. Go upstairs and lock yourself in the bathroom."

I yank free of his grip. "We're stronger together. I'm not hiding while you face him alone."

Rowland's eyes search my face. His features war between his need to protect me and his recognition that I'm right. That two of us have a better chance against Rochester than one. That I've already proven I can handle myself.

Finally, his shoulders sag. "You're right. But stay by my side. No heroics."

We reach the end of the lawn, cross the patio and push open the kitchen door. Rowland leads me down the hallway toward the cellar stairs, where the grandfather clock ticks in the silence like a countdown. My heart pounds at the prospect of Edward surviving the fire, but I tell myself that there are two of us, and we're armed.

Rowland pauses at the cellar door. Sweat beads on his forehead, and his breaths are rapid and shallow. Just as he reaches the handle, the doorbell rings.

We turn to each other and freeze.

"Edward?" I mouth.

He shakes his head and points toward the basement.

Then who?

The bell rings again.

"Police! Open the door."

My pulse kicks up several notches. I grab Rowland's arm, hoping the cops aren't here for me.

"It's Morrison," says the voice. "I know you're in there, Rochester. Open the door, now!"

Morrison. The cop who called Edward about Blanche's death. What the hell is he doing back here?

Neither of us moves.

"Edward Rochester! Open this door right now!"

Morrison's voice carries through the house with an authority that won't be ignored. He's not going away. More pounding echoes from the front door, sharp and insistent.

"I swear to God, Rochester, if you don't open up, everyone will know the truth about Blanche Ingram!"

My breath stutters. What truth? Morrison knows something about Blanche's death. Something that could expose Rochester. Which means he could expose us if we're not careful.

But more importantly, Morrison isn't leaving. He'll keep escalating until someone opens that door. If he calls for backup and if more cops show up, it might jeopardize our plan to have Rowland replace his brother.

I place my hands on Rowland's bicep. "Hide. I'll answer the door."

"Absolutely not." His grip tightens on the knife. "You can't face a policeman alone."

"I can handle Morrison. You can't be seen. God knows what this is really about."

The pounding intensifies. Morrison's getting angry, which means he's getting dangerous.

"Trust me," I say, already moving toward the front hall. "I've been lying to cops my whole life."

And I'll lie to Morrison, too. Because it means protecting the only person who's ever bled for me.

FORTY-FOUR

I stand behind the front door, my pulse hammering loud enough to muffle the racket. Morrison continues knocking as if the house is on fire, and I race through what the hell I'm supposed to say.

If I act too nervous, he'll know I'm hiding something. Too calm, and I'll look suspicious. I need to play the part of the confused servant who knows nothing about her employer's business. Just the help. Just another girl who cleans floors and minds her business.

But what on earth does Morrison know about Blanche's death?

"Rochester! I'm not leaving until we talk!"

More pounding echoes through the wood, making me flinch. Each blow sounds like it might splinter the frame.

Hands trembling, I glance over my shoulder. I can't let him see Rowland. Not just because everyone thinks he's dead. The last thing I want him to think is that I'm hiding a dubious character. But I can't delay. He'll break down the door or call for backup.

"Hello?" I say, my voice trembling.

"Open this fucking door."

"A-all right."

I smooth down my dress. Remind myself to think like a servant who's worried about her job and terrified of authority. That's who Annalisa Burlington is supposed to be.

With a sharp inhale, I turn the lock.

Morrison barrels inside before I can even get the door open. He's bigger than I remember—shoulders like a bouncer, neck like a tree trunk, and cheeks mottled with fury. And the way he stares down at me like a suspect makes him all the more menacing.

"Where's your boss?" he demands, his gaze scanning the foyer like he's cataloging every detail.

"Mr. Rochester hasn't yet returned," I say, keeping my voice steady. "Would you like to leave a message?"

"Answer my question," he says, his gaze snapping back to me.

"I don't know where he went. He doesn't tell me his movements. I just keep the house running while he's away."

Morrison's eyes narrow. "Why are you so banged up?"

My stomach lurches. There wasn't time to get changed. I shift on my feet, trying to drum up the most plausible lie. "I had an accident."

His gaze sweeps up and down my ragged form, taking in the bruises on my neck, my torn dress, the blood and cuts and dirt. "What kind of accident?"

"There was a fire in one of the outbuildings," I rasp. "I tried to put it out before it spread, but I fell and got scraped up. Should've called for help, but I couldn't find my phone."

Seconds pass, and he continues glaring down at me like he's trying to decipher my bullshit. One wrong glance and he'll tear the lie apart. I hold my face steady, but my heart slams hard enough to wake the dead.

Eventually, he curls his lip. I can't tell if he can imagine me bumbling through a fire or if he no longer gives a damn. "When did you last see your boss?"

My throat dries, but I stick to my original story. "The morning he and his new bride left for their honeymoon."

"Bullshit." He strides past me toward the back of the house like he owns the place.

I follow him, wringing my hands. "Is everything alright? Has something happened to Mr. Rochester?"

Ignoring me, he strides into the study, walks over the papers strewn across the floor, and sits on the edge of the mahogany desk. "Call him."

"Excuse me?"

"Call Rochester. Tell him Detective Morrison needs to speak with him about his wife."

My throat tightens. My breath turns shallow. "I don't have his number. Mrs. Fairfax handles all the contact information, and she's away on the mainland."

Silence stretches between us, broken only by the tick of the grandfather clock. Morrison watches me with the cold calculation of a predator sizing up a target. Every hackle on the back of my neck rises, and I pray to whoever's listening he doesn't scrutinize me too closely.

"You know what I think?" Morrison says, his voice low and menacing.

"What?" I rasp.

"You're covering for that bastard." He shifts off the edge of the desk and steps toward me, his glower forcing me to skitter backward.

I shake my head, not wanting to say anything incriminating.

"Stupid of you to protect a sicko who'll run you around in circles before putting you in the ground." He stands so close, I breathe in his coffee-scented breath. "Because you'll end up just like the others."

My back hits the wall. "What others?"

"Other girls worked here before you. Pretty little things, looking for work, thinking they'd landed a dream job with a rich gentleman." His gaze drops to my cleavage.

Nausea surges in my gut. He knows. Knows Edward Rochester is a serial killer. Knows he murdered Blanche.

"What happened to them?" I ask.

"They disappeared." He shrugs as if he's talking about misfiled paperwork. "Vanished like smoke."

I flinch at the matter-of-fact way he tells me about Rochester's murders. The contemptuous tone an officer of the law would use to identify me as his next victim makes my back stiffen. Even more disturbing is this entire situation. He isn't here to arrest a serial killer. He came alone because... Oh, shit. Because—

"You've been helping him." The words slip out before I can stop myself.

Morrison grins, showing molars in serious need of dental work. "Smart girl."

The pieces click into place with sickening clarity. Why nobody ever arrested Rochester. Why he thought he could get away with murdering Blanche. Because Morrison helped him cover up the disappearances. Made sure no one looked too hard for missing servants. Took payoffs to keep his secrets buried.

"How many?" I rasp.

"Does it matter? They were nobodies. Runaways, orphans, women with no familial ties. But I'll give him one thing. Rochester has fantastic taste." Morrison grabs my arm, his fingers digging into my flesh.

I try to pull away, but his grip tightens. "Let go of me!"

His hot breath fans against my ear. "Relax. This'll be quick. Much better than what Rochester's planned for you anyway."

I glance around, my mind scrambling for a weapon. The brass letter opener on the desk. A glass paperweight. My knee. If it comes to it, my fucking teeth. I suck in air, ready to scream loud enough to wake the dead.

But before I can move, the door slams open and Rowland charges inside. He hits Morrison like a freight train, his fist connecting with the cop's jaw. The impact sends Morrison staggering backward, blood spurting from his mouth in a crimson arc.

"Nobody touches what's mine!" Rowland roars, his face twisted with animalistic rage.

Morrison hits the wall and lunges for the gun at his hip. His fingers close around the grip, but Rowland slams into the cop's midsection, driving them both into Rochester's desk. The heavy furniture overturns, sending out a spray of papers and pens.

"You fucking psycho!" Morrison yells, holding the pistol.

Rowland grabs Morrison's wrist, slamming the weapon against the desk edge until it goes flying. It skitters across the hardwood floor and spins under a bookshelf. The fight continues, with Rowland pounding the other man with his fists, and Morrison reaching for his beard.

I look from side to side for a heavy object to smash over the cop's head, but they both move too quickly for me to assist. Morrison is bigger, but he's slow while Rowland lunges with a desperation bordering on feral. They crash into the bookshelf, sending leather-bound volumes tumbling to the floor in clouds of dust.

Morrison gets his hands around Rowland's throat, squeezing hard enough to make his veins bulge. Face darkening, Rowland drives his elbow into Morrison's solar plexus. The cop lurches backward with a gasp, and Rowland breaks free.

Then Rowland grabs a fallen lamp and wraps its extension cord around Morrison's neck.

The cop's eyes bulge. He claws at the cable with one hand, making awful choking sounds that turn my stomach. With the other, he reaches for Rowland's face, only for him to jerk back. I raise my hands to my throat, my pulse pounding so hard its reverberations reach between my legs.

I'm not getting turned on by the sight of a man garroting another for my protection. Despite this, something in my heart flutters. Rowland is choking out a cop for me. Morrison's face turns red, then purple as his legs kick frantically against the desk.

"Please," Morrison wheezes, but Rowland's grip only tightens.

"Annalisa belongs to me," he growls, every word serrated like blades.

I pant through parted lips. I should be horrified, but my heart thrums with something darker. Somewhere in the madness, I feel safe. But this is beyond twisted. I press my hands to my ears, but nothing can block out the gurgling. Or the desperate scrabbling of a man dying because he hurt me.

Morrison's death throes grow weaker. More desperate. His kicks fade into feeble twitches. He turns to me, his lips moving as if to deliver a final curse. But I turn around. Can't bring myself to look. Can't face that bone-deep sense of satisfaction of finally having a man who fulfills his promises. Instead, I stare at the wall, counting my breaths, trying not to think about what's next.

I wait for the nausea, the terror, the guilt, but I feel nothing. Morrison is just another corrupt cop, like Callahan. Both men were violent. Both tried to use me as a pawn. Both died because they couldn't stay on the right side of the law. I feel nothing, save for the slow, sinking weight of the fact that Rowland kept his promise.

He said he'd protect me.

And he did.

Moments later, strong arms wrap around my waist from behind, pulling me against a chest that rises and falls hard with exertion. I inhale Rowland's familiar scent beneath the sweat and blood—salt and cedar and something uniquely him that makes me feel safe even in the middle of carnage.

"He's dead, Annalisa," Rowland says, his voice rough from the fight. "That bastard will never be able to touch you again."

I turn in his arms and bury my face in his shirt, my entire body shaking. "What are we going to do now?"

He strokes my hair, his touch heartbreakingly gentle. He just killed a man... for me.

"You understand why I did it?" he asks.

I swallow hard, my mind already spinning through

the consequences. Another dead cop. Another potential manhunt. Another reason to run.

"He would have hurt you," Rowland says, drawing back to cup my face. "That man helped Edward cover up his murders and would have done the same to you. I couldn't let that happen. You're mine to protect, and I'll kill anyone who tries to take you from me."

His possessive words should be terrifying. Any sane woman would turn tail. But what Rowland just did for me is the closest thing I've ever felt to love. I lean into his embrace, taking comfort from his protection, his strength, until the panic subsides, giving space to reality.

Rowland just killed a cop. We'll both be hunted. Even if we can prove it's self-defense, that still puts the spotlight on me for my past. I pull back to look at Morrison's body sprawled face-down across the study floor.

"His colleagues will come looking for him," I whisper.

Rowland follows my gaze to the dead cop. "I'll put him with the others. But first, we need to check if Edward's underground. If he managed to escape the fire, he'll be trapped in the passageway between the cottage and the basement."

My blood chills at the reminder of Rochester being alive. That bastard threatened to put me in a prison I could never escape. If he finds out we've killed a cop, he'll use it as a weapon in his arsenal of psychological torture.

I meet Rowland's dark eyes. Eyes that shine with love and concern. Gathering my courage, I raise my chin. "Then let's finish this. I'm tired of running."

Rowland nods. "Stay close. If Edward's down there, he'll be desperate. And desperate men are the most dangerous kind."

FORTY-FIVE

The adrenaline's gone. All that's left is dread.

All I can think about is what we'll find when we dispose of Morrison's body. Rochester could be in that passageway, already recovered from his head wound.

Rowland drags the corpse through the hall. I follow, eyes on the marble, relieved to see no streaks of blood. At least that means less cleanup.

My hands still shake. I've never helped cover up a murder before, but that bastard got what he deserved.

"Do you want me to take the legs?" I ask.

"No," Rowland grunts.

Morrison's dead weight makes Rowland's movements awkward, and sweat beads on his forehead with the effort. The dead cop's head lolls at an unnatural angle, his pale eyes staring sightlessly at the ceiling.

"Apart from being a psycho rapist, what do you think he wanted?" I ask.

"Probably an advance on the Ingram inheritance," Rowland mutters.

"Did they ever share victims?"

He hesitates, his grip on Morrison slipping. "Some-times. But only after Edward had broken the woman and wanted her dead. If I'd known the officer would attack you, I'd have never allowed you to answer the door."

"What does that mean?"

"I thought you'd be safe so early in my brother's killing cycle."

A shudder races down my spine. "Cycle... right."

He adjusts his hold on the dead body and continues walking. "I love you too much to let you fall into the hands of a brute."

My chest clenches almost painfully. Now that he's killed for me, his declaration of love takes on new meaning. It's nothing like the hollow words of manipulation I've heard my entire adult life. Every confession I've endured before was a chain, a trick, a cage. This feels dangerous but real.

We reach a section of wall that looks identical to every other panel in the hallway. It's a long stretch of mahogany wainscoting, nothing to suggest anything special. But Rowland drops Morrison to the floor and runs his fingers along the wood molding until he stops at something I can't see.

"What are you doing?" I whisper.

"Opening the passage to the basement."

A soft click echoes through the hallway, and the panel swings inward to reveal a narrow staircase descending into darkness.

"Shit. Does this house have any more secret doorways?"

Rowland glances back at me, his dark eyes shining with warmth. "Of course. Hiding places like these kept our ancestors safe when the authorities came sniffing around."

I shake my head. Rich families always have their dirty secrets. Corruption, smuggling, murder and whatever else Rowland hasn't yet revealed. At least now those passages will serve a useful purpose.

He grabs Morrison under the arms again and steps through the opening.

"How deep does this go?" I ask as Rowland descends the steep stone steps.

"This set? Two stories." His breathing is labored from hauling dead weight. "But there's another that leads down to the cliffs."

Shuddering at the reminder of being so close to the ocean, I follow behind with a hand trailing along the damp wall for balance. The air grows colder and mustier with each step, and I try not to think of how the tunnel leads to those murdered women.

Or possibly Rochester himself.

At the bottom, we reach a heavy door even thicker than the one I had to smash through to get into the attic. Even in the dark, I can tell it's reinforced with iron bands and a lock that looks medieval.

Rowland drops Morrison's arms and leans against the wall, breathing hard. "If Edward's anywhere, this is where he'll be."

I stare at the imposing door, my pulse quickening. Anticipation, nausea, and fear battle for dominance in my gut. If Rochester really survived the fire and is waiting for us, now's our time to finish him.

My fingers tighten around the cleaver. If he's waiting on the other side, I need to be close enough to protect Rowland.

Rowland reaches into his pocket and pulls out a ring of keys. "Step back. I'm opening the door."

"I'm not moving from this spot," I reply.

Rowland fixes me with a look, though I can't tell if it's with pride or exasperation. When he offers me a crooked smile, I shift backward, giving him space. He turns the lock, making a grinding sound that echoes off the stone walls. With a groan, he pushes open the heavy door, revealing a long corridor stretching into shadow. We both peer into the darkness, muscles tensed for an attack.

Silence stretches until my nerves are pulled to the point of snapping. I wait for signs of Rochester, but there's nothing. No movement. No sound of breathing or shuffling feet. Just quiet.

Relief loosens my lungs, and we both exhale.

"Maybe your brother really is dead," I say, my voice trembling with hope.

Rowland grunts and picks up the corpse by the arms. "Step aside. I'll take it from here."

"Let me come in with you. I should watch your back."

"No need. This won't take long." He straightens, Morrison's weight making his arms shake.

I step back, letting him haul the corpse into the corridor. The darkness swallows them both, leaving me alone on the stone landing. That's when I notice a small notebook on the floor that must have slipped from Morrison's jacket.

Curious, I pick it up and flip through the pages. Most of it is police notes, dating back several weeks. But then I see my name written in capitals.

Below it, I scan details about my background: My birth name: Mary-Jane Reed. Mom and Dad's names:

Janet and James Reed. He even dug up the names of my sisters and brother, Diana, Mary, and John.

I continue reading to find the date I married Matthew Eyre. The date of the fire and a list of casualties. Then he lists names of old lovers and sugar daddies, with the last one being Gilberto Agostini. I shake my head. I had no idea that was even his full name.

But it's the conclusion at the bottom that makes my blood run cold:

Subject has been a missing person for nine years, eleven months, with no family ties. Background suggests she will not be missed by law enforcement or civilian contacts. Ideal candidate.

A sharp breath hisses from my teeth.

I was always prey. A profile, not a person. Just another ghost girl with no future, no one to miss her. My whole fucking life was a checklist on a predator's clipboard.

So that's how it worked. Rochester didn't randomly hire and dispose of desperate women. Morrison researched them first to make sure no one would come looking when they disappeared.

I wasn't just unlucky. I didn't just stumble into this situation. I was specifically selected.

Jaw clenching, I flip the page. Morrison wrote a bunch of lies about my past. Details about supposed escort work. He paints me as a woman who fucked for money, when what I was looking for was support. Most of it is distorted bullshit designed to make me look like nothing but a prostitute.

What the hell would Rowland think if he read this twisted version of my history?

A shiver runs down my spine. I can't let Rowland see

this. Chest tightening, I glance into the darkness, checking for signs of his return. He doesn't need to know about my long list of lovers. Doesn't need Morrison's corrupt little notes poisoning our relationship.

The sounds of dragging grow fainter as Rowland moves deeper toward that terrible graveyard Edward built down there. I have possibly two minutes before he returns.

I rip out the pages from the notebook, tear them into small pieces, and stuff the evidence into my pocket. Morrison can rot with his lies in hell.

Minutes later, footsteps echo from down the corridor. I arrange my features into a calm mask and get ready to show Rowland what's left of the notebook.

Some secrets are worth keeping.

FORTY-SIX

I'm still twitchy when Rowland's footsteps approach.
Maybe because it's my turn to lie by omission. The ripped
pieces in my pocket feel like they're fused to my skin, but
I remind myself it's best for both of us if he doesn't know.
He steps out from the darkness of the corridor, his weary
features turning bright. Then he pulls me into his strong
arms.

All the tension escapes my lungs, and I melt into his
embrace. Rowland squeezes me tight against his chest like
he's afraid I might disappear.

"It's over," he says, his voice rough with exhaustion.

Pulling back, I meet his dark eyes. "Your brother's
really gone?"

"He wasn't in the tunnels. And the basement's empty
except for..." Rowland doesn't need to finish. I already
know he's talking about the bodies Rochester collected
over the years. Now, Morrison's keeping them company.
"You were right. He really did die in that fire."

"Are you sure?" I ask, my voice breathy with hope.

Rowland nods, his eyes fluttering shut. With an

outward breath, he murmurs, "Edward is gone. We're finally free."

The next few days blur together in a haze. We clean the study and hallways of all traces of the fight, dispose of Morrison's car in a nature reserve on the other side of the island, and settle into the routine of two lovers learning to live without looking over our shoulders.

Rowland and I spend hours talking, touching, discovering each other without the constant threat of his brother's return. We make love in Rochester's bed, in his study, in every room where he once held power, claiming the space as ours.

But our fragile peace doesn't last long.

Three days after Morrison's death, letters arrive from Blanche's attorney requesting meetings to discuss Rochester's inheritance. Her will left everything to her husband, and the estate is still in need of rescuing from bankruptcy.

The solution is obvious but terrifying. Rowland must become Edward Rochester legally, financially, and socially to claim Blanche's money and save the estate. It's the only way we can stay here and build a life together.

Which is why I'm standing outside the bathroom, listening to his labored breathing through the door.

"Rowland," I press my palm against the wood. "You need to come out."

"I look monstrous," his voice is thick with revulsion and shame.

"You don't know that until I see you."

Silence stretches for several seconds, broken only by his pained sobs. My heart squeezes. I picture Rowland's face crisscrossed with the same scars marring his chest. It's hard to imagine what manner of torture he endured.

No matter what, my love for this man won't waver, even if he's disfigured.

"Rowland. Come to me. Please."

"Alright," he says with a sigh.

Moments later, the lock clicks, and the door swings open. Rowland emerges naked, save for a white towel around his hips. He bows his head as if walking to his execution, his shoulders drawing up to his ears. The beard is gone, and his hair is slicked back with water, but I still can't see his face.

"Look at me," I murmur.

He jerks his head to the side.

I place both hands on his scarred chest, frowning at the frantic beat of his heart. "What are you afraid of? We've seen each other at our worst. You can't turn away from me now."

Throat bobbing, he finally straightens and looks me full in the face. The man staring back makes every fine hair on my body stand on end.

Rowland's resemblance to his brother is so strong that I reel on my feet. He has the same aristocratic nose, the same sharp cheekbones, the same cruel mouth.

"You didn't tell me you're twins," I whisper.

He grimaces, his lips tightening with distaste. "Not identical. Not really."

My chest squeezes at the denial. They're so similar, it's painful. But Rowland probably hasn't seen his own face since he started growing facial hair.

I place both hands on his cheeks, forcing him to stay still, and I look past the shock of recognition. Rowland is right. He's not his brother. But he could wear that face like a glove. Besides, his features are more weathered, with lines bracketing his mouth from years of pain. The posture is also different—more guarded, beaten down, less entitled.

Rochester moved through the world like he owned it. Rowland is a man barely clinging to survival. Rowland might have looked identical to his brother if he hadn't lived a hard life instead of one cushioned by privilege and wealth.

"Do I look monstrous?" he whispers.

"No," I blurt. "Never."

Rowland glances away, breaking eye contact. The shame rolling off his shoulders is palpable, and I understand why. He isn't just wearing his brother's face. He's becoming the murderer who tortured him for decades.

"Look at me," I say, injecting my voice with command.

He sucks in a deep breath as though gathering his courage before returning his gaze to mine. Fear shines in his dark eyes, reminding me so much of how I felt before I finally escaped my previous life.

"You are not your brother," I say, meaning every word. "After everything we've endured together, everything you've done to protect me, I could never see you as a monster."

He starts to turn away again, but I catch his face in my hands, forcing him to maintain eye contact.

"But you saw me murder Morrison," he mutters. "Doesn't that sicken you?"

"We're both killers," I say with bite. "We did what we had to do to survive."

Rowland doesn't reply. But from his shallow breathing, I can tell he's fighting an internal battle. He isn't like me. I burned two men alive. I didn't hesitate. Didn't flinch. Just let the flames do my work. Both threatened me with something worse than death—a lifetime of hell. If I'd stayed married to Brother Matthew, he would have kept me enslaved and pregnant. Rochester would have worked me to death, then choked me for sport.

So if Rowland endured thirty years of that without killing, I would never judge him for slaying a cop for my protection.

Rising on my tip-toes, I press my lips to his. He stiffens for a heartbeat, then melts into the kiss with a deep groan.

"I need you, more than air," he murmurs against my mouth. "You're the only person in the world who makes me feel human. With you, I'm no longer a caged beast. I can finally be a man."

He slips his fingers through my hair and kisses me again with desperate hunger, pulling me closer as if I can chase away his demons.

We tumble backward into the bedroom, the towel slipping from his hips, revealing lean muscles and that long, thick cock. I run my hands down his shoulders and chest, my fingers tracing decades-old scars. Burn marks, slashes, grooves lie beneath body hair as luxuriant as silk.

"I love you, Annalisa Burlington," he says, his voice breathy with need.

I whisper it back. Not because I should. Because it's the truth. "I love you, too."

Rowland stiffens, his eyes widening. "Say it again." His voice is rough, like he's barely holding back. "Slower."

"I... love you."

"Don't say it unless you mean it," he growls. "Because if you do, I'll never stop wanting you. Never."

My pulse quickens. The hunger in his voice should be terrifying. After years of men who threw me away, I need to be wanted this desperately. I slide a hand over his scarred chest, meeting eyes that burn with need.

"Rowland, it's you I love. Only you."

His breathing becomes ragged, his grip on my waist tightening. I can feel him fighting for control, the decades of deprivation warring with his need to be gentle. "You have no idea what your love does to me. I've lived a hundred lives in agony, and you undo them with three words."

"Deal with it," I murmur against his lips. "Because you're mine, forever."

A sharp breath whistles through his teeth. Drawing back, he gazes down at me, his eyes blazing. I meet his stare, communicating everything I failed to say with words. Rowland means everything to me, and my heart beats only for him.

With a groan, he yanks me against him with bruising force, his mouth claiming mine with desperate intensity. His kisses travel down my chin, down the sensitive column of my neck, making me shiver. He roams his hands over my body like he's memorizing every curve, every hollow, every place that makes me gasp.

"Mine," he snarls against my throat, dragging his teeth along the pulse hammering beneath my skin. "Say it. Say who you belong to."

"You," I say with a gasp.

"That's right. Every inch. Every breath."

"Yours," I moan, arching into his touch. "Always yours."

"And I'm never letting you go." He throws me onto the bed. The air rushes from my lungs as I hit the mattress. Then he's on me, eyes dark with hunger. "After thirty years of having nothing, I want everything with you. I want to create something that's ours."

My head spins. I'm so breathless for this man, I barely hear his words.

"I want to fill you up, make you mine completely," he growls into my ear.

"Yes... please."

"Open those legs for me, little pet. Prove you deserve this cock."

My gaze roams down his chest. Light streams in from the window, cutting across his pecs. Rowland is all lean strength and controlled power, utter perfection. White lines criss-cross his skin, meeting darker patches where he was burned. Some would see flaws. To me, he's unbreakable.

Beneath his chest are tight abs with a smattering of dark hair. The scars over his abdomen tell the same story. His thick cock lies flush against the ridges of his stomach, leaking, heavy with need. Breath quickening, I part my thighs.

He gazes down at my pussy, and his eyes darken. Then he looks up at me, nostrils flaring. "Good girl, showing your master what's his. You're dripping. Eager. Good enough to eat, but I won't give you my mouth. Not yet."

"What?" I say with a gasp. "Why?"

"Because I need you to beg for it," he snarls. "Tell me you want to be bred like a good little slut."

My pussy clenches before I can even process the words. Everything about this man is intoxicating, and the thought of him taking me so thoroughly has me crying out, "Breed me, Rowland."

His breath catches. For a heartbeat, he stares down at

me like I've said something sacred. Then a low growl rises from his chest, rough and satisfied, the sound dragging over my skin like heat.

"First, I'll fill you up. Make you take it to the hilt. I'll put my seed so deep inside you your belly will swell with my children."

The possessive words flood my veins with heat. I buck my hips, wanting more. "Yes," I say with a gasp. "Give me everything."

Rowland positions himself between my spread legs, his hands pinning my wrists to the headboard. Feral intensity burns in his eyes, making every fine hair on my neck stand on end. My heart skips several beats. Without the beard, he's all sharp edges and danger. A monster. An unrelenting beast. I have to remind myself that he belongs to me.

I wrap my legs around his waist, pulling him close, until the head of his cock grazes my opening.

"Tell me your safe word," he growls.

"Why?" I whisper.

"Because once I start, I won't stop. Not until you're full of me. Not until you're bred." He presses in closer, voice rough. "I want to hear you sob when you take it all. Want to feel you clench around me when you break, saying my name."

"It's red."

"Good girl." His eyes flash with something dark. Could be satisfaction. Maybe control. Then he thrusts into me, hard and deep, and I cry out, the sound raw and helpless.

He fills me completely, making my inner muscles stretch to accommodate his size. I gasp as his grip on my wrists tightens, holding me in place. Building up a punishing rhythm, he fucks me without mercy or restraint, all the while growling filthy promises that make my toes curl.

"You'll take this cock like you need it to survive. I'll pump you full of cum until your belly fills with my heir. Then everyone who sees you will know how well you take it." He pants against my ear, his breath hot and urgent.

The thick head of his cock brushes back and forth against a spot that makes me jolt like a live wire. I rock my hips, on the verge of climaxing, desperate for more friction, but he changes position.

"Do you want to come, little pet?" he asks, his voice thick with lust.

"Yes," I cry.

"Then tell me how much you want it," he says through clenched teeth.

"Please," I moan, arching beneath him. "Let me come."

"Tell me how much you want to carry my babies. Tell me you'll stay here forever."

Euphoria floods my heart. Rowland wants me as much as I want him. I finally have security. Love. A future.

"I want it all," I say through panting breaths.

"Tell me what you want."

"Please, breed me," I beg, my voice hoarse with need. "Make me pregnant."

His eyes flare. Something inside him snaps. He slams into me harder, his thrusts wild, hungry, raw. "Such a good girl, begging for my seed. I'll fill you so deeply, you'll be dripping for days."

His words send electricity through my core. I've never wanted anything more than this: to be claimed, filled, owned so completely by this man who killed to protect me.

"The estate needs a mistress. And an heir. And you're going to give me one. I'll make you so round and full that you can't leave me even if you wanted to."

"You have me, Rowland," I say with a gasp. "I'll never leave."

"That's right. Because you'll be tied to me forever." His rhythm falters as he gets closer to the edge. "I'll make those glorious tits heavy with milk, make your belly stretch tight with my baby. Everyone will know you're mine."

The image he paints of us together forever pushes me over the edge. I come apart beneath him, crying out as waves of pleasure crash over every nerve ending. Rowland follows seconds later, burying himself deep as he fills me with hot fluid.

Afterward, we lie tangled together, our breathing slowly returning to normal. His hand rests on my stomach, as if he's already imagining the life we might have created.

"We're going to be happy here together," I murmur against his chest.

"More than happy," he replies, his arms tightening around my waist. "We're going to have everything. The money, the estate, the life we deserve."

I smile into his chest, already planning our future. With Blanche's inheritance and Rowland's new identity as Edward Rochester, we'll have wealth, security, respectability. But more than that, we'll have each other.

Two killers bound by love. And by what we've done to survive. And if anyone ever threatens what we've built, we've already proven what we're willing to do to protect it.

FORTY-SEVEN

EPILOGUE

SIX MONTHS LATER

I wake up in the master suite of Rochester Manor. Sunlight pours through the tall windows overlooking the gardens, penetrating the silk curtains. The bed I'm lying on is wide enough to accommodate four and a hell of a step up from the old servant's quarters.

Rowland shifts at my side, his arm pulling me closer, his lips grazing my neck. These past months have been blissful beyond belief. Each day, he brings me something new, whether it's flowers from the garden, jewelry that belonged to his grandmother, or a wonderful dish he conjured up in the kitchen. He even brings me his favorite books, wanting to share the happier moments of his childhood.

And the sex is incredible.

We fuck like animals, twice or three times a day, as if he's making up for decades of enforced celibacy. He's possessive. Primal. Feral. I've never in my life felt like I've belonged to a man so completely. He touches me like he's starving, like I'm his only salvation.

"Good morning, my beautiful little pet," he says, kissing my shoulder. His hard cock settles between my ass cheeks, sending a shiver up my spine.

"Morning," I start to say, but my stomach heaves. Bile shoots up my throat like I've been poisoned.

I bolt out of bed, race for the bathroom, and barely make it to the toilet before I'm puking so hard my ribs ache. Tears gather in the corners of my eyes. What the hell did I eat?

Rowland appears behind me and gathers my hair off my face. As I throw up, he rubs my spine in time with my convulsing stomach. "Easy, pet. Let it out."

I barely hear him through my retching. I can't even remember the last time I felt so awful. It subsides, and I lean against the toilet seat, panting and spent. When the worst passes, I slump against him, wiped out and shaky.

"Must be food poisoning," I say with a groan.

Maybe it was the lobster bisque. Maybe that rooster finally poisoned me with one of the eggs. My mind spins with crazy possibilities. It isn't like me to feel queasy.

Rowland pulls me to my feet, his large hands cupping my cheeks, his brow creasing with concern. "Are you alright?"

"I can't believe you saw me with my head down the toilet."

Eyes shining with warmth, he studies my face. "When was your last period?"

The question hits me upside the head. When was it? I've been so caught up in this fairy tale that I haven't been keeping track. Days blur together when you're finally happy.

"I..." I frown. "I don't remember."

He grins. "Are you pregnant?"

I laugh, but the sound is hysterical. Brother Matthew tried to make me have his babies from day one, but nothing stuck. The old bastard kept calling me barren.

Throat closing, my mind echoes with his insults: barren, worthless, cursed. All those years, he had me thinking I was defective.

"Well, are you?" Rowland breaks me out of my thoughts.

"Not to my knowledge." My teeth worry at my bottom lip. "I'd know, wouldn't I?"

But my mind's already racing. We've fucked every day since Rowland met with Blanche's attorney and received the inheritance, sometimes twice or three times a night. I've been too happy to even recall something as trivial as bleeding. Shit.

"Stay there." He leans me against the wall and opens the bathroom cabinet.

I'm so mesmerized by the scars on his back that it takes a moment to notice he's extracted a pregnancy test. My stomach flips again. Of course, he's been planning for this. Every time we fuck, he growls about getting me pregnant.

"Pee on this," he says.

I take it with trembling hands. The plastic feels strange, like I'm holding a grenade. Rowland watches me perform the test, and we both stare at the little window in silence.

Minutes crawl by like hours. The plastic stick sits between my fingers like a loaded gun. My heart drums so hard I can feel it in my throat. I stare at the display, unable to stand still. Rowland hovers at my side, his gaze burning the side of my face.

The second line appears, and my jaw drops.

"I'm pregnant," I whisper.

Rowland falls to his knees and grabs me by the hands. I glance down, my breath catching, to find his eyes glistening with tears. Reverence shines in his gaze, pure admiration as he looks up at me like I'm the answer to every prayer.

"Marry me, Annalisa," his voice breaks. "Be mine forever. Make me the happiest man in this world."

The words hit me like lightning. This is real. This isn't a delusion, a dream or a desperate fantasy. Rowland is offering me forever. My throat closes. This is it. The moment I strove for during all those years of running from one disaster to the next. A man who wants me forever, not just for the night. The answer comes to me as easily as my next breath.

"Yes."

Rowland pulls me down to his level and kisses me like I'm oxygen and he's drowning. "Today," he murmurs against my mouth. "I can't wait any longer. Not when you're carrying my child."

"What? How?"

"There's a church nearby. If you can drive us, I'll make it happen."

"O-okay." I laugh through tears.

He jumps to his feet and rushes to the bedroom. I follow, still dizzy from the pregnancy news, finding him rummaging through the wardrobe. Moments later, he extracts a flat box and places it on the bed.

"What's that?" I ask.

"Open it," he says, his voice breathy.

I pad across the room, my hand on my belly, not quite believing I'm growing a new life. A child equal parts of Rowland and me. A baby made from devotion and love.

Rowland hops from foot to foot, wringing his hands. I've never seen him look so excited.

With trembling fingers, I lift the lid and push apart the tissue paper to find a delicate white dress.

"I made it especially for you," he says.

"You did?" I ask, lifting the garment from the box. It's made of the softest silk, simple, elegant, and shaped exactly to my figure. The tiny stitches forming the seams are more delicate than anything I could ever make. "This must have taken hours."

"I worked on it at night while you slept," he says, his cheeks turning pink.

Sighing, I shake my head, awestruck by his talent. It's beautiful. Clean lines, no fuss, nothing like Blanche's elaborate minidress. But then this garment was made with love instead of money. And only for me.

I think of the morning of my first marriage, when Mom shoved me into the wedding dress she'd been forced to wear when she married Dad. Grandma had also been forced to wear it when she was a child bride.

"It's perfect," I whisper, my chest filling with warmth. "Thank you."

We dress quickly, both giddy with excitement. The dress fits like he measured me in my sleep, but then he's already memorized every inch. Rowland knows my body better than I do.

I'm too nauseous for breakfast, so I drive us through the countryside in a sports car Edward parked in a hiding spot within the grounds the day he ambushed us. Rowland rests a hand on my thigh, his gaze warming the side of my face.

"Are we meeting the same priest who married Edward and Blanche?" I ask.

"St. John's is the only church on this side of the island." He pauses, his hand stilling on my thigh. "And Father Henry's been with the family for years."

Cold shivers down my spine. "Won't he think it's strange that Edward's getting married again so soon?"

"The Rochester family owns the church's land. And the vicarage." His tone shifts, becoming cultured and cold. It's the voice he uses when he's being his brother. "Father Henry knows not to ask questions."

I hold back a grimace. No matter how many months have passed since Rochester's death, that voice always gives me the creeps. I had nightmares the first few weeks about Rochester lurking beneath the house, waiting for the right moment to attack.

Each night, I would wake up in a cold sweat, screaming that the monster was here. They only stopped when Rowland took me to the cottage's burned remains and showed me his brother's charred corpse.

We arrive at the church, a one-story building of stone walls thick with ivy. An elderly man in black meets us at the door. He's stooped and gray, looking like he was once as tall and robust as Rowland.

"Edward!" He frowns, his gaze sweeping up and down Rowland's form. "You've lost weight, dear boy. Are you eating well?"

Rowland strides toward the priest with his chin raised and his shoulders pulled back, looking every inch the entitled rich bastard. "I didn't come here for a discussion on my health, Father. I'm here to get married."

The priest rears back. I can't tell if he's startled by the harsh tone or the thought of another wedding. "Of course, my son. Though isn't this a little rash—"

"Would you like to continue having a roof over your head?" Rowland says.

My stomach dips. I guess this is precisely what a psychopath like Rochester might say.

Father Henry nods like he's used to the Rochester family's demands. "Well, you'd better come this way."

He sweeps his arms toward the empty church and limps inside. The ceremony is quick but beautiful. I'm so nervous that I barely pay attention to the religious preamble.

"'Do you, Edward Rochester, take this woman to be your lawfully wedded wife?" asks the priest.

My stomach clenches so hard I nearly double over. Even though it's Rowland playing the role of his brother, hearing that name again feels like jumping from the roof.

"I do," he replies.

Father Henry turns to me and asks the same. Rowland squeezes my hand as though sensing my dry mouth, my fluttering pulse, the way my gut churns with unease.

It doesn't matter which name Rowland uses. I know it's him. This is about transcending survival. About remaining hidden from the outside world. About building a life from the ashes of our combined misfortunes.

"I..." I clear my throat. "I do."

"By the power vested in me, I pronounce you man and wife," says the priest. "You may now kiss the bride."

Rowland's mouth crashes into mine, urgent and unrelenting. His lips claim me like he's sealing a blood pact, his hands tangling in my hair to keep me close. I return the kiss with equal passion, because I finally have somewhere to belong.

The kiss is hungry, claiming, possessive, as if he's

marking territory. When we break apart, he's breathing hard, chest rising and falling like he's been running.

"You're finally mine in every way that matters," he whispers against my lips, his breath urgent and hot.

Father Henry clears his throat and takes us into the vestry to sign the marriage license. Rowland barely shakes the old man's hand before walking me back to the car with an arm around my waist. I haven't felt this light in over a decade.

"Want a honeymoon?" he asks as I start the engine.

I laugh. "Every day with you is a vacation."

He squeezes my thigh, offering me a dazzling smile. "Happy, pet?"

"Ecstatic." I pull out and drive through the country roads leading back to Rochester Manor.

Rowland shifts on his seat, his hand drumming against my leg, his breath coming in quick bursts.

"You okay?" I ask.

"We need to make preparations for the baby."

"Like what?" I ask with a smile.

"Set up a nursery, for starters. The space behind the mirror would be perfect. I can convert it this week."

I blink, my gaze darting across the front seat. "Wait. What's behind the mirror?"

"A hidden room." He grins like he's sharing a delicious secret. "There's a latch on the side of the frame. It's the perfect size for a nursery, and we can keep an eye on the baby without needing a nanny."

"How many other spaces are in this house that I don't know about?" I ask.

"Countless," he replies with a chuckle. "Our children will have plenty of places to play hide and seek."

"You've been looking forward to this baby, haven't you?"

He leans across the seat and kisses me on the temple. "I pictured breeding you from the moment I decided you'd be mine. You won't need to lift a finger. I'll build everything. A changing table, a crib, a rocking chair. Our baby will never want for luxuries."

When we reach the manor, he carries me across the courtyard and over the threshold. I expect him to charge up the stairs or to the nearest surface to consummate our marriage but he sets me on my feet and presses a kiss on the tip of my nose.

"Meet me in the dining room in thirty minutes for brunch."

"Will there be bucks fizz?" I ask with a smile.

"Absolutely not." He places a hand on my belly.

Giggling, I race up the stairs to check out this hidden space. At this time of the morning, the master bedroom is drenched in light. Dust motes dance in the air, making the space look magical. I, Annalisa Burlington, am the lady of this entire manor.

I walk to the mirror and pull back the fabric of my dress around my waist. Now that I'm scrutinizing myself, my belly is rounder. All this time, I thought being in love and free from persecution had made me gain weight. Now, my heart swells at the thought of having a happy little family.

Although by the way Rowland talks in bed, he wants me constantly pregnant.

I feel around the mirror's edge, my fingers finding a metal lever. When I press it down, the entire frame springs forward, and a doorway opens with a click.

The space is around nine feet by twelve. Large

enough for a crib and a changing table. Sunlight streams in from a tall window, illuminating a set of shelves at the back.

This is perfect for our needs. I can already picture it painted in pastel colors, filled with toys and books.

As I turn to leave, my gaze catches a leather-bound book on the shelves. Curious, I walk to the end of the room and flip it open to the first page.

It's a photo album, containing a picture of a stern-looking man dressed in a dark suit, waistcoat, and cravat. His stern features are framed with sideburns so thick, they look fake. Beneath the image, in neat handwriting, is the name:

EDWARD FAIRFAX ROCHESTER.

"Must be an ancestor," I mutter.

The next page is a wedding photo. Old Rochester wears a top hat with his black suit and cravat, while the woman behind him is in a long, white dress with a high neckline and a veil covering her features. The only writing at the bottom says WEDDING 1847.

"So, his great-great-great-great-grandparents?" I shake my head, unable to calculate the distance.

The next several pages contain pictures of their children, of the eldest sons growing up to be haughty looking gentlemen who marry nameless women who bear their heirs. They go on and on from black-and-white to color. I tune out until I reach a man who looks startlingly like Edward Rochester, but wearing clothing from the seventies or eighties.

The text below reads HENRY ROCHESTER.

"Their father?" I whisper. "Has to be."

I study his sharp features, noting the same cheekbones and aristocratic nose. This was the monster who locked up Rowland for supposedly murdering his sister while the real killer went on to kill and torture innocent women. His eyes are even colder than his son's.

When I flip to the next page, the portrait on the other side makes my breath stutter. Henry Rochester stands behind three kids in front of a massive fireplace. Adele is easy to spot with her blonde ringlets and pale skin. She's about five years old, grinning with a missing tooth, alive and smiling instead of the horror I found in that locked room.

Edward is about ten, looking like his father's mini-me. Same stern features, identical cold eyes, looking like the perfect predator in training.

But the third child makes my heart skip.

He's the same height as Edward, with curly red hair, freckles and a smile as bright as the sun. His eyes are the same pale blue as his sister's. The text below reads: HENRY, EDWARD, ADELE AND ROWLAND ROCHESTER.

Rowland?

I frown, my pulse picking up speed. Fingers trembling, I flip through more pages. Birthday parties. Christmas mornings. Every photo shows the same small family. Sometimes together, other times alone, but the red-haired boy is always labeled ROWLAND ROCHESTER.

And always with hair as curly and red as Orphan Annie's.

My breathing shallows. I keep going. The final picture stops my heart. Edward and Henry stand by two familiar gravestones on the grounds. A woman weeps in the background, burying her face in her hands. She wears the same black uniform I used to wear, the identical one belonging to the skeleton in the attic.

The headstones are child-sized. I can't read the names. It doesn't matter because Rowland already told me the story of how his father faked his death.

But I can't stop thinking about that red-haired boy.

The only other family photos I saw around the house were in Adele's room, from the time Rowland directed me to her corpse. I have to see them again. I have to know. Heart pounding, I set down the album, step through the mirror, and head for the door.

I haven't been back to that room since I discovered the truth about Adele. Now, the thought of seeing her again makes my skin crawl, but I have to check those photos. I need to compare.

The hallway stretches ahead, with dead Rochesters watching from their frames. The pulse between my ears pounds so hard it muffles the echo of my footsteps.

My feet stop outside Adele's door, not wanting to take me any further. I clutch my belly and groan. If I see that grotesque thing again, if I look into those glass eyes...

But the red hair on Rowland doesn't make sense.

I turn the handle and step inside.

Adele still sits in her chair in the corner, a nightmare in lace and ribbons. I don't linger on the sight. Turning away, I force my focus on the photos lining the walls. They're the same family portraits from the album. Same three kids. Same labels.

Same red-haired Rowland.

Stomach roiling, I move from picture to picture, checking and double-checking. Every single photo shows a boy with flame-bright hair. Nothing like the man downstairs.

Nothing like the man with black hair who calls himself Rowland.

Nothing like the man I just married.

Panic claws up my throat and grips tight. There has to be an explanation. Hair dye. Photoshop.

Something.

Anything.

After reaching the end of the photos, I turn toward the door, carefully avoiding the sight of Adele. But my gaze catches what's on the bed, and I freeze.

The curtains are drawn around it, hiding whatever's on the mattress. But I can see the outline of a small figure. Dread sinks into my gut like lead.

I should run.

I should hide.

I should wipe the sight from my mind.

But my legs keep moving me forward.

My heart thrashes so hard that my sinuses fill with the scent of blood. I walk to the four-poster bed on legs that feel like water and pull back the curtain.

A small body sits propped against the pillows, arranged like a doll. Sunlight bounces off his red curls, and his glassy blue eyes shine bright. On the chest pocket of an old-fashioned white shirt is an embroidered monogram that reads:

ROWLAND.

I stumble backward, my hand flying to my mouth. The room spins like a broken ride. My stomach heaves. My eyes squeeze shut. I press a hand to my chest, my mind spinning back to the church.

When Father Henry pronounced us man and wife, my husband said I was finally his in every way that mattered. I drop to my knees, my palms hitting the floor.

What did Edward Rochester say before I left him to burn in that cottage?

"You won't die like the others," I whisper, my voice rising with panic, my hand clutching my pregnant belly. "Your prison will keep you at my mercy until the end of your days."

Nausea hits me in the gut. The man I married, the man who put this baby in my womb never existed. It was Edward. Edward Rochester all along.

ALSO BY GIGI STYX

Morally Black Series

Taming Seraphine

Snaring Emberly

Breaking Rosalind

Stalking Ginevra

Pen Pal Duet

I Will Break You

I Will Mend You

ABOUT THE AUTHOR

Gigi lives with her husband and two cats in London. When she's not crafting twisted dark romances with feisty heroines and the morally grey villains who love them, she's cuddled up on the sofa with a cup of tea and a book.

Sign up for Gigi's updates at:
www.gigistyx.com/newsletter